Uncharted Waters

By

Lynnette Beers

Paperback ISBN 978-1-61929-571-1

Hardcover ISBN 978-1-61929-573-5

Cover Design by AcornGraphics

Publisher's Note:

Dedication

To everyone who has a battled life-threatening illness—whose grit and grace have inspired family, friends, and often strangers. In life and beyond...you are the bravest people I have the privilege to know.

Prologue

Morro Bay, California: September 2014

Atop her surfboard, Maddie scanned the misty surface of the ocean. Behind her, Morro Rock towered over her and the other surfers as they waited for the perfect swell. Thick bands of fog sat on the horizon, making it difficult to see past the breakers, but behind her, strobes of sunlight forced their way through the clouds. Morro Rock glowed in the golden light of morning. Maddie squinted at the piercing light as she studied the building swell. Several yards away, the silhouettes of other surfers floated just inside the surf break. Nearby, her daughter, Taylor, sat on a foam surfboard while Maddie instructed her on how to prepare for the incoming set of waves. This was a forgiving break, and a ride at the Rock on a beginner board would get Taylor used to the feel of a wave.

"Make sure you stay right where we are," Maddie yelled to Taylor without taking her eyes off the approaching breakers. "You never want to get stuck in the whitewash close to shore."

Taylor paddled closer to her mom, her ponytail swinging with her movements. "But it's boring here. There aren't even any waves in this area."

"Taylor, one day you'll realize that surfing requires patience while you wait for the perfect wave. If you get caught in the whitewash, you'll see how difficult it is to paddle out to the surf line." Maddie continued to study the waves magnifying in the distance.

"We should've gone to Montaña de Oro, where you go with Grandpa Kai when he's in town. The waves are way better there." Taylor frowned and slumped forward, acting more like a small child than a pre-teen.

"Montaña de Oro isn't the best surf spot for beginners. Only experienced surfers go there, and we don't go alone. That's why I only go there with Grandpa Kai." Not to mention the recent shark sightings at Montaña de Oro, which reinforced Maddie's decision to never surf there by herself, much less allow her twelve-year-old daughter to enter the water in that area.

"Can I go there with Grandpa Kai?"

"Let's see how you do today first. Then you can ask him the next time he visits, okay?"

Kai Tamamoto was Maddie's mom's long-term boyfriend and the person who introduced her to surfing eighteen years ago. He'd patiently taught her how to ride the waves and conquer even the largest ones. Born and raised in Hawaii, Kai instilled in Maddie a love of the ocean and eventually coached her to win a few surf competitions when she was a teenager. It was so long ago, and yet it still felt like yesterday that she was first learning how to stand up on a surfboard. She'd mastered so many big waves since then, and yet there were way more surf breaks she wanted to explore, especially since Taylor could join her once she got comfortable with a board.

Taylor looked toward the lineup of surfers and kicked the water with both feet, creating a whirlpool of froth. "Why can't we go way out there where the other people are?"

"Honey, it's too dangerous out there for your first time. Plus, it'd likely be hard for you to get out that far. Trust me, if you get stuck between the whitewash and the approaching waves, you'll end up expending a lot of energy as you battle the surging water, and you'll never catch a wave."

Taylor rolled her eyes and shrugged.

This was the best morning to teach Taylor to surf since the forecast predicted only two to three-foot peaks, and Maddie had the day off from teaching. She looked toward the horizon to see if the swell had increased in size. It hadn't, but the sun's rays made her wince. A bad headache put a slight damper on her time in the water this morning, but she hoped the fresh air would revive her.

The waves were less dangerous and easier to ride in this area, and with Taylor on a beginner foam board, she could more easily paddle out and possibly stand up and ride a few waves. Plus, if she fell off her board and it happened to hit her, she wouldn't get hurt. They'd surf for a couple hours, relax on the sand for a while, get some lunch, and then head home where Maddie would get ready for her evening out. After two coffee dates, she'd finally asked the woman from the local art gallery out on a real date—dinner at an upscale restaurant.

In a thick neoprene wetsuit and with the ocean only in the mid-fifties, Maddie basked in the warmth of the sun and waited for the next set. But a sharp pain flashed in her left temple, causing her to gasp and hunch forward. Daily headaches had plagued her for weeks, diminishing her energy and making it hard to focus on the classes she taught at the local college, but today's headache was much worse.

Taylor paddled closer to Maddie. "Another headache?"

"Just a little one. Probably eye strain from grading too many papers." Since she didn't want to reveal the severity of the headache, Maddie splashed water on her face and studied the building swell.

Taylor drifted closer and set her hand on Maddie's shoulder. "Mom, you said you'd see a doctor this week. A headache for a full month isn't normal. You rush me to the doctor even if I've got a sore throat for only a couple days."

"Honey, it's nothing. Let's just enjoy the waves. There's a set approaching. Get in position." Maddie watched the breakers headed their way, but an intense wave of lightheadedness overcame her—the same sort of dizziness that'd been plaguing her all week. The wooziness caused her to lean forward and set her forehead on the board. She hoped it would subside before a rideable wave came her way.

A few deep breaths steadied her. Maddie slowly sat upright and brushed the damp strands of hair off her shoulders. The swell magnified in the distance. She glanced at Taylor to make sure she remained within shouting range, and then Maddie lay flat on her board and sliced her hands through the water to get closer to the line-up. The whitecap continued to build in momentum, the peak swelling as it approached. At the base of the wave, Maddie stroked the water and attempted to drop into the shoulder, but she couldn't propel her board fast enough to catch the wave since the dizziness had left her unexpectedly weak. With Maddie now on the outside of the wave, the breaker shriveled down to fine mist over the surface of the ocean.

Maddie sat on her board and watched the waves in the distance, but the pain in her head intensified. The headaches had been sapping her energy lately but nothing like this. Maybe Taylor was right about getting to a doctor. She closed her eyes and rubbed the back of her head as she hoped the pain would subside. When Maddie heard the breakers crashing nearby, she opened her eyes to find the cusp of a wave swelling and moving closer.

"Taylor, make sure you face the shore," Maddie said when Taylor paddled closer. "Remember, your back should be to the approaching wave, but always glance back to keep an eye on the surf." Maddie cupped her hands in the cool ocean and splashed water on her face. The pain in her temples now radiated from her forehead to the top of her skull.

Several surfers rushed toward the cresting wave. While other waves built in momentum, more people paddled to the surf zone. In the distance, a huge wave began to peak. Maddie and Taylor paddled to get closer to the face. Full of adrenalin, which dulled the pain, Maddie charged toward the massive breaker. With her daughter next to her, Maddie eyed the crest and stroked her hands through the water until the board caught the momentum of the wave. She then popped up on her board. To the left, Taylor dipped into the face and stood within seconds.

Just like her mother, Taylor opted to surf goofy-footed, the placement of her body atop the board exactly like Maddie's when she'd first started surfing in Southern California. "Maybe next time I can ride a real surfboard," Taylor yelled, riding the curl of the wave as if she'd been doing it for years. "This foam board sucks. It isn't fast enough."

Maddie laughed and shook her head while riding the whitewater next to Taylor. "You might look like you know what you're doing, but you're still just a beginner!"

The severe headache returned, causing her to wince.

They popped off that wave, but Taylor quickly padded back out to the line-up and caught another one.

Maddie waved a fist in the air. "That's my girl! Move your feet a little farther apart like we practiced on the sand. That's it! You got it." While she kept a close eye on Taylor, who rode all the way to shore, Maddie caught another wave. The mist from the tumbler washed over her face, the cold spray slightly diminishing the pain in her head.

Elated that she finally caught a decent wave, Maddie attempted to step forward in order to gain momentum, but her left leg suddenly felt as if it were made of lead. Her foot wouldn't budge, and her hands trembled. Maddie shifted her hip forward, but her lower leg still wouldn't move. Her vision became fuzzy, and the intense pain in her forehead now radiated to the back of her skull.

The wave decreased in power. Maddie lost her balance and fell face first into the frothing water, her body tumbling in the whitewash. With the leash attached to her ankle, the surfboard lunged forward, yanking her body into the churning surf. Try as she might, Maddie couldn't move her legs or arms to tread water. Then her jaw went rigid, her teeth sliced her tongue, and blood pooled in her mouth—the coppery taste causing her to gag. Her entire body then began to convulse. Trapped between the shoreline and the breaking waves, Maddie struggled to stay afloat as the whitewater surged over her—completely helpless against the current.

Inside her head, she screamed for help. It'd been years since she'd been caught inside the shoreline and the crashing waves. Normally able to swim to safety, right now she couldn't even tread water. Her buoyant wetsuit kept her limbs afloat, but she couldn't raise her arm to notify the lifeguard that she needed assistance. Small tumblers washed over her. She moaned, hoping Taylor or a nearby surfer would hear. Saltwater entered her mouth, mixing with the blood that gushed from her tongue, and Maddie coughed.

Over the slapping of the waves came the sound of distant screams—the kind of shrieks that indicated to other surfers that something was terribly wrong. More calls for help. No Taylor in sight. Breakers rolled over her; seawater burned in her nose and down her throat. She coughed and was able to clear her mouth of saltwater, but the coppery taste of blood quickly pooled in her mouth as her tongue continued to bleed. Maddie closed her eyes and prayed she'd be able to keep her head above water.

"Hold tight!" someone yelled.

Maddie opened her eyes to see a woman paddling toward her. The woman reached her a few seconds later and immediately wrapped her arms around Maddie's convulsing body.

"You're gonna be okay," the woman said. "The lifeguard's on his way with a rescue board. I'm Jenny, a retired lifeguard."

Maddie tried to relax in Jenny's arms, but her body continued to shake. The chilly water surged over her face, once again making her cough. As each breaker washed over her, the leash from the board yanked her body forward.

Jenny steadied Maddie's surfboard, preventing it from lunging forward. "Your daughter flagged me down and said you were having trouble. I sent her to shore to get help. I rushed over to get to you as fast as I could." Jenny quickly but gently bent Maddie's leg at the knee and removed the leash from her ankle. "Look out! Board loose!"

Words formed in Maddie's head. Complete sentences. But nothing exited her mouth.

Jenny kept a firm grip around Maddie's body, keeping her head above water. "Looks like you hit your head pretty bad. The lifeguard's almost here. He'll get you to shore as fast as possible."

I didn't hit my head, Maddie wanted to say. Something's not right in my brain. Is this an aneurism? Did I have a stroke? Is Taylor okay? Call Drew Richards. He's Taylor's father, my ex. She needs him right now. Maddie tried to move her lips to form sentences, but the words remained lodged somewhere deep inside her brain.

A new voice spoke. "She looks pretty bad." It was a

male voice, one of the young lifeguards often working at this beach. "We need paramedics here as soon as possible."

Paramedics? Just how injured am I? Maddie thought. More blood poured from her mouth. Intense pain pressed into her skull like a vice.

The young lifeguard cradled Maddie's back and neck and kept her afloat. "I got you now. You must've hit your face on your board. You've got a lot of blood coming from your mouth."

Jenny lay atop her board a couple feet away and faced toward shore. "I bet I can make it back to shore fast and call 9-1-1." She paddled away and headed to shore.

Maddie's injured tongue still flowed with blood. Alert and aware of her surroundings, Maddie opened her lips and allowed the saltwater to enter her mouth, washing away the metallic taste of blood.

"Careful," the lifeguard said. "Don't want you swallowing any seawater. I'll help you keep your head up."

This kid couldn't be more than eighteen, but Maddie completely surrendered to his aid. "Buh," she said, her sliced tongue making it impossible for her to clearly say the word "blood." More words formed in her head, but she couldn't utter anything coherent.

The guard hoisted Maddie onto a rescue board and secured an arm around her body to prevent her from jostling in the waves. He expertly guided them through the churning tumblers to the shallow water where only small breakers sloshed over the board.

Someone tromped loudly through the water, and Maddie opened her eyes to see the red trunks of another lifeguard. Then another one approached. The guards carried her to dry sand where Taylor rushed to her side. Sirens wailed in the distance.

Taylor crouched in the sand next to Maddie. "Dad's on his way." Taylor's voice was shaky. She was clearly terrified.

Maddie attempted to reach for Taylor's hand, but her arm went rigid, and her eyes filled with tears. A kid shouldn't have to see her mother go through this. The lifeguards kneeled by her side, and soon, a team of paramedics rushed down to the sand.

"Come on, Taylor," Jenny said. "We need to give them room to work. Don't worry, your mom's got a good team helping her."

"I'm still here, Mom," Taylor called out. She sounded like she was trying not to cry. "Don't worry about me. Dad will be here soon."

Several people dressed in dark blue crowded around Maddie—first responders clothed in crisp uniforms way too hot for summer. A female paramedic used cold scissors to cut through the neoprene of Maddie's wetsuit, exposing her chest and abdomen. The cool air on her bare skin made her shiver. Someone strapped a rigid brace around her neck, making her entire body stiff. Others cut the rest of her wetsuit off, and Maddie was hoisted atop a backboard and lugged across the sand. Voices came from all around. In her distress, Maddie couldn't distinguish one from the other. Paramedics poked and prodded at her body. Why couldn't she move?

"Possible head injury," someone said, followed by muffled voices over a radio.

"ETA to Maple View Hospital…twenty-two minutes."

"We need to transport her faster than that."

"Thirty-two-year-old woman. Apparent seizure. The patient's daughter told us her mom is otherwise healthy except for chronic headaches. Says her name is Maddie Fong Richards. No history of seizures or epilepsy."

Maddie tried to turn her head to search for Taylor. A paramedic stabilized her body, preventing her from locating Taylor.

"It'd be too hard to get life flight here in the parking lot. Might as well go by ambulance."

"Give her point-four milligrams of diazepam."

Atop a gurney, Maddie had no choice but to stare at the hazy blue sky overhead. Someone raised the top of the stretcher, which gave her a clear image of the sand and breaking surf at the Rock. The fog had dissolved into thin clouds over the horizon. In the distance, whitecaps formed on the surface of the water while breakers surged toward the shoreline.

"Taylor, we're taking your mom to Maple View Hospital," the female paramedic said. "A trauma team is on standby."

"Can I at least say goodbye to her?" Taylor asked.

"Really fast, okay?" was the paramedic's reply. The gurney had begun moving across the bumpy dirt, but Maddie was soon brought to an abrupt stop. The morning sun shone in her eyes.

"Mom, I'll see you at the hospital. Dad's almost here to take me." Taylor slipped her hand in Maddie's. Twelve years old, the kid acted more like twenty right now. She needed Drew here with her, someone to tell her it'd all be okay. But would everything be okay?

"Don't worry, Maddie, I'll stay with her till her dad gets here," Jenny said.

Maddie pursed her lips and attempted to speak, but the words remained lodged deep inside her brain. Someone tightened a blood pressure cuff on her left arm, followed by a needle puncturing a vein in the crook of her right arm. Cold liquid stung as it coursed through her veins, the muscles in her legs and back relaxing within a couple minutes.

Sirens wailed, an engine rumbled, a hollow metal door slammed shut. Only the second time in her life that she'd been transported by ambulance, fear washed over her. Maddie's vision blurred, and she soon couldn't tell the difference between sunlight and the glaring lights inside the vehicle. Drowsiness flooded her body, her muscles relaxing even more. Not sure if the vehicle was moving or if this was her body once again convulsing, she closed her eyes and prayed this would all be over soon.

Chapter One

Big Sur, California: October 2018

Under the night sky, the ground was barely visible as Maddie and her friend, Dot, trekked down the walkway. Several bright stars blanketed the sky. Since the ocean air was so crisp, Maddie had secured a knit beanie on her head and scrunched a fleece scarf up to her chin. She gripped the handle of her wooden walking stick, carefully placed each foot on the stone steps, and followed the steep incline down the path until they reached level ground. Maddie linked an arm through Dot's, and they hiked across the gravelly footpath.

Maddie's life over the past four years had been consumed with doctors' appointments and hospital stays. Her time was divided between medical exams, work, and family. This weekend, she'd come to Monarch Bluffs to finally do something just for her: a writing workshop focusing on personal storytelling. And though the medical stuff wasn't all in the past, Maddie was hoping to not dwell on it for the weekend.

Maddie looked ahead but couldn't see where the path led. "How much farther?"

Dot halted her stride and adjusted the bright orange shawl over her shoulders. "Not much farther, hon. Probably around ten minutes from here, I reckon."

"Where exactly are we headed?"

"Buckeye Hall."

Maddie tilted her head. "What kind of name is that?"

Dot chuckled. "Haven't you figured out by now that every structure at Monarch Bluffs is named after a butterfly?"

Maddie nodded in acknowledgement. "That's pretty clever. Now it makes sense why our room is called Painted Lady." She let out a loud sigh.

"You okay?"

"Just a little winded, I guess. Haven't walked this much in a long time." Years ago, when Maddie lived in Southern California, she would've never asked about the distance of a hike or a trek along the beach to a perfect surfing spot, but lately she got winded walking only a few yards. This weekend, she was determined not to let the neuropathy win and at least appear to be a typical woman in her thirties.

"We can take a break if you'd like."

"No, I refuse to slow either of us down this week-end." Maddie picked up her pace. They had to get to the other side of the property before the opening session started.

While Maddie stepped across the gravel, she kept a tight grip on her cane, the handle worn down since Dot made it a few years ago. Carved out of dark snakewood, the walking stick had a unique design in the shape of a serpent's head. From afar, the patterned snakewood staff looked just like a rattlesnake and often startled passersby, but she rarely went anywhere without it.

With her hand gripped on the serpent's head and the other on Dot's plump arm, Maddie marched across the path. Their feet crunched on the coarse walkway, the only other sound coming from the clunky metal bracelets jingling on Dot's wrists.

A sharp pain abruptly radiated to the back of Maddie's head, and she staggered. Used to these fleeting headaches, she closed her eyes and waited for the pain to subside.

"You sure you're okay?" Dot gripped her hand on Maddie's arm.

"Yeah, fine. Just got a little out of breath." Fortunately, the pain vanished quickly, and Maddie opened her eyes. A dimly lit pool at the edge of the bluff reflected the moon overhead, although it didn't illuminate much of the dark grassy area. "So, is this the famous lawn where you drummed naked in your younger years?"

"I didn't drum naked. I'm not that wild." Dot laughed as she realigned the chunky beaded necklace over her ample bosom. "Besides, this isn't a nudist camp. Nudity is only allowed in the hot springs."

"I suppose that pool is clothing optional, too?" Maddie pointed to the glowing teal waters of the pool. Over the past four years, she hadn't done much more than go for a quick dip.

"Nudity is allowed in the pool area, but it's only open in the daytime. The water's warm, probably around eighty. More of a wading pool than anything, it's perfect for someone like me who doesn't know how to swim."

Again, a sharp pain flashed in her left temple but quickly subsided into a dull ache.

They stepped onto the lawn and were met with the crashing of waves far below the cliff. Soothed by the sound, Maddie stepped closer to what looked to be a dark garden. "I can't believe I'm finally at a writing workshop at Monarch Bluffs. Always wanted to come here."

"Maybe you'll write the opening chapter of your memoir. Good idea to start working on it before—" Dot halted her words and stared at the ground.

"Before what? Before I die?" Maddie rarely minced her words since her diagnosis. Again, a sharp pain flashed in her left temple but quickly subsided into a dull ache.

"Mad, no, I didn't say that. Before...well, before Taylor has the baby."

Maddie still couldn't believe her sixteen-year-old, straight-A daughter was four months' pregnant. The last thing she'd ever wanted was for her daughter to follow in those particular footsteps. "I doubt I'll have time to do any writing before the baby's born. I've got two sets of papers to grade this weekend and more coming in next week. I also need to prep for a class at the penitentiary that starts in a few weeks."

"How about making it a no-grading weekend? We're here to write, soak in the tubs, drink wine, and enjoy the slower pace at Monarch Bluffs."

"Even though Doctor Lau lowered my anti-seizure meds, it still makes me foggy-headed. It takes me twice as long now to grade a paper than it did before my surgery. You know I've gotta keep up on my grading. I have to show the English department I'm capable of handling the workload, especially since I submitted the application for the full-time position."

Dot took a few slow steps down the walkway. "You sure you're up for a full-time job? I thought you'd...given up that goal."

"It was my goal before I got sick. I think I can handle it." Maddie shined the flashlight on the pathway and squinted to try and see where to place her feet.

"You gonna pay for a ride any time you need to get to campus to teach a night class? Or continue to have Drew or Taylor drive you?"

Maddie focused on the dark ground and slowed her pace. The thunderous waves pounded on the rocks far below the cliffs. The ache in her temples radiated into her forehead and behind the eyes. Maddie hadn't driven at night since before her surgery, and rarely drove farther than a few miles during the day. Although her neurologist gave her the all-clear to be able to drive as much as she'd like, Maddie continued to get rides from others.

"They might not even call me in for an interview, but I figure I shouldn't slack on my duties as an English professor. I'll just grade a few papers each morning. Maybe I'll come across more funny student errors. It'll keep us entertained this weekend. I might find some good ones to post."

"Those were some doozies from the last set of papers. When are students gonna learn the difference between 'defiantly' and 'definitely'?" Dot stepped farther into the dark garden and followed the path under the moonlight.

"Or 'asses' and 'assess.'" Maddie laughed but was privately daunted by how many more papers she needed to grade by Sunday. Before she got sick, she could easily teach five classes, including one at the prison, as well as a night class. Would her health ever allow her to return to that?

Dot picked up her pace slightly. "Fortunately, most of my grading consists of scantrons and creative projects. Don't know how you do it, making your way through such rubbish that college students write these days. But, it might do you some good to take a break from those dreadful papers this weekend. You can finally do some of your own writing for a change. Why not create something for Taylor to read before she's a mum? Maybe pen some sort of piece about what it was like for you to be a young parent."

Hardly anyone knew about Maddie's teenage daughter being pregnant, but more people would find out soon enough. "That's not a bad idea. Can't believe I'm gonna be a grandma in my mid-thirties, though. I just hope I live to—"

"Hush, there will be none of that kind of talk this weekend. Look, you lived to see Taylor learn how to drive. You lived to see me finish that mural at the senior center in Monterey. Remember when your goals were marked only by the week or the next holiday? Now that you've beaten the odds, you can finally start enjoying life."

"Dottie, you know the odds."

Dot stopped walking and turned to face Maddie. "Mad, it's time for you to realize that you're a walking miracle. You might as well enjoy being a grandma. Taylor's gonna need your support."

"My God, only sixteen and a mother even before she's out of high school." To say the entire situation was stressful was an understatement. Drew had been furious, and Maddie had felt let down. Not by Taylor as such, but by life. She'd done her best to prevent her daughter from also becoming a teen mother. But all the sex ed and protection in the world didn't matter if the birth control failed, which was what had happened. Taylor had been adamant about keeping the baby, despite everyone's private and not-so-private views otherwise. Maddie was worried about how Taylor would handle being a mom at such a young age, but even more than that, she grappled with being a grandmother while in her thirties.

Dot plodded forward through the dark garden. "You were barely out of high school when you had Taylor, and your mum was also young when she had you, right?"

"Apparently, young motherhood runs in my family, but at least I was a legal adult when I had Taylor. Right from the start, I had Drew to help raise her. My mom was nineteen when she had me but raised me all on her own."

Dot paused on the pathway. "You certainly turned out fine being raised by a single mum."

Maddie was always grateful for how hard her mom worked after they left Mississippi and relocated to California, but she had been sad to not have two parents around during much of her childhood. "Mom worked seven days a week in order to give me a good life. She taught five days a week and worked most nights and weekends at Royal Palace. But she wasn't always a single mom."

"For the most part she was. She had a baby with no father around."

"It's not like she didn't know my dad, and she wouldn't have been a single mom if my dad hadn't died in the war right after I was born. Besides, Kai was a great father figure to me."

"Not until you were, what? Fourteen? Fifteen? Your mum never actually married him, did she? Good on her, keeping her independence for a woman her age."

"I was fourteen the day Mom met Kai, but she and I didn't move into Kai's house until I was sixteen. He was a great father to me when I was growing up. Or like a father. He's made my mom very happy over the years and has always been there for her…and for me."

Kai always remembered the important things: birthdays, anniversaries, allergies, likes, and dislikes. He was unfailingly polite to Maddie's grandmother, no matter how grumpy she was. There was no better shoulder to cry on than Kai's. Ever since he'd wandered into Maddie's family's Chinese food restaurant, he'd become part of their family, and they'd become his.

Dot nodded. "He has been there, that's for sure. What I'm saying is that your mum did a fine job raising you by herself when you were in your formative years. With your help, Taylor will figure things out just fine. Might as well accept it, Mad. Before you know it, you'll be in the delivery room watching your grandchild enter the world. In the meantime, I say your next goal should be to find yourself a new girlfriend."

Did she really just say that? Maddie huffed. "Dot, I came here to write. The last thing I need is a long-term relationship, anyway.”

“Yeah, it certainly has been a while since you've been in a long-term relationship. I wouldn't call two coffee dates with that woman from the gallery long-term. Or the fling with the history professor. Then there was Callie. Never did quite reach girlfriend status, did she?”

“Not when she saw me as nothing more than her mistress.” Maddie's body tensed after she said that word. It had been many years, but what happened with Callie still hurt.

“Maybe we'll find you someone new while we're here at the workshop. Oh, maybe another English professor!” Dot became so excited and enthused, as if this was her project for the weekend—to find women for Maddie to meet.

In contrast, Maddie just wanted to relax this weekend and not follow any sort of schedule or be pressured into socializing with others. “Meeting women this weekend isn't really on my agenda.”

“Never say never. When was the last time you actually went on a real date with a woman? Or slept with one,” Dot added quietly.

If anyone else had asked that question, Maddie would never have answered. “It's been a little over four years since…well, since my last date.”

“Four years? Oh Lord, like I said, you'll meet lots of women this weekend.” Dot waggled her eyebrows. “Especially if you go down to the baths.”

Maddie couldn't help laughing at Dot's ridiculous expression. “No! I'm not gonna strip down in front of anyone.” The humor vanished from her voice. “Not with all the scars on my body.”

“I certainly don't have the body I had in my twenties. After having three kids, lots of places on my body sag. But at fifty-six, I don't give a shit what anyone thinks of this body. Besides, it's so dark at the hot springs at night that no one is gonna notice anything.”

Maddie didn't know that. She assumed they'd be lit, much like the pool they'd just passed. Dot had given her something to consider, but Maddie didn't reply. They had reached a paved incline and were no longer alone. Now they were part of the stream of people heading to the opening session. A few muted lights at the base of a wooden fence guided them across a narrow bridge. The waves roared, and Maddie caught a glimpse of the dark ocean where the full moon cast a strobe of light over the black water.

Once they reached the entrance to Buckeye Hall, Maddie and Dot kicked off their loafers and left them next to rows of other shoes. The carpet leading into the entryway was soft. Inside were well over a hundred people sitting in rows of plastic chairs. Buckeye Hall looked like a huge makeshift tent for some sort of traveling circus. Most of the structures at Monarch Bluffs were made of dark wood and reminded Maddie of an exclusive camp for adults, but the location of the opening session for the writing workshop seemed temporary and makeshift. The contrast only enhanced Maddie's excitement, and she eagerly took in every detail. It was as if the tent had been set up just for her.

Although she'd driven by Monarch Bluffs numerous times, Maddie never had reason to venture past the front gates, given she always associated it with hippies and new agers. It was only when Dot told her about *New Moon Magazine's* writing retreat that Maddie knew she had to make the trip. It was exactly what she needed to start writing again. The magazine called this workshop "Rising Phoenix," the sessions focusing on poetry and memoirs. In a few months, Maddie would be teaching a class on autobiographical writing at a men's prison. Preparing the lessons had sparked a desire to write about her own life. Since she got sick, she hadn't written anything more than an email, but this afternoon she jotted down a thirty-word bio as the details on the workshop website instructed—a mere few words to sum up her life thus far. With a bit of luck and inspiration, they would be the start of many.

The tent was nearing capacity, but they found seats way in the back. Maddie sighed in very audible relief at finally being able to sit down. With the high ceiling and canvas walls, the tent lacked proper acoustics. The chatter roared in Maddie's ears—the combined voices of over a hundred attendees making her head throb. Maddie still experienced occasional seizures, especially when under intense stress, so she tended to avoid large crowds. But the medication worked well at keeping the seizures to a minimum. However, with her immune system still compromised, a huge room full of people meant exposure to germs, viruses, and bacteria. Any of these could set her back for weeks, but she wasn't going to think about that right now.

A young woman stepped onto the stage and hushed the crowd. Members of the audience quieted within seconds. The crash of the waves sounded nearby, and Maddie was momentarily soothed. She wrapped her arms around herself and leaned forward, determined to drink in every word.

"Good evening, my name is Natalie. Welcome to what we hope will be a wonderful weekend." Her voice was gentle, similar to Maddie's favorite yoga teacher. "We invite you to immerse yourself in poetry, essays, and short stories. This weekend, we'll celebrate the power of the written word. We're fortunate to have six writers from *New Moon Magazine* who'll share their expertise with you. First, a quick reminder of the workshops being offered tomorrow." Natalie quickly ran through them, and Maddie knew she absolutely had to attend the one about connecting to your audience through food. When Natalie was done, she gave the audience a warm smile. "All right, now it's time to introduce yourselves to the room and read your thirty-word bios."

An older woman in the front row took the microphone from Natalie. "Frequent visitor to Monarch Bluffs, Charlene Griffith is a psychologist by day and a poet by night. She lives in Monterey with her husband of thirty-six years and their bulldog." She handed the microphone to a young guy next to her and returned to her seat.

The young guy stood and smiled at the room. "Matt Evans lives in Northern California where he enjoys surfing and mountain biking. He's an EMT and a pre-med student. He frequently visits surf locations all along the California coast." He handed the microphone to the person next to him and sat down as they started speaking.

The mention of surfing piqued Maddie's interest, even though she hadn't taken out her board in four years. There were a lot of things she'd given up a few years ago: surfing, hiking, driving, pedicures, dating, sex.

People of various ages sat in the audience. Some were probably barely twenty; others were well into their retirement years. There was a young woman who had a bandana snug on her head. Maddie felt a pang of sympathy for her. She could always spot cancer survivors in a crowd. Even though her hair had grown back, albeit brittle like her nails now, Maddie was always self-conscious of the two-inch scar on her scalp. Then the radiation seared the area so badly that it killed the hair follicles and left a huge bare spot. She'd tried combing the hair over the bald area, but because her hair grew back so thin, she never could completely hide the scar. Always wearing a beanie or a scarf was out of the question because they made her head itchy after wearing them for too long.

A woman in the second row with long dark hair and wearing a bright floral dress stood. "Leilani Kamaka is originally from Kauai. She speaks Hawaiian and Japanese, and has published a few poems and stories. She wants to write a memoir about growing up in Hawaii."

Now that really piqued Maddie's interest. She made a mental note to look up Leilani's work. Kai would definitely be interested in reading it as well.

The man next to Leilani faced everyone in the room. "Max Carter discovered *New Moon Magazine* when he was incarcerated. After getting a narrative essay published, he decided he wanted to write about his past, especially his addiction to heroin."

A heroin addict? Max couldn't be more than twenty-five. That must have been rough. Good for him for beating his addiction. Six years ago, Maddie started teaching at the men's prison in San Luis Obispo, or SLO, as the city was often called. It had become her favorite place to teach because of how well she connected with the inmates. Fascinated with the narratives the prisoners wrote, she unfortunately hadn't taught there since her diagnosis. She'd only taught two courses in the past year—an online composition class and one critical thinking class that met on campus. Now, with clearance from her doctors, she was ready to return to the prison to teach an autobiography class and a poetry workshop. The extra income would help pay some of her medical bills. Though no longer on the harsh chemo that made her hair fall out and caused her to vomit for several days in a row, she still got a round of bevacizumab once a week, or B-vac as her oncologist liked to call it. It held the cancer at bay, but the co-pay of that alone was a hardship each month.

Although no longer together in the traditional sense, Maddie stayed on Drew's insurance and continued to live in the same house. His benefits through the high school where he taught allowed her to see the best doctors located along the Central California Coast, including Doctor Cho, one of the top oncologists in San Luis Obispo. The cancer halted Maddie and Drew's plans for divorce, but it made much more sense financially for them to not legally separate. He'd recently gone on a couple dates with a French professor from a college in SLO, who apparently wasn't bothered about Drew still being married to Maddie.

The hum of a fan in the front of the room lulled Maddie into an even more relaxed state. While an entire row of people read their bios, Maddie zoned out, but she leaned forward when an elderly woman stood with the help of the young man next to her.

"At ninety years old, Evelyn Hastings wants to write an autobiography about growing up in Brooklyn. She has four children, sixteen grandchildren, and eight great-grandchildren. She enjoys whiskey every night."

The crowd erupted into laughter as Evelyn took her seat. Maddie smiled. Perhaps she should ask Evelyn whether that was the secret to being a good grandmother and living a long life. Whiskey wasn't Maddie's favorite drink, but it was worth a try, although her doctors might disagree. Maddie relaxed back into her chair as the next woman stood to read her bio.

"After battling breast cancer, Kendra Sanchez started writing romance novels and mysteries. She's published three sapphic romances and one award-winning mystery novel, and has another story brewing in her head."

Maddie leaned forward to get a better glimpse of this fascinating woman. Kendra couldn't be more than in her mid-thirties. And four books published? Those had to have taken her a few years to write. Kendra had creamy skin and thick auburn hair. Either that was a great wig, or she'd long since battled cancer and was in remission. Or close to it. Maddie had a year to go until Doctor Cho could say she was in remission, but she knew the odds. Oncologists were resistant to say that patients with her type of cancer ever went into remission. It was always a matter of when the cancer would return, not if.

Now the people in Maddie's row were reading their bios. As the microphone made its way closer to Maddie, her heart sped up. She never got anxious speaking in front of her students, but this was different. To lecture about James Joyce or Virginia Woolf fueled her passion and never caused her to feel nervous, but rarely did she ever speak to a huge crowd about anything personal.

Dot stood and spoke loudly into the microphone. "Dorothy, or Dot Campbell, sometimes called Dottie by her closest friends, is originally from a small town just outside London. She's an artist and often displays her paintings, wood carvings, and sculptures in Monterey and Big Sur galleries. She teaches art history and studio art at a couple community colleges."

"That sounded like way more than thirty words," Maddie muttered and smirked.

"You didn't expect me to follow the rules, did you?" Dot laughed and passed the microphone to Maddie.

With her fingers gripped around the mic, Maddie stood and focused on the slip of paper shaking in her hand. She took a deep breath and began to read each word slowly and with emphasis. "Given six months to live, Maddie Fong is kicking brain cancer's ass. At four years post-diagnosis, she's got gnarly scars from brain surgery, a fighting spirit, and a hopeful future."

Though she didn't believe the last three words of her bio, Maddie did her best to adopt the motto of "fake it till you make it." No one noticed her self-doubt because everybody burst into cheers and applause, only slowing down once Maddie passed the microphone to the woman next to her.

Maddie's heart continued to thud hard as she sat down in her seat. But not from nerves. She really didn't feel right. Lightheaded and weak, she took a few deep and slow breaths, but her entire left side started to feel heavy. Then she couldn't move her arm, and her left cheek tingled. She tried to nudge Dot, but her elbow wouldn't move from her side.

Maddie attempted to get something to exit her mouth—just one word to get Dot's attention. Maddie's cheek became leaden, and she couldn't utter more than a few soft grunts, but she managed to gently fall into Dot's shoulder and huff out a muddled "Help."

In an instant, Dot wrapped her arm around Maddie like she did a few weeks ago when she had a mild seizure when they were out for coffee. "Deep breaths, hon. I got you. I can see if there's a doctor in the crowd."

"No," Maddie managed to say. This was supposed to be her writing weekend. These weird neurological moments happened at the most inopportune times but rarely escalated to the point of her needing to get medical attention.

Dot held Maddie tighter and continued to whisper to her while the people in the back row read their bios. Maddie closed her eyes and went to her happy place—the location she hadn't visited for real since before she got sick. More relaxed now, she imagined the cool water lapping over her feet while she clenched her surfboard under her arm. With this image in her mind, the heaviness in her left side dissipated. Maddie opened her eyes, glanced at Dot, and smiled. Then she reached her right hand up to her lips, relieved that her smile was symmetrical on both sides.

While Maddie tuned out the words of the conference attendees, she concentrated on the waves pounding on the shore below the cliff. As she focused on the sound of the surf, Maddie wiggled her toes, relieved she could move her feet, but the piercing pain in her head concerned her. Dot's arm held her tighter, and Maddie relaxed into the embrace, afraid to tell her what was happening—terrified of what these symptoms might indicate.

Chapter Two

Big Sur: October 2018

"Madelyn Fong Richards." The young man read Maddie's nametag out loud. "Can you tell me where you're at?"

"In Big Sur with my blabbermouth friend." Maddie resisted the urge to correct the man's grammar error and glared at Dot, who stood nearby. Several people filed past while Maddie remained slumped in a wheelchair near the doorway. "I'm at a writers' workshop at Monarch Bluffs. I'm in Buckeye Hall, in front of way too many people."

Natalie, the young woman with the gentle voice, stood nearby and pointed to the exit. "Please, we need everyone to head outside." As if herding sheep, Natalie spread her arms and paced behind the crowd while they funneled out of the tent.

Thick plastic flaps hung over the exit, and a huge metal fan whooshed each time someone passed through the doorway. The frequent exiting of workshop attendees and the accompanying loud fan drowned out any signs of the surf far below the cliff. All Maddie wanted to do was get outside to smell the ocean air, hear the crashing waves, and head back to her room to sleep.

Natalie set a hand on Maddie's back. "We've got a golf cart waiting at the top of the walkway to take you to the bridge and another one waiting on the other side to take you to your room."

Maddie mustered up the energy to give her a grateful smile. "Thank you."

"You can call security any time this weekend and ask them to give you a ride." Natalie ushered more people out the door and stood by the exit to wait for the others to leave.

"Madelyn, my name's Matt. I'm an EMT." Matt set

two fingers on the inside of Maddie's wrist and checked her pulse. "Can you tell me what month this is?" Tall and muscular, he folded his arms and awaited her response. Despite the chilly air, Matt was dressed in a tight, short-sleeved T-shirt.

"October." Maddie repositioned herself in the wheel-chair. "Please, call me Maddie. They got my nametag wrong when I registered. I use my maiden name now, anyway."

"Maddie, I think we oughta call 9-1-1 or have your friend drive you to a nearby hospital."

It was hard, but Maddie managed to restrain her annoyance. "Nearby hospital? Isn't that, like, two hours away?" All she wanted to do was get back to her room and lie down.

"Depends on if you're going north or south on High-way One." Dot paced in front of the wheelchair.

Maddie ignored her friend and studied Matt's face—the chiseled jawline, the kind smile, the blue eyes. "You're the pre-med student, right?"

"Yes, ma'am, good memory."

"My short-term memory is still intact. Never had any issues with that after brain surgery." A figure standing nearby caught Maddie's attention, and she saw Kendra Sanchez pausing in the doorway. Their eyes met for a moment, and Kendra smiled reassuringly before pushing through the plastic. Something about Kendra's smile put Maddie at ease. She'd locked eyes with several cancer survivors over the years, but Kendra's eyes carried more depth and understanding than most of the other people who fought or were fighting this terrible disease.

"What type of brain cancer did you...or do you have?" Matt's brow furrowed, and he bit his lower lip.

"Grade four glioblastoma multiforme." Maddie slouched in the wheelchair and glimpsed at Dot, who continued to pace back and forth down the middle aisle of the room.

Matt's eyes widened in shock. "I think you men-tioned you were diagnosed with GBM four years ago, right? That's remarkable that you're—"

"Still alive?"

"That you're doing so well and that you're so active." Matt reached for her hand.

Maddie was used to these sorts of astonished reactions, especially from medical personnel. Relieved that no more onlookers gawked nearby, Maddie breathed out a loud sigh but wouldn't have minded if Kendra had lingered behind. Out of everyone in tonight's crowd, Kendra would have understood how exposed and vulnerable Maddie felt right now.

At the sigh, Matt let go of Maddie's hand. He maintained eye contact but now with such a pitiful look on his face.

There was no getting around it. Maddie would have to waste time making conversation with Matt so he'd leave her alone, but he reminded her of Drew, at least in the color of his eyes and his kind smile. Maddie softened a bit. "So, Matt, in your bio you said you surf all along the California coast. I used to surf...well, years ago."

"That's cool. Longboard or short? Or both?" Matt ran a hand through his shaggy hair, the ends bleached from saltwater and sun.

"I surfed with a longboard and a shortboard in Southern California where I used to live, but I always used a shortboard when I competed."

"Competed? Wow, that's impressive. Whereabouts did you live in Southern California? My parents live in Laguna Beach."

"I lived in San Clemente when I was a teenager but left Southern California when I was twenty. I moved to Morro Bay with my husband and ended up switching to a longboard, but I haven't surfed in about four years."

"Hopefully you'll take your board out again soon. The swell has been a blast lately. Lots of long rides with good form."

"Yeah, maybe one day." Maddie gave him a small nod. There, that should be enough small talk. "Matt, I appreciate your concern, but I'd like to get to my room. I'll be fine after a good night's sleep. It's kind of you to make sure I'm okay, but there's no need for me to go to a hospital. I just want to enjoy myself this weekend."

But Matt wasn't so easy to shake off. "Your friend

tells me you occasionally have seizures since you had brain surgery four years ago. How long since you last saw a neurologist?"

"I see Doctor Lau about every six months. He lowered my anti-seizure meds, but maybe we need to up the dose again. And actually, my neurologist doesn't even think these are seizures. My last EEG came back totally normal. He says they're some sort of—"

"Mad, I really think I oughta take you to the ER," Dot said, her voice tinged with irritation.

Maddie matched it. "Dottie, you remember what they told me the last time I had one of these minor seizures. Doctor Lau said they're technically not even seizures, that they're some sort of neurological misfire or something."

"When was the last time you had an MRI?" Matt set a hand on Maddie's shoulder.

Irritated with Matt's questions, Maddie kept her answers short and hoped she could just get to her room. "I go every four months. I'm due this week."

"You still need to make that appointment." Dot gripped both hands around Maddie's walking stick and tapped the end a couple times on the ground. "I'll make the appointment and drag you there myself if Drew doesn't take you."

"Dottie! I'll call on Monday." Maddie hated raising her voice, but Dot's insistence was so frustrating.

Matt took out his phone from his back pocket and shined the light into Maddie's eyes, causing her to flinch when the glaring flash hit her pupils. Since Matt stood only a few inches from her face, Maddie recognized his cologne as patchouli or some other musky scent. His face and hands were tanned, but his arms were white—typical of a surfer in this area where the waters rarely went above sixty and required a full wetsuit. At one time, Maddie used to have that same odd tan: face and hands bronzed but arms and legs pale. She'd considered selling her boards and wetsuits but held onto them for now in case Taylor wanted to return to surfing after she had the baby.

Matt continued to stare at Maddie's eyes. "Have you

been experiencing any dizziness lately? Headaches? Slurred speech?"

Maddie averted her eyes from Dot's. "I've had bad headaches lately."

Dot flailed her arms. "Ah, jeez, Mad! You didn't tell me about any headaches. How bad have they been?"

Maddie kept her eyes focused on Matt and didn't bother to answer Dot's question. That same dull pain continued to press into both sides of her head. No longer sharp or sudden, the headache had now turned into a consistent ache in her skull. Despite the headache, she wanted to stay at Monarch Bluffs and try to have a good time. If she could get a solid night of sleep, she'd likely be okay to go to the writing sessions tomorrow.

"How about you squeeze both my hands a couple times?" Matt reached out his hands.

Obediently, Maddie squeezed Matt's calloused hands. He leaned over so that his face was close to hers. As she gazed into his steel blue eyes, she again gripped his hands with all her might.

"Good grip." Matt laughed and took a couple steps back. "Now, let's have you smile."

"I haven't had a stroke," Maddie said louder than she'd intended. She offered him a quick smile to appease his need to do a thorough neuro eval. "It was just a small seizure. Probably never even got to the point of it being a full-on seizure. I'm used to these weird neurological misfires by now. I've learned techniques to halt the progression of a full-on seizure. I was totally fine by the time Natalie made her closing remarks."

"Yeah, while I kept a tight grip around you the entire time." Dot thumped the walking stick on the ground.

"Dottie, you saw that I was fine after a few minutes. You didn't need to find an EMT and have him examine me." Maddie glared at Dot, who glared right back.

Right after her surgery, Maddie had become annoyed with the neuro checks every two hours in the hospital. The nurses, doctors, and physical therapists spoke to her like she was an idiot. Obediently, she'd tell them the date, where she was, her birthdate, and what'd happened to her. She'd long since recovered from nearly all neuro deficits since brain surgery. The neuropathy was just a minor inconvenience and only slowed her down occasionally.

Matt crouched down at Maddie's knees and clasped both hands around hers. "Neurologically, you seem fine, but I think you should get checked out by a doctor. We should probably notify your husband. There's no cell service anywhere on the property, but I can ask someone here with a land line to call him."

"Or we can do a video chat with him once we're back in the lodge where there's Wi-Fi," Dot said.

"Drew doesn't need to know about this." Maddie leaned forward and studied Matt. He never released her hands and remained crouched at her knees. At the start of her treatment, she initially hated when anyone doted on her. The hatred became resignation and then acceptance that people were just doing their jobs. However, someone being genuinely kind, like Matt was right now, always softened her. "Matt, I'd rather you not call my husband. He's not...well, it's kind of complicated."

Matt's smile was understanding and sympathetic. "No worries, I get it."

"I don't even need to be in this wheelchair. I'm thirty-six, not eighty. I do fine with my walking stick." Maddie pushed herself up from the chair but got dizzy when she started to stand. Before she could manage to sit back in the wheelchair, her body involuntarily swayed to the left.

"Whoa, here, lemme help you." Matt gripped her arms and eased her back into the wheelchair.

"Just lost my balance, is all," Maddie muttered.

"For fuck's sake, Mad, stop being so goddamned stubborn." Dot nudged Matt. "Told you she'd be resistant to your help."

"I'm just tired, Dottie. Hand me my cane, and we can head back to our room."

Dot refused to give up. "I really think I oughta drive you to the hospital tonight."

"Dottie, can't you see I'm fine? I didn't have a stroke, I'm fine neurologically, and I want to enjoy the weekend at Monarch Bluffs. I'll call my doctor first thing

Monday morning, and I'll set up an appointment for the MRI."

"How about this?" Matt said. "Let me escort you to your room. Once there, I'll make sure you get settled and are steady on your feet."

"I guess that sounds reasonable." It wasn't, but Maddie was tired of arguing.

"But I'd like to see how you're doing tomorrow morning," Matt said. "Check your vitals and see how you're feeling. I've got a blood pressure cuff in my truck and—"

"I don't think that's necessary." Maddie tried to make the line sound friendly but wasn't sure she succeeded. "It's nice of you to be so concerned, but I don't need you to do any more medical assessments."

Matt didn't seem offended and only gave her a friendly smile. "Then how about we just have breakfast together? We surfers gotta stick together, right? I'll tell you about my epic experience a couple years ago at Mavericks, and you can tell me about your favorite surfing spots along the California coast."

Now that was a reasonable request. Maddie nodded and fought off the tears that brimmed at her eyes. Matt released the brake on the wheelchair and pushed her toward the door. At this point, the entire left side of her body was less heavy, but hiking up the steep walkway to get to the golf cart would be a feat her body couldn't endure. Every time she had one of these neurological misfires, it left her lethargic. Being driven around in a golf cart all weekend would be embarrassing, but if that was how Maddie would get the most out of her time at Monarch Bluffs, she'd do it. When Matt pushed her through the doorway, she shut her eyes and once again surrendered to the care of a medical professional.

Chapter Three

Big Sur: October 2018

Monarch Bluffs' outdoor eating area was a wooden deck, which meant Maddie could enjoy the fresh morning breeze. It was seven-thirty, and breakfast would be served in an hour, but Maddie was able to get a cup of coffee to start her day. She relaxed in a chair next to a glass-top table facing the ocean. Next to the deck was a koi pond full of orange, white, and black fish. Far below the bluff, breakers pounded on the rocky shore. Beyond the swells, the water reflected the morning sun. Aware that distant squalls could be brewing several miles offshore, Maddie studied the ripples on the water and watched each wave grow in size as it approached the shoreline. Even though she might never again surf, she still got a rush whenever she observed a wave gaining momentum and crashing onto the rocks.

Although she still had several papers to grade, Maddie allowed herself a few minutes to skim passages from *To the Lighthouse*—the first Virginia Woolf book she'd ever encountered. Her initial exposure to Woolf happened the summer she turned fifteen. Smitten by a cute girl from high school named Ally Flores, Maddie wanted to read anything her crush was reading, including difficult novels written by Woolf. Several years later, Maddie immersed herself in Woolf studies when she was in graduate school. *To the Lighthouse* always called to her, no matter her age or place in life. Maddie had one more sip of coffee, then skimmed a section that always resonated with her:

What is the meaning of life? That was all—a simple question; one that tended to close in on one with years. The great revelation had never come... Instead, there were little daily miracles, illuminations, matches struck unexpectedly in the dark.

Maddie regarded the last line of this excerpt and considered her own little daily miracles. The cool morning breeze off the ocean made her shiver. A blue jay fluttered its wings in the birdbath next to a giant tree, its branches like arms reaching to the Pacific. Wisps of fog sat over the ocean. The blue jay splashed in the water once more, then flew to one of the tree limbs and warbled in tune with another bird on the same branch.

The cold air stung Maddie's skin, so she scrunched the scarf closer to her neck and took a sip of coffee. The headache had subsided into a mild ache behind the eyes, nothing like the intense pain she'd experienced last night. Now on her second cup of coffee, the caffeine was kicking in and easing the headache even more. Maddie hoped to grade a few papers before everyone showed up for breakfast. Although she and Matt hadn't chosen a specific table for this morning, he'd be able to easily locate her on the deck.

Maddie opened her laptop and skimmed the opening paragraph of a student's paper. Beyond the intro, the body paragraphs consisted of nothing but superficial summary. What a disappointment. This girl had decent insights in class but couldn't write a good essay, no matter how much guidance Maddie gave her. Even worse, she still couldn't be bothered citing her sources properly! It was so easy to create a works cited page. When Maddie was a student, she'd had to type out each source individually, checking to make sure each one was perfect. Today, the process was mostly automated with easy-to-use online works cited generators, but students still couldn't be bothered. This was the eighth paper out of twenty that only provided a scattered list of URLs and nothing more. Did they seriously expect Maddie to visit every link and confirm it was legitimate? She shook her head as she pored over the next couple paragraphs and inserted a few comments. The online grading program the college used provided easy-to-use features for reviewing a paper, but Maddie had developed a bank of customized comments over the years to fit any type of assignment.

Maddie made a few more comments and identified the grammar errors and typos, then opened a dialogue box at the top of the paper to type the final overview—words that would hopefully get the student to understand why she got a low grade on the paper.

Before turning off her computer, Maddie decided to spend a little time on social media. As was now a weekly tradition, she selected three or four noteworthy errors from her students' papers and posted them on what she called the Wall of Shame. She only had around four hundred followers, many of whom were fellow professors and teachers, but they all got a kick out of these typos and misspellings. From the essay she just graded, she found many errors worth sharing but chose the funniest one to post:

Here's this week's Wall of Shame winner from the last batch of papers: "quince dental." I'm not sure what sort of dental procedure that might be, or if this is some sort of new fruit I've yet to try!

It was so tempting to share the error on other platforms that weren't as private. People there loved this kind of thing even more than her colleagues. Maddie resisted the urge, though. While she loved getting responses from her followers, she didn't want to hurt her students and would be mortified if they found out about the Wall of Shame. Her social media account was set to private, and many of her friends were other college professors who understood the intent of her posts.

Maddie decided to include a couple bonus student errors in this week's social media posts. The next error was especially funny. A grandmother who'd come back to school late in life, Phillis Nunley sat in the front row and made insightful comments during class discussions, but her essays contained numerous grammar errors and typos. Maddie was shocked that someone of Phillis's age didn't catch such obvious errors, and this one definitely had to go on the Wall of Shame:

Okay, so here's a doozy. From a student's paper (who happens to be a seventy-six-year-old reentry student): She mentioned that a reputable NY newspaper is a notable news source with numerous "pullet surprise awards" for their noteworthy articles.

Within a few minutes, responses flooded onto her

page:

Terri Smith: OMG! That's one of the best ones you've posted all semester. SHE should win a pullet surprise award for her unique use of language!

Miryam Abdullah: Does quince dental have anything to do with a Quinceañera???

Evie Huang: How could this student have not caught that error? Maybe it was a coinci-dental oversight?

Jamie Miller: These actually look like speech recognition software errors. It's no excuse for not proofreading, but you might want to ask the students if they use those types of software.

Dennis Vanderhof: My 7th grade son writes better than that. Eee-gads!

Vivi Chandramurthy: Voice recognition software or not, they should proofread.

Isaac Goldberg: Wow, it's shocking that a seventy-six-year-old woman doesn't know it's called a Pulitzer Prize and probably has no idea how prestigious that is to a writer. Sad she's so sheltered.

Maya Lopez: Maybe students are using voice-to-text on their smart phones to write their papers? If so, give the "smart" phone an F!

Diego Estrada: Kudos to grandma for going back to school at her age. Maybe talk to her about not just relying on spell check on her computer?

Maddie pursed her lips. Diego was missing the point. He was a great instructor but always only looked at the positives in his students and tended to give way more A's in his classes than other English professors. Maddie typed a quick reply to him:

Trust me, I've advised her to not rely on spellcheck, but grandma also writes this way in her in-class essays and on her quizzes. Unfortunately, she has a sour attitude and blames me for her lack of success in the class. It's sad that her writing is sometimes incoherent.

Maddie reread her reply and started to delete the part about Phyllis's sour attitude but then stopped. Her reply was rather harsh, but the truth of the matter was that Phyllis did have a bad attitude. More comments trickled in, but Maddie simply liked the other responses and didn't type any more words of retort. She then scrolled through previous papers she'd graded, looking for the one written by a student who'd analyzed hyper-masculinity and violence in recent blockbuster films.

Once Maddie found the paper, she copied the sentence that made her laugh out loud earlier this morning:

This student error deserves honorable mention: "Well-paid male actors who are buff and handsome fulfill a need that many viewers seek when watching a movie: They prefer the well in doubt men on screen no matter their acting ability."

Maddie laughed and entered the post. Others nearby glanced her way, so she stifled her laughter. She continued to grin and snicker quietly when she heard heels clicking across the wooden deck.

"You look like you're having a fun morning," someone said to Maddie's right.

Maddie looked up from her computer and saw Kendra, the woman from last night who introduced herself as a breast cancer survivor. Kendra smiled and stood there with a mug of tea in her hand and a notebook wedged under her arm.

"I guess you could say I'm having as much fun as a person can have while grading papers." Maddie pointed to her computer screen. "I came across some typos and errors that were...well, noteworthy. Did you know that some male actors today are well in doubt?"

Kendra leaned down to view the computer screen and cocked her head. "Well in doubt? I bet a lot of men think they're well in doubt, though it's been a while since I've actually...um, seen that firsthand." Kendra laughed and sat in the chair next to Maddie. "I don't think I've ever used the phrase well-endowed, now that I think about it, not even when I used to write mainstream hetero romances."

Kendra's eyes were a lovely shade of blue—brighter than the ocean. She only wore a bit of mascara and lip gloss, but she looked radiant. Last night Maddie caught a glimpse of Kendra's auburn hair and creamy skin, but now with her only a couple feet away, she was taken aback by Kendra's natural beauty. Self-conscious of her own ruddy complexion and the dark circles under her eyes, Maddie kept her head down. Still in a beanie, she tucked loose strands of hair behind her ears. At least she'd taken the time to put on mascara and eyeliner this morning.

Kendra set her notebook on the table and picked up the Woolf book. "You a fan of Virginia Woolf? I've only read *Mrs. Dalloway* and *A Room of One's Own*."

"I studied her in college. I might use one of her books in my class next semester, but I'm afraid Woolf might be too complex for a lower division composition class."

Kendra raised her brow. "So, you're an English professor? I don't recall you mentioning that in your bio last night. But, with only a thirty-word limit, there's only so much we can say."

"I probably could've added a line about being an English professor and a lesbian cancer survivor with a teenaged daughter, but I figured I should adhere to the strict thirty-word limit." Maddie's palms immediately began to sweat. Had she really just outed herself to a complete stranger? She tried to discreetly wipe her sweaty palms on her pants.

"Well, you sound even more interesting now." Kendra smiled and glanced at the coastline but then looked back at Maddie.

Maddie's heartbeat sped up, but she gathered up the nerve to comment on Kendra's bio. "Your bio caught my interest last night…for a number of reasons."

"I tried to pick the best thirty words possible. You know, the key words that best describe me at this point in my life."

Maddie nodded. "For me, it made most sense to tell people about my cancer story, but it's hard to convey in only thirty words just how difficult it's been. I left out how horrible those first few months of treatment were."

Kendra's face filled with compassion. "Wait'll you hit the five-year mark. Your entire perspective changes when you realize the awfulness is behind you. Like, you start thinking about an actual future."

The waves pounded on the rocky beach below the

cliff. Maddie peered down the coast as far as she could see and wrung her hands. Though uncertain about her future and fearful her cancer would one day return, she gathered the courage to continue this conversation. "I hope the awfulness is behind me. Any new symptom—a headache, a bout of dizziness, even a slight cough— makes me scared the cancer is back. Recently, I've had swollen ankles and feet. What was my first thought? That this means the tumor is back."

"I know what you mean." Kendra set her hand on Maddie's arm. "One week at a time."

Kendra wore a shiny band on her ring finger, some- thing probably purchased at a high-end jewelry store. The diamonds sparkled in the morning light, sending the strong message that this woman was off-limits.

Maddie dragged her gaze back to Kendra's face and shrugged. "I sometimes still struggle with taking it one day at a time."

Kendra squeezed Maddie's arm once more and pulled her hand back. She gripped her mug of tea as she took a slow sip. "I know how scary it can be. When I got diag- nosed with breast cancer, I knew right away that my situ- ation was pretty dire since the cancer had spread to surrounding lymph nodes. I was facing my mortality in what should've been the best time in my life."

Both women got quiet and turned to view the shore- line. Always comfortable anywhere next to the Pacific, Maddie took a deep breath and closed her eyes as she rubbed the back of her neck. When she exhaled, she opened her eyes and glanced at Kendra—again struck by her beauty. Something about the soft morning light reflected in Kendra's eyes touched a part of Maddie she hadn't realized was still there. Even though they were talking about cancer and mortality, Maddie felt a connec- tion she hadn't experienced with a woman in a long time. Kendra was so vibrant. Surely, she had many years left.

"Did they give you any sort of…prognosis when you first found out you had cancer?" Maddie asked, her voice barely audible.

"My doctor told me if I didn't go through aggressive treatment, I wouldn't live to see my thirtieth birthday. It was the worst couple years of my life. Then, being the online medical sleuth I'd become, I read that women with my type of breast cancer had a higher risk of death within five years of diagnosis."

"You've surpassed the five years, right? Is there…still a risk of death after those five years?" Maddie still found it so hard to use that word: death. It was impossible to shake the irrational fear that saying it might make it come true.

"After the five-year mark, the risk goes way down, but I still have my fears." Kendra got quiet, and then her eyes filled with tears.

"I know a bit about fear." Maddie gave her an understanding smile.

Kendra dabbed her eyes with a tissue but quickly composed herself and sat upright. "One day at a fucking time, right?"

Maddie usually only talked about her family to people she knew well, but something told her Kendra would appreciate this. "Way before I got sick, I learned how important it is to face my fears. When I was a kid, my mom and I moved to California, and then she met an amazing man from Hawaii named Kai. His real name is Kenny, but he goes by Kai, which means ocean in Hawaiian. He helped me get over my fear of water and taught me to surf."

The pain melted away from Kendra's eyes and was replaced with curiosity. "I've always been impressed with how surfers handle big waves, especially in the Central California Coast area where there are sharks. That's gotta take some guts to surf."

"It definitely does take a lot of guts. When I was first learning how to surf, Kai told me about *maka'u*, which means fear in Hawaiian, and told me to never let it get in the way when I was in the ocean. Didn't realize it at the time, but he was right that there'd be much scarier things in life than rough waves. It's been hard not letting *maka'u* get in the way as I've gone through treatment for brain cancer."

Kendra nodded, looking sympathetic. "I know what it's like to live daily with that sort of fear. When I first felt the lump in my breast, I figured it was just a cyst. The possibility of cancer never even entered my mind. Didn't think much of the lump until it was too advanced to ignore."

Maddie gave Kendra a subtle smile. "I ignored horrible headaches and dizzy spells. I mean, who thinks a bad headache is a brain tumor? Getting diagnosed with brain cancer turned my world upside down."

"Most cancer survivors say the same thing—that the cancer blindsided them. I was in my twenties and going to gay pride and lesbian bars. Next thing I knew, I was having a double mastectomy and facing chemo and radiation. Then after treatment and after the cancer was gone, I went through reconstructive surgery. I felt vain to want my breasts back, but...I wasn't even thirty at the time and knew I'd eventually want to be intimate with a woman again. I mean, scars are sexy, right?" Kendra laughed quietly and leaned forward but abruptly became pensive.

Maddie was struck by what Kendra said. So, Maddie wasn't the only one to feel this way. It'd been about four years since she'd been intimate with anyone. For the past few years, she hadn't even had a tinge of longing for a woman. The radiation, chemo, and various medications sapped her energy but also stripped away what used to be a healthy and eager libido.

"For me, the cancer pretty much halted my coming out." Maddie looked down at her lap. "I got sick right as I was ready to leave my husband and...finally live life as a lesbian."

Kendra cocked her head. "You have a husband?" She looked more shocked than intrigued.

Maddie couldn't help smiling at Kendra's shock. Her situation was definitely unique. "Legally, yes. I actually never intended to marry Drew. Right after I had his baby, I got back together with my high school sweetheart—a girl named Ally who totally captured my heart when I was a teenager."

"You and Drew had a baby together, but then you ended up with your girlfriend from high school? This all sounds pretty complicated." Kendra gave Maddie's arm a quick squeeze and laughed quietly.

Maddie waved a hand. "Nah, not that complicated. I was only nineteen when I got pregnant. Even though Drew and I were having a baby, I originally decided to not marry him because I knew I wanted to date women."

"So, is Ally still the love of your life? Do you and Drew have an open relationship?" Kendra looked at Maddie as she fumbled with a napkin on her lap.

Surprised at Kendra's bold questions, Maddie's eyes widened, but she also smiled as sweet memories of Ally, her first love, filled her head. "My relationship with Ally is way in the past. Haven't been in a steady relationship for years, but when I was much younger, Ally taught me how to open my heart to love. We were so young at the time. Things between us were pretty amazing after we got back together, but right after Taylor was born, I vowed to make sure she had two parents who were there all the time, which meant I never wanted to be far from Drew. That ended up being hard on my relationship with Ally."

"I can imagine." Kendra took another sip of tea and smiled. "You and Drew sound like great parents, though."

Not ready to reveal she'd somehow messed up by raising a teenager who ended up getting pregnant, for now Maddie kept things vague about Taylor. "It's not always easy raising a kid, but I do my best. When Drew accepted a really great teaching job up here, I didn't want Taylor to be away from her dad, so I decided to move to Morro Bay with Drew."

"So, you and Ally moved there?"

"No, she needed to stay in L.A. because of the gallery she owned. We tried the long-distance thing, but we eventually realized it'd never work to have her be in L.A. and me four hours away. Plus, right after I moved to Morro Bay, Ally opened a gallery in Chicago and was planning to open another one in New York. It's one thing to be in a long-distance relationship in the same state, but to have her be out of state for several weeks at a time would have never worked." Maddie took a sip of coffee and gazed at the wispy clouds over the ocean.

"I wasn't as lucky as you to find love at such a young age, but I know what you mean about someone opening up your heart to love." Kendra squinted up at the trees, the morning light filtering through the leaves and throwing soft shadows on her face.

"I'll always love Ally, but...we're so different now. For a variety of reasons, I did end up marrying Drew. He's an amazing man, and I love him dearly. But, not in any sort of romantic way. He's been my rock throughout my cancer treatment."

"You're lucky to have someone help you through it all." Kendra stared at the coastline. Without looking at Maddie, she said, "In the darkest times through surgeries, radiation, and chemo, you learn a lot about your partner and whether they're in it for the long haul. You know, in sickness and in health and all that other wedding vow bullshit."

Taken aback by Kendra's sudden bitter tone, Maddie paused before responding, curious to ask about her wife but hesitant at the same time. "Yeah, I'm definitely fortunate. Anyway, to answer your earlier question, I'm a part-time English professor. I only teach a couple classes right now, but two more start up soon at the men's correctional facility in SLO—so long as I'm still up for taking on a couple more classes."

"A correctional facility?" Kendra appeared impressed. "That's really interesting. It must be a challenge, though."

Maddie shrugged. "I like giving back. The only challenge is going through security. Otherwise, it's just like teaching any other college class."

"My niece just started college and is taking a writing class right now. She shared one of her papers with me, an essay about LGBTQ rights. She's obviously proud of her auntie." Kendra tucked a strand of hair behind her ear. "She's joined me a couple times at gay pride and was so supportive throughout my treatment. We even did a breast cancer walk together. Since I don't have a kid of my own...and will likely never be able to get pregnant after all the chemo and radiation I've been through, she's always been special to me. Love the girl to pieces, but I don't think she can write anything that doesn't sound like a social media post or a text." Kendra chuckled. "We certainly need people like you to teach the young people how to write well."

Maddie beamed at the compliment and looked into Kendra's captivating blue eyes. "It's not just the young students who need to improve their writing skills. One of the errors I came across was from a paper written by a grandmother in her seventies."

"Maybe she never had a chance to go to college when she was younger?"

"Perhaps, but you'd think at her age she'd know what a Pulitzer Prize is and not think it's called a pullet surprise. She's mentioned how her kids and even her grandkids all went to the same college and how she's following in their footsteps. But the woman has such weak writing skills and has a sarcastic and negative attitude about everything we do in class."

"I'd give anything to win a pullet surprise." Kendra laughed and shook her head as she gazed at the ocean.

The clock in the bottom right of the laptop screen now read just after eight o'clock. It was time for Maddie to take her morning meds, so she reached into her pocket for the bottle of pills. In addition to her anti-seizure and blood pressure medication, she'd been taking two extra strength acetaminophen for the headaches. They dulled the worst of the pain, but it would be back later today.

"Who knows, you could still win one. I heard you say last night that you've written four books. Sapphic romances and mysteries?" Maddie swallowed one of the pills with a sip of water but kept the others in her hand.

"Mostly romances with a bit of intrigue and mystery." Kendra glanced at the pills in Maddie's hand. "I also do some freelance editing. I'm supposed to be working on my fifth book right now. My publisher wants it finished by January, but the story isn't flowing yet. How about you? You teach writing, so I assume you're also a writer?"

"I used to write poetry and essays but haven't done any writing in a few years." Though ready for more coffee, Maddie didn't want to leave Kendra, even for a couple minutes, so she decided to be fine sipping the rest of the lukewarm coffee.

"Hopefully this weekend will inspire you. I mostly came here to get away, to figure out a few things. I also thought maybe surrounding myself with other writers would get the creative juices flowing. Well, I need to get the juices flowing for my two lesbian characters, if you know what I mean." Kendra suppressed a quiet laugh, her expression softening into a warm smile.

Maddie averted her eyes from Kendra's and swallowed the rest of her pills, the bitter residue lingering on her tongue. Her heart sped up as she considered a flirty response. "Maybe this weekend you'll discover ways to get those juices flowing."

"A girl can certainly hope for that." Kendra smirked and took another sip of tea. The playful look in her eyes took Maddie by surprise, but then Kendra went right back to being serious and inquisitive. "So, what sort of essays do you write?"

"Mostly lyrical essays and narratives. I'm just now easing back into it. I thought I was ready to start writing a few months after my surgery, but then about eight months after the initial diagnosis, there was a tiny spot that showed up on the MRI. So, a specialist in radiology oncology did a special type of non-invasive robotic radiotherapy."

"Is that a type of radiation?"

"Actually, much stronger than regular radiation and more targeted to the precise location of the tumor. It got rid of the new growth with a laser."

"Wow, lasers and robots?" Kendra raised her brow and smiled. "Very futuristic."

Maddie laughed in genuine amusement. "That's what I called it too but was very quickly corrected and told it's actually a linear accelerator."

"Not as catchy, though. Please tell me you at least told the cancer, 'I'll be back.'"

Maddie laughed again. "I wish I had! I didn't think of it at the time. I was just so happy the treatment worked."

Kendra gave Maddie's arm yet another quick squeeze. "It's amazing how much treatments have advanced. But that's all in the past, right? I mean, the cancer treatment."

Acutely aware of the odds for brain cancer, Maddie knew she was living on borrowed time. She cleared her throat and leaned forward. "No, I still get treatment once a week." Maddie provided a rundown of the IV drug bevacizumab and how it blocked a particular protein that prevented growth of new blood vessels, including those that fed tumors. "My oncologist and I call it B-vac. Much easier to say."

Kendra gave her an affirmative nod. "It definitely is. So, they're trying to starve your tumor. Hopefully there aren't too many side effects." Kendra didn't take her eyes off Maddie, her tone so earnest and caring.

"Just some occasional nosebleeds, bleeding gums, and high blood pressure. Sometimes bad diarrhea." Maddie lowered her head, her face quickly getting hot. Did she really just tell Kendra about her occasional diarrhea? Maddie was sure Kendra noticed that she was blushing. "But, it's nothing like what I went through when I was on the harsh chemo. This drug doesn't cause hair loss like the other chemo did."

Kendra nodded slowly. "That's good. Losing my hair was hard emotionally at first, but I finally didn't give a fuck that I was bald since I just wanted to be cancer-free. Fortunately, my hair grew back thicker than before." She laughed quietly. "That's good the side effects aren't too bad."

Maddie took another sip of coffee. Normally pretty private about her cancer treatment, she was so comfortable sharing these details with Kendra since she too had been through the same thing. "The long-term effects can potentially be bad, but…most patients with my type of brain cancer don't live long enough to reach the point of the drug causing any serious long-term effects. At least that's what I read online."

Kendra reached over to clasp both hands around Maddie's. "One day at a time. Sometimes I think we should stay off the Internet and not read about the scary stuff. I don't know about you, but I scoured the Internet to read everything I could about my cancer. We should have medical degrees after all the information we've learned, huh?" Kendra squeezed Maddie's hands again.

"Yeah, I became really good at deciphering the information in medical journals." Maddie inhaled the fresh ocean air and smiled. Kendra's hands were so soft and warm. "And maybe you're right about not reading about the scary stuff. What I first read about my type of cancer terrified me. The average survival rate of people with grade four glioblastoma is about a year and a half, and there's only a thirty percent chance of living more than two years. As of right now, I've far exceeded the original prognosis for patients with this type of brain cancer." Maddie pulled her hands away from Kendra's and gripped her coffee mug.

"That's amazing! When I was first diagnosed, I searched the Internet for the best treatment options for my type of breast cancer. When my doctor said I had triple-negative breast cancer, I thought maybe that was a good sign, like it meant I didn't test positive for a really bad kind of breast cancer. Turns out triple-negative is much more aggressive. I was only twenty-seven when I was diagnosed, which is never a good sign when it comes to breast cancer. The younger the age, the worse the prognosis. But, after being brought to death's doorstep, I survived."

"That's wonderful. So, you're in remission now?" Always comforted to hear about someone beating cancer, Maddie wanted to know more about Kendra's success story.

"Pretty much. I still see my oncologist for check-ups. I'm in the clear for the most part, but you know the odds. Anyone who's had radiation for cancer has a higher risk of developing a different type of cancer years later." Kendra twirled the ring around her finger a couple times, then clasped her hands together.

"Like you said, one day at a time." Maddie grinned.

They moved onto the subject of travel and, from there, to food, family, and their favorite seasons. It turned out they both loved summer, but Kendra equally loved winter when she could wear cute boots and sweaters.

"It's also the best time for hot cocoa by the fire!" Kendra said with a laugh.

"For me, winters usually meant really awesome surf conditions." Maddie looked at Kendra and smiled. "But hot cocoa by the firepit was always nice after getting out of the chilly ocean." She rested her elbows on the table and relaxed her chin in her hands. Out on the ocean, breakers formed in the distance. Huge waves tumbled onto the rocky shore. In the tree above the deck, the blue jays squawked and flitted down to the bird bath while a couple squirrels scurried over the roots of the tree.

Several people gathered around the entrance to the lodge where meals were served. Matt was among them, standing by the door and chatting with a young woman. Maddie waved to acknowledge him. It was nearly eight-thirty and the breakfast line would open soon, yet Maddie didn't want this time with Kendra to end. Although she'd spoken with many cancer survivors, she'd never connected with any of them like this.

As the sun ascended in the sky, the morning quickly lost its chill. Maddie removed her beanie and fluffed her hair in an attempt to hide the scar. She loosened the scarf from her neck and unzipped her sweatshirt. Likewise, Kendra opened up the front of her jacket, revealing a tight-fitting V-neck shirt—the thin cotton material snug across her chest. Maddie noticed Kendra's perky breasts but quickly averted her eyes. It'd been a long time since she'd been attracted to a woman, let alone admired one, because her life was consumed by cancer treatments. Long before she came out, she had a thing for large-breasted women, but here she was checking out a breast cancer survivor's reconstructed breasts and felt really awkward for having appreciated her ample bosom.

Kendra peered at the coastline, then looked at Maddie and smiled. "You've picked a perfect spot to enjoy such a beautiful morning. I love the ocean. Never like to be far from the coast."

A huge smile crept across Maddie's face. "Same with me! I can't ever see myself living anywhere not by the beach. The views here are breathtaking."

"I've always loved staying here. Is this your first time at Monarch Bluffs?"

"Yes, but hopefully not my last. In some ways this

place reminds me of a camp for adults," Maddie said, her thoughts drifting back to being a kid and going to camp in Mississippi. She'd never forget the last time she stayed there—the memories much too vivid to ever fade. "Are you here with anyone?"

"Nope, I'm here all by my lonesome. My dad paid for my trip and insisted on putting me up in Chrysalis Cottage right on the cliff, overlooking the ocean."

Maddie only barely remembered her manners and kept her surprise in check. Luxurious Chrysalis Cottage was one of the most expensive lodging options here. At well over two thousand dollars for the weekend, it was a stark difference to the eight hundred or so dollars Maddie spent to share a room with Dot.

"How about you?" Kendra asked. "You here with anyone?"

"I'm here with my friend Dot. She teaches at one of the colleges where I work, but we met several years ago at a conference. We're in one of those shared rooms up past the garden."

"That's right. I did see someone with you last night after they cleared the tent and assisted you."

"You mean when Dot embarrassed me by summoning a paramedic in the crowd?" Maddie shook her head and rolled her eyes.

"You two seem close. I thought she might've been your partner or your wife."

"My wife? Oh, God no. She's just my kooky friend. You'll meet her soon when she brings me my breakfast. I texted her earlier to ask her to fill a plate with whatever they're serving today." Maddie glanced at the crowd to see if Dot was there. "Even if she did date women, I don't think I could handle being around her all the time. She's a hoot, but the woman wears on me after a while. Plus, she's twenty years older. I'm not attracted to women that much older."

"Well, I wish I wasn't." Kendra pursed her lips and examined her hands. "Ended up in a relationship with an older woman. Much older, actually."

Now that was an intriguing statement. Should Maddie ask for more information? Or was it too soon in their friendship? Before Maddie could decide, the door to the lodge thudded open and shut a few times as people exited carrying plates heaped with scrambled eggs, toast, roasted potatoes, and grits. Maddie eyed the creamy grits on a woman's plate as she passed by. When sick from the chemo, Maddie had only been able to tolerate a few things: toast, saltine crackers, scrambled eggs, and cheesy grits like her mom made. Drew attempted to make Southern grits for Maddie, but they turned out watery and bland. When her mother came up to care for Maddie during the worst part of her treatment, she'd made this for her every morning. The warm grits had filled her stomach and eased the nausea a bit.

"If you want to get something to eat," Maddie said to Kendra, "I'll save your seat so no one takes it."

"Thanks for the offer." Kendra's smile became mischievous. "But if there's one thing I've learned from coming to Monarch Bluffs, you need to be first in line for food or wait until the crowd has thinned. Otherwise, you'll be standing for longer than you'll be eating."

A swarm of people clomped across the deck and set their plates on the glass-top tables. The tinny sound of metal utensils on the glass surface was grating, and Maddie immediately craved the serenity she had moments ago with Kendra. Soon, nearly every table was full. A hand clasped Maddie's shoulder, and she looked up to see Matt and the young woman to whom he'd been speaking.

"How are you feeling this morning?" Matt set his plate on the table and settled in the chair next to Maddie.

"I feel pretty good today. No headache at the moment, no lightheadedness, only the usual tiredness."

"You and me both." Matt laughed and glanced at the woman next to him. "I didn't get to bed until three."

"Oh? Fun night?" Maddie whispered then nudged him in the shoulder.

"Not what you think, but I'm hoping," Matt whispered back and grinned. "In case we don't get much of a chance to chat later today or tomorrow, I wanted to give you my email address and phone number." He handed Maddie a folded piece of paper. "I know I barely even know you, but I'd really like to hear how your next doctor's appointment goes and find out about your MRI results."

"Thank you. I'll keep you updated." Maddie slipped the folded paper with Matt's information into the side pouch of her laptop case. Another young guy approached the table to join Matt. Soon, the conversation got lively as everyone wolfed down their food. The savory aroma from the grits and roasted potatoes wafted up from the table, and now Maddie's stomach growled.

Dot approached with two plates and a bowl in her hands. She set a plate of food in front of Maddie, who fervently thanked her, and plopped down in a chair at the end of the table.

"I got your favorites—cheesy grits, roasted potatoes, and scrambled eggs." Dot retrieved napkins and utensils from her pocket. "I wasn't sure if you also wanted oatmeal, so I got that just in case. Added some honey and raisins. I must've looked utterly piggish as I loaded up two platefuls of food and a huge bowl of oatmeal. But I got myself as close to an English breakfast as I could find. Also stopped by the gift shop to get some of that strawberry-rhubarb jam they make here." Dot set a jar of preserves on the table, then cracked a soft-boiled egg, mashed it onto a piece of toast, and added salt and pepper.

Maddie shoved a forkful of grits in her mouth. "This is a lot of food. Maybe Kendra would like some of these oats?"

"Sure, one of my Monarch Bluffs favorites." Kendra mixed the honey and raisins into the oats, and then savored a big spoonful.

Dot picked up her toast. "How ya doin', Mad? Having a nice morning?" She took a loud, crunchy bite off the corner.

Maddie looked up to find Kendra smiling at her. "It's been a great morning. Perfect, actually."

Dot laughed quietly. "Told you this place was amazing. I went to the baths early this morning. Absolutely divine! You really oughta venture down there today."

"I plan to head down there again tonight," Kendra said, not taking her eyes off Maddie. "The full moon over the ocean is beautiful from the hot springs, a sight you won't want to miss while you're here."

Maddie didn't say anything and instead continued to savor her grits while the conversation at the table increased in volume. Kendra had already devoured most of the oats, and many of the plates at the table were scraped nearly clean.

With six people crowded around the table and a few of them gabbing at the same time, Maddie couldn't closely follow any of the conversations, but Matt mentioned something about a huge swell headed this way next week. When he described a storm way out in the ocean and massive waves headed to the California coast, Maddie peered at the horizon. Ever since she was a teen, she could predict the rising swell and anticipate when the surf would magnify in size. With only a slight ripple on the surface of the water in the distance, Maddie guessed the swell wouldn't be here until late next week.

Matt and the others continued to chat while they finished their food, which reminded Maddie of mornings at the kitchen table in San Clemente when she was a kid. While her cousins talked about school, sports, or the beach, the adults also carried on their own conversations all at once. The mix of Chinese and English spoken during mealtimes often created frenzied chatter. Maddie learned early on to be more of an observer than a participant in those discussions, similar to how she behaved in school.

Right now, Maddie tried to follow three conversations at once, still missing the mellow vibes she and Kendra shared moments ago. With the first writing workshop session about to start, several people filed out of the dining area and up the steps to one of the meeting rooms. And just like that, Maddie's serene morning with Kendra was over.

The fog had dissipated into wispy clouds far above the horizon. Below the cliff, the ocean shimmered from the morning sunlight. Mesmerized by the glint of light on the ocean, Maddie became drowsy now that the anti-seizure medication had entered her bloodstream, but a sharp pain at the base of her skull jolted her awake. It was strong enough to cause her to gasp. Maddie leaned forward and rubbed her neck. Worried about what these headaches might indicate, she took a few deep breaths—her exhales matching the rhythm of the waves as they surged closer to shore.

Chapter Four

Big Sur: October 2018

"But she's married." Maddie gripped her walking stick as she took careful steps down the steep ramp leading to the baths. With the fog overhead, the moon barely peeked through the clouds, making it hard for Maddie to see the path.

"Mad, so are you." Dot shone her flashlight on the ground, barely illuminating the walkway.

"That's different. You don't see a ring on my finger." After so many people had raved about soaking in the baths, Maddie decided to give it a try, despite being nervous about stripping down naked in front of strangers. Kendra might even be there, but whether that would make things easier or harder, Maddie didn't know.

Dot huffed and flailed an arm in the air. "Ah, these days, rings don't mean a damned thing. You ever see me wear mine?"

"That's because you've got your hands in paint or clay all the time."

"I stopped wearing that ring way before I was an artist. Besides, after nearly thirty years with Peter, it's not like we need wedding bands to prove our commitment."

"Looks to me like Kendra wears her ring with pride, like she's making a clear statement." If Maddie wore a wedding ring, it'd be because she wanted to show the world that she had a life partner—someone she adored and who cherished her in return.

"So what if she's married?" Dot threw her arms apart, and the ring of light zoomed sideways, leaving the path in darkness. "You don't see her wife here, do you? That's rather telling, isn't it?" Dot pulled in her arms, and the flashlight returned to its original position. "And besides, why not just enjoy yourself? You two looked mighty engaged this morning at breakfast and again this afternoon after the poetry workshop, like you were having a marvelous time. If I had to guess, I'd say you're quite smitten with this woman."

"Smitten? We were just comparing cancer stories, sharing the highs and lows of being cancer survivors." How odd it was to refer to herself as a cancer survivor. Maddie had never used those words before to describe herself, but right now, she was living with brain cancer and not dying from it.

"Bonding over cancer." Dot nudged Maddie. "At least you've got something in common. Look, I know you well enough to recognize when you're smitten. You gotta admit she's quite attractive."

"Dottie, I am not smitten."

"Sure, that's definitely not why you changed your mind about going to the baths."

Maddie didn't need light to know Dot looked very smug right now, although she was glad the darkness hid her blush.

The beam of the flashlight zig-zagged as Dot adjusted her scarf. "We've been friends for a long time now, and this is only the third or fourth time I've seen you this intrigued by a woman you just met. Why not have a little fun this weekend, if you know what I mean."

Maddie knew exactly what Dot meant, but she was not usually the type to have one-night stands or sleep with someone without feeling the first stirrings of love. There would be no hooking up with Kendra. "She is very attractive, and we do have a lot in common, but you need to understand that I'm not about to get involved with a married woman again. You know how disastrous that was for me before."

"Yeah, especially since you were also married at the time." Dot shook her head and laughed.

"That was different. For the most part, Drew and I were essentially separated."

"But still married back then as you are now."

"You know our situation is different. Drew may not be my soul mate, but I did love him at one time…as much as a closeted lesbian could love a straight man. He's been a loving father to Taylor and a good husband, the type of person anyone with terminal cancer could hope to have by her side."

"Mad, for God's sake, you're not terminal. Your MRIs keep coming back clear, and you've more than exceeded all the doctors' prognoses."

"But it's probably just a matter of time until the cancer—"

"Right now, you're cancer free, right? Just enjoy yourself once we get down to the baths. With any bit of luck, you'll see Kendra there tonight. You're just here to have fun. Kendra is different than Callie. For one thing, she's a lesbian. Callie didn't know which way she wanted to go."

"I do feel ready to be in a committed relationship again, but it has to be with someone who's a hundred percent available."

"Who said Kendra has to be someone you end up with in the long-term?" Dot removed a flask from her satchel and took a long slurp, then handed it to Maddie. "Here, have some merlot. It's from that winery in Napa that you like. Anyway, married or not, you can at least enjoy time with her this weekend. Or what's left of it."

"Liquid courage, huh? I'll need it if I'm actually gonna strip off my clothes and sit naked in a hot tub with you and God knows who else." Maddie paused next to a fence and took a couple sips of merlot. They were now only a few paces from the stairway leading to the hot springs. The nearby coastline was a misty blur since the fog still hid the moon overhead.

Dot retrieved the flask and took another long slurp. "Mad, I bet you'll find the experience liberating."

"Who cares about it being liberating? I'm doing this because it might help with the neuropathy." Maddie grabbed the flask from Dot and took a couple more sips of wine, the alcohol loosening the tight muscles in her shoulders and neck, and easing her headache a bit. Far below the cliff, crashing breakers pummeled the shoreline. "I do enjoy long soaks in a bathtub. Just not with lots of other naked people around."

"Trust me when I say no one gives a shit about what your body looks like. But I've got something else that might help you." Dot retrieved a small bottle of whiskey from her satchel and handed it to Maddie. "Go ahead and put this in your bag. It's all for you. I'm gonna lay off the hard stuff tonight. The marinara sauce from dinner gave me awful heartburn."

"Maybe we oughta head back to the room. I've got antacid in my medicine kit. Besides, I'd like to work on that essay I started at tonight's workshop." Winded and lethargic, Maddie winced from the intense pain in her feet. Be it neuropathy or edema, the discomfort slowed her down more than usual tonight. It might be best if she returned to her room to work on her narrative essay. The workshop had been about using food as a way to connect to readers. Bubbling with enthusiasm, Maddie had started to write about working at Royal Palace, her family's restaurant, when she was a teenager.

"We can write later tonight or else in the morning. You can't very well be at Monarch Bluffs and not have the full experience if you don't soak in the baths. The heated water comes directly from the earth and is said to be healing to the muscles, the circulatory system, and the endocrine system." Dot let out a belch and patted her chest.

"What about the digestive system? Can the waters help with that?" Maddie smirked.

Dot chuckled. "I bet it's a cure-all for many issues. You'll feel like a new woman after a good soak. Let's get to the baths before the best one gets too crowded."

Dot was right. Maddie could work on her essay later tonight. They continued down the uneven terrain to the stairs. The air coming from the hot springs area was humid. Maddie gripped the handrail and trudged down the stone steps—the smell of sulfur so pungent it made her eyes water.

The changing area was barely lit, thankfully. Maddie and Dot hung their hoodies on hooks and scooted their shoes under the wooden slatted bench. The roof was made of stone, but much of the sea-foam green sliding wall was open to the ocean, with only a sturdy metal fence between them and the waves. It was so quiet here, with the roar of the surf much louder than any sound made indoors.

A few feet away, two women rinsed off in the open-air showers. Maddie lowered her gaze to the floor, but marveled at everyone's openness while they showered or tromped through the changing area totally naked. When no one was in the near vicinity, Maddie reached into her canvas bag to retrieve the bottle of whiskey and took a swig. The whiskey burned in her mouth and down her throat. She furtively looked around to make sure no one was watching and took another couple sips. Although Doctor Lau said drinking alcohol in moderation was fine with the meds she took, Maddie knew her limits and usually restricted herself to one glass of wine a couple evenings a week. It'd been a while since she'd had hard liquor.

Within seconds, Dot stripped down naked and wedged a towel under her arm, not even bothering to cover up. She marched over to the showers and rinsed off. From only a few feet away, Maddie smelled the lavender liquid soap that Dot pumped from the dispenser.

Tipsy and foggy headed, Maddie slipped out of her sweatpants and hid them under the ledge by her flip-flops. Sufficiently buzzed, she sat down and leaned her head against the wall as she listened to the crashing waves. A cold draft wafted through the open-air showers.

Maddie finally peeled off her T-shirt and set it on her sweats. While she waited for Dot to finish showering, Maddie gazed at the dark ocean and set her fingers on the scar above her left breast. She palpated the port under the skin. Used for blood draws and the administration of IV meds, the protrusion from the portacath and the scar were reminders of how much her body had changed in the past four years. When she had the harsh chemo, the first drug they tried gave her a severe rash all over her chest and neck. After a round of prednisone and antihistamines for two weeks, the rash disappeared but left her skin mottled and prone to irritation from soaps and overly hot water.

Although Maddie was still slim like she'd been all her life, cancer and chemo had taken a toll on her body. Her dry and flaky skin sagged in some places, and her muscles weren't as firm as they used to be. Her feet and ankles were swollen. Each toe looked like a Vienna sausage, and the skin on top of her feet was shiny and taut. Her toenails were thick and yellow, similar to her grandmother's. In her eighties now, Popo walked hunched over and often limped, much like Maddie these past couple years. In what should be the prime of her life, Maddie often felt older than Popo. Maybe the magical baths of Monarch Bluffs could restore some of her energy.

Dot returned to the changing area. Maddie took a deep breath. It was now or never. She quickly removed her bra and panties, then just as quickly wrapped a towel around her body and followed Dot out of the changing area. When Maddie took a step on the hard cement floor, intense pain shot through both feet. She really hoped the baths had actual healing properties. "How far of a walk is it to the hot tub?"

"The best one's way past this first hot tub and down some stairs." Dot stopped at a water fountain and filled two paper cups with water and handed one to Maddie. "Here. I know from experience that the baths make you thirsty."

Once they maneuvered past a hot tub on the left, they descended the stairs. There was nothing over their heads now. The only roof was the open sky. With her hand gripped on the railing, Maddie looked up to see moonlight forcing its way through the fog and casting bright strobes onto the crashing surf. The steady rhythm of the surging waves below the cliff soothed Maddie as she peered at the moonlit ocean. Dot walked ahead a few paces. Maddie headed down the stairs until she reached Dot, but there next to the fence was Kendra!

And she wasn't wearing a stitch of clothing—the moonlight casting soft rays of light on her bare skin. "Maddie!" Kendra's smile was warm and welcoming. "Glad you decided to come down to the baths."

Maddie swallowed hard. "Hi," was all she managed to say. Her heart was thrumming wildly, and her knees got weak. She dropped her gaze to the floor and pulled the towel tighter across her chest.

Dot headed back toward the stairs. "This heartburn is getting worse. I'm going to pop back to my room and get some of those chewable cherry-flavored antacids. Kendra, you'll take care of my girl here, won't you? If she gets dizzy, make sure she gets out of the water. She's a stubborn one, but she'll listen to you. And call security for a golf cart to get her up that hill if she's too weak to walk."

Maddie glared at Dot. So that's why she'd been so insistent about coming to the baths. Maddie opened her mouth to deliver a scathing lecture, but Dot took off before she could respond.

Kendra lightly brushed her hand against Maddie's. "The tub over here is the best one. It's got a stunning view of the moonlight over the ocean." Kendra motioned toward a stone wall next to a square bath, then took the cup from Maddie's hand. "The water is really hot. Let me know if it's too much for you. You need help getting in?" Kendra stepped into the water but remained close to the steps.

Maddie's knees shook. "No, I should be okay, but thanks." She dropped her towel and quickly entered the water, the heat causing her to gasp as the scorching temperature scalded her skin. Maddie winced but managed to situate herself on a ledge a couple feet away from Kendra. The coarse stone was rough against her butt and legs.

As the surf crashed on the rocks below the cliff, Maddie relaxed a little. Kendra was quiet. Be it the booze or the hot mineral springs, the tension in Maddie's neck and shoulders melted away, but the water was unbearably hot. Sweat poured from her face. "This water feels like it's a hundred degrees," she said, the words coming out in a gasp.

Kendra scooted closer to Maddie. "Actually, right now it's probably around a hundred and five. This is usually the hottest tub since it's got the biggest spigot directly connected to the thermal hot springs from deep under the earth. The water comes out of that thing at a hundred and nineteen degrees."

"No wonder I'm so overheated." Maddie let out a nervous laugh and reached for her cup of water and took a few sips.

"It helps to sit up and let the chilly ocean air cool you

down." Kendra sat up on the ledge with just her lower legs in the water.

Lightheaded and woozy, Maddie took another sip of water and hoisted her body up on the ledge. Kendra was right. The breeze cooled her face, making her feel less hot. A gentle breeze chilled her arms and chest, causing her nipples to harden. The surf pounded on the shore far below the cliff. By now the fog had completely lifted, leaving the sky dark but clear. With the moonlight reflected on the dark ocean, Maddie could see the phosphorescent breakers crashing onto the jagged rocks. "Wow," she said under her breath. Kendra was right about the view. Maddie was less overheated, but between the wine and the whiskey, her head spun.

Maddie leaned forward and folded her arms to try and cover her breasts, but the gesture did nothing more than make her look awkward and contorted. She felt exposed and vulnerable with the moon shining on her nakedness, so she plopped back into the water, and Kendra did the same. It'd been so long since she'd been naked with a woman in a tub, but this situation was far different than anything she'd ever experienced. She couldn't bring herself to look at Kendra. They hardly knew each other, and yet here they sat naked in a hot tub. Maddie hadn't been this nervous in a long time.

Maddie kept her gaze on the dark sky. "You were right about the full moon on the ocean. Definitely worth it to come down here tonight." She took a deep breath and let it out slowly.

Kendra scooted closer to Maddie, so close that her arm brushed against hers under the water. "Couldn't ask for a better night."

"I love hearing the waves crash on shore." Maddie was a little dizzy. The wine, whiskey, and 105-degree water had turned her into a limp noodle. But Dot was right. It was so dark that no one could really see much here in the tub. To be naked under the moonlight while the waves crashed below the cliff was something she never imagined experiencing. Rather than feel exposed and vulnerable, Maddie suddenly felt carefree. The lack of clothes had a strange effect on her—as if most of her worries had been stripped away. Plus, it was thrilling to be here with such a gorgeous woman.

"Glad you made the trek down the hill," Kendra said.

"Me too." Maddie found herself with a silly grin on her face. Didn't matter that Kendra couldn't see it.

"After all we've been through with our various treatments, it's the simple pleasures like this that mean the most."

As Maddie formulated a few words in her head to reveal to Kendra more about her cancer, three women tromped down the stone steps and plunked into the hot tub. Rotund and raucous, the ladies quickly turned the serene evening into a gab fest as they talked loudly about the government. Disappointed to no longer be alone with Kendra, Maddie acknowledged the women's presence with a quick nod, aware that her scowl couldn't be seen in the darkness.

While the women blathered on about the ineptness of the current president and his as-inept administration, Maddie schemed of ways to slip out of the water and back to her room. Sweat poured from her face; her heartbeat increased. Still buzzed from the wine and whiskey, Maddie knew she had to get out of here soon. It was disappointing she couldn't stay and enjoy the healing effects of the mineral springs, but Maddie had to get out of here before things got worse. The intensely hot water and loud chatter were too much. Her headache had returned, so she leaned forward and rubbed her neck.

"You okay?" Kendra asked, her voice full of concern.

"My headache is back. Well, it probably never went away entirely." Maddie closed her eyes and continued to rub her neck, but was startled when Kendra set her hand on her head and massaged her scalp. The pressure was firm yet nurturing—the gentle touch easing the pain a bit.

"Hope you don't mind. Sometimes a little neck and head massage will make the pain go away fast."

"I don't mind. It feels nice, thanks."

"I used to get horrible migraines after chemo." Kendra moved her hand a little lower, somehow knowing the spot above the nape of Maddie's neck needed an extra massage. "Nothing would relieve the pain. Between the headaches and the vomiting, I thought I'd never get through it. In fact, there were times when I didn't think I'd wake up the next day."

"I've had many of those sorts of moments. More than I could ever count." Maddie was lightheaded and weak, but her headache wasn't nearly as bad now.

Kendra dropped her hand and scooted closer to Maddie, their hips and thighs touching. While Kendra's bare skin against her own was startling, Maddie resisted the urge to move away. The truth was she did want Kendra's touch. She glanced at Kendra, unwilling to tell her the heat was making her feel sick and weak. Maddie didn't want Kendra to see her as an invalid, someone who couldn't even walk up a flight of stairs, but this was a cancer survivor next to her—someone who'd likely experienced many moments of weakness.

As if by magic, Kendra knew exactly what to say. "Let's get out of here," she whispered in Maddie's ear.

"I'm not sure I can get out of the water without help," Maddie managed to say, her voice so faint.

"I'll help you." Kendra slipped her hand in Maddie's and guided her out of the bath until they were both at the metal railing. "We can call security to have them drive us up the ramp in a golf cart."

The night air immediately began cooling Maddie's overheated skin. The dizziness subsided, but the weakness remained. "I hate that I can't even walk back to the lodge or to my room without assistance."

"It's okay. It'll get us up there faster. Plus, I've got an idea for what we can do later." Kendra kept her hand firmly grasped in Maddie's.

"That sounds intriguing. What do you have in mind?" Maddie let go of Kendra's hand, then retrieved her towel from the railing, noticing Kendra's smooth, shimmering skin—the moonlight on her wet body so beautiful in the dim light.

"You'll see." There was a mischievous tone in Kendra's voice. Not at all modest, she stood there naked while she leaned on the railing and looked out toward the ocean.

Maddie turned her back and secured the towel around

her body. With no warning, another bout of weakness flooded her body. Be it the alcohol or the 105-degree water, Maddie didn't know, but she lost her balance once again and gripped the railing. Kendra reached out a hand to help steady her. Hand-in-hand, Maddie and Kendra returned to the changing area where they quickly got back into their clothes.

The cool, salty ocean air was bracing and chased away any lingering weakness. Maddie savored the warmth of her hoodie and wondered what the rest of the night would entail. Kendra had refused to reveal her plan, although her eyes had glimmered in mischief. But for the first time in a long while, Maddie didn't fret about the intense headache or the results of her next brain scan. Maddie would simply enjoy whatever the night brought her way. At four years post-diagnosis, she was living well beyond borrowed time. She and Kendra had tonight, and for now, that was all that mattered.

Chapter Five

Big Sur: October 2018

The security guard dropped off Maddie and Kendra at the top of the ramp. Kendra offered Maddie her elbow, which Maddie gratefully accepted since she was still feeling light-headed. They walked down a dirt path and then past the koi pond until they got about ten feet from the outer ring of benches around a big fire pit. Even from this distance, Maddie could feel the heat radiating from the embers. Beyond the cliff, huge waves crashed onto the shore. The moon illuminated the breakers as they moved closer to the beach, reminding Maddie of the times when she surfed under the moonlight in Southern California.

Winded from the trek along the path, Maddie stopped to catch her breath while Kendra talked about her new book. Less buzzed now and steadier on her feet, Maddie released her grip from the crook of Kendra's arm.

"I might branch out a bit and have the book take place somewhere other than California." Kendra zipped up her hoodie and shoved her hands in the pockets. "I'm considering Hawaii, maybe one of the smaller islands. My dad's company is opening a new hotel on Maui. He says he'll fly me out on his jet so I can spend a little time learning about Hawaiian culture. But I'm not sure Maui is where I want my novel to take place, since it'll be a historical romance with lots of details about old Hawaii."

By now, Maddie had figured out Kendra was a rich daddy's girl—the type of woman she usually avoided. Kendra was clearly interested in learning about Hawaii, though, so Maddie took the opportunity to share some knowledge. "Maui's becoming much more commercialized with all the new hotels, especially in Kapalua and Kaanapali where your dad is likely opening a hotel. Those areas of Maui aren't the best representation of Hawaiian culture, especially if you're planning to focus on old Hawaii." Maddie pulled her scarf closer to her neck.

"That's good to know." Kendra shrugged. "Even though my dad can be somewhat of an asshole, I'm grateful for his financial help, especially when I went through my treatment. Might as well take him up on his offer to fly me over to Hawaii. My dad's not too keen on me writing a sapphic historical romance, but for now I don't have to tell him much." Kendra waved her arm toward a bench near the fire pit. "Let's sit for a bit. There's an empty spot over there."

Maddie gave her a sideways glance. "So, I take it he's not your biggest fan?" She sat on the bench, facing the fire.

Kendra sat next to Maddie—so close that their bodies were touching. "He's never read anything I've written. Says he'd rather not know any details about what I write. He had a hard time when I came out but eventually got to a point where he tolerated it, but he'd rather me not have a career focused on queer-themed books. He'd prefer that I help him run his business."

"Sounds like job security to me."

"It was always my goal to someday take over his company. I even got a degree in business administration and another one in finance since I figured that was my career path. My dad was pushing me to get my MBA, said he'd pay for grad school like he paid for my undergraduate degrees. Then I got breast cancer, and my priorities radically shifted. But now that I'm cancer-free, my dad seems to think I've got my whole future ahead of me and that I should follow in his footsteps and be a hotel developer." Kendra scoffed and glanced at the flickering flames from the fire pit.

"It's interesting that even when we're adults, our parents still seem to think they know what's best for us."

"We'll always be their little girls, huh? Now that I'm done with treatment and am well past the scary years, I'm not sure I want my dad to continue overseeing my life. But, I'd definitely like to go back to Hawaii, especially since my dad will be there a lot in the next couple years. Might as well catch a ride in his jet. I'm the type of writer who has to get a good feel for the setting of my story before I start to write it, but my guess is there aren't a lot of places on the islands that still look like Hawaii in the 1940s."

Maddie had never known anyone who flew on a private jet. At best, Maddie upgraded to business class if she had enough frequent flyer miles, but she'd never even flown first class. "Must be nice to just hop on a private jet and soar on over to Hawaii. You might as well island-hop while you're there. But places on the north side of Oahu still have the old Hawaii feel to them, especially if you go to some of the old towns." Kendra obviously lived a life of privilege—so different than the frugal life of a part-time English professor who struggled to make ends meet. But right now, there was no harm in Maddie enjoying some time with Kendra. She'd already placed her into the friend category—a fellow cancer survivor, someone who could relate to the long-term effects of chemo, radiation, and surgery.

"Oh?" Kendra raised her brow. "That's interesting. I went to Oahu once with my ex. Wasn't all that impressed with the busyness of the island. For the setting of my book, I'm thinking about something more isolated, maybe one of the smaller islands, but I guess a little town in a remote part of Oahu might work for the story I have in mind."

"What do you have in mind?" Maddie asked.

Kendra's eyes lit up, just as they did when describing her ideas in the short story workshop. "I really want to write about someone who loves where she lives and never wants to leave. I see her as being really into music, maybe jazz, especially since the book will be set in the post-World War Two era. A tight-knit community would work well since she's a bit of a wild woman who thrives on excitement and goes against the grain. I've always been a California girl, so I have no idea what it's like to grow up in Hawaii."

The crisp autumn air stung Maddie's skin. Tall flames and red embers glowed from the fire pit. Assuming they were here to sit by the fire, and possibly get a cup of tea from the lodge, she was less nervous about whatever plan Kendra had in mind. Earlier, Maddie had visions of seductive embraces under the moonlight—things she'd normally never do with a woman she just met—but right now she just wanted to chat next to the warm fire.

"If you need information about Hawaiian culture, I can connect you with some of the locals over there. I've got family on a couple of the islands. Remind me to give you my number and email address before we leave tomorrow." Maddie felt somewhat forward in saying that, but she reasoned that this was just one writer to another assisting in gathering information for a book.

"Thanks, I'll definitely take you up on that. Are you Hawaiian?" Kendra leaned closer, and a lock of hair fell across her cheek.

Maddie laughed softly. "I get that a lot. No, my mom's Chinese, and my dad is…or was a blond-haired guy from the south. He died when I was a baby, killed in a war. My mom never liked to talk about it."

"That must've been hard, not having a dad when you were a kid."

"No, not really," Maddie lied and kept her gaze on the embers. "As a child, I used to look at the one and only photo I had of him and wonder if I was anything like him." She took her phone out of her back pocket and scrolled through the photos until she found the one of her father. "It's not the best resolution, but I took a picture of the photo I used to keep in my desk drawer as a kid. That's my dad, Lance Corporal Ben Rudolph of the U.S. Marines. This was taken shortly before he died in combat."

Kendra leaned in close to get a good look at the photo, her arm brushing against Maddie's and her face incredibly beautiful in the flickering light of the fire. "Handsome guy. Looks like you got your smile and height from him."

"That's probably all I got from him. I always thought that if my father had lived, life would've been a whole lot different for me."

A serious look washed over Kendra's face. "My parents split when I was eight. For most of my childhood, my dad was never around. He reentered my life when I was a teenager, but we've never had a close bond. He's always been the type to think he can buy my love. As a teenager, I certainly didn't turn away any of his gifts, but I missed having a fun and loving father like most of my friends had."

That sort of upbringing sounded lonely. At least Maddie had received a lot of love from Mom and Kai over the years. "It's sad your dad wasn't around for the fun stuff. When I was a child, I got used to not having a dad, but Kai was like a father to me during my teenage years. His family quickly became my *ohana*."

"*Ohana* sounds Hawaiian." Kendra cocked her head and laughed. "I oughta be taking notes right now if I'm really gonna have my next book be set in Hawaii."

"*Ohana* means family, but it doesn't necessarily only mean blood family. For example, sometimes someone will decide to informally adopt someone into their family. That person becomes their *hānai* son or daughter. I've been Kai's *hānai* daughter since I was a teenager. I wrote about this at the afternoon workshop but didn't feel brave enough to read it out loud."

"That's really cool. I'd love to read it."

"Sure. It's mainly about the first time Kai took me surfing and focuses a little on his Hawaiian background."

"Sounds intriguing. I've always been interested in Hawaiian culture. I recently did a bit of research and came across some interesting details from the forties, but obviously I've got a long way to go to understand Hawaiian culture and language. The extent of my Hawaiian is *aloha* and *mahalo*."

"Kai taught me a bit of Hawaiian. Mostly basic phrases and words. One of the first words I learned was *keiki*, which means child, but Kai still calls me that once in a while. You might consider visiting Molokai, one of the smaller islands in Hawaii. I went there with Kai to visit his cousin Mark when I was a teen. You'll likely find it to be most reflective of old Hawaii."

"Thanks for helping me to get the creative juices flowing. Lots to consider. Maybe a trip to Hawaii is in my near future." Kendra grinned.

In the dim lighting, Maddie admired Kendra's creamy skin and blue eyes. When the moon hid behind the clouds and she couldn't see Kendra's face, Maddie was drawn to the sound of her sultry voice. So perhaps Dot was right—maybe Maddie was smitten.

But she quickly sobered up enough to realize what could happen with Kendra tonight. Or what shouldn't happen. Kendra had a wife. Maddie would not repeat the mistake of getting involved with a married woman. The relationship with Callie had lasted several months, each day filled with infatuation and longing, only to result in Maddie's heart being broken when Callie said she'd never leave her husband.

The fire continued to burn and crackle, the heat radiating onto Maddie's face. "You wanna move inside and have a cup of tea? Maybe they've got some of that apple cobbler left over."

"I've got a better idea." Kendra stood and reached for Maddie's hand. "I know of a place where we can be totally alone."

The dizziness Maddie experienced at the baths had diminished, leaving her clear-headed and aware she needed to be honest with Kendra and convince her instead to enjoy some chamomile tea and cobbler. Although the gorgeous woman holding Maddie's hand awakened a part of her she'd long since thought was dormant, Maddie had vowed to never get involved with a married woman again, even just for the weekend or for one night.

Maddie let go of Kendra's hand. "I'm not sure we should follow through with your plan. I don't think it's a good idea to—"

"How do you know it's not a good idea? You haven't even heard my plan." Kendra laughed, her voice soft but flirtatious. There was a mischievous look in her eyes, a look that scared Maddie.

Sober enough to realize it'd be best if they stayed here, where others sat and conversed, Maddie refused to look away. She had to do whatever she could to not give Kendra the wrong idea. "It's late, nearly midnight now, and I really oughta get some sleep."

"I won't keep you up too late," Kendra said, her voice low and sultry. "I wanna do something I've always wanted to do. Just haven't had the nerve to do it until tonight."

Perplexed, Maddie had no idea what Kendra meant. Firm in her conviction to not cross any lines, she tried again to convince her that this was a bad idea. "Really, I should get to bed. I'm sure Dot is wondering where I am." Right when she was ready to be fully honest about why she wanted to cut the night short, Kendra intercepted the moment.

"Are you a rule follower...or a rule breaker?" Kendra cocked her head and stepped closer.

"I guess I'm usually a rule follower." Speaking of following rules, Maddie really should go, but then she noticed Kendra wasn't wearing her wedding ring. Maybe she left it in her room since the Monarch Bluffs brochure mentioned the sulfur in the hot springs could damage jewelry.

Kendra looked deep into Maddie's eyes and smiled. "Maybe it's time to change that."

It was time for Maddie to be direct. "Look, I know you're married. I saw your ring. Earlier, I mean. You're a really nice person, but I don't think we should—"

"I wear the ring to keep people from asking me out or hitting on me." Kendra wrung her hands and stared at her feet. All the humor had left her face.

Now that was a possibility Maddie had never considered. "You're not married? I just thought, with the ring and all."

"My wife left me when the cancer treatment got bad. She couldn't handle the whole...in sickness and in health thing. She broke up with me after my third chemo treatment, right when I was at my sickest." Kendra fell silent and sat back down on the bench.

Maddie gasped, appalled that a partner would be so heartless and leave when things got that rough. She sat next to Kendra—her body so warm next to Maddie's. "That must've been difficult, to go through a breakup while getting treatment for cancer. I can't imagine someone leaving when you were so sick."

"We still lived together during most of my cancer treatment. Separate rooms, of course. At that point, it felt like I had a roommate, but Bree was always a good provider when it came to covering the bills when I was too sick to work. She sometimes took me to my appointments, but she was never all that caring, which is odd because she's a doctor. Well, a pathologist. She works in a lab and rarely has contact with patients. Probably why her bedside manner sucks."

"I don't know what to say. That's awful." Maddie gave her an understanding smile as she thought about how Drew stepped up when she was at her sickest. There was no way she could have continued to teach. Mom and Kai helped out the best they could, but if it wasn't for Drew taking on extra music lessons beyond his usual teaching duties, Maddie wouldn't have made it.

Kendra got serious and stared at the flickering flames. "You know the piece I wrote this afternoon? About feeling alone even while you're with another? That was about Bree. A year or so after I found out I had cancer, Bree met someone. I didn't feel hurt or jealous, but I knew it wasn't right for her to live with me yet be involved with someone else, so that's when I moved in with my sister and niece. But, Bree leaving me right when my cancer got bad has left me tainted as far as ever getting married again."

"Ever?" Maddie's question came out louder than she'd intended, her tone tinged with disbelief.

"Yeah, ever." Kendra's shoulders slumped. "See, it wasn't just that Bree left me at the worst time in my life when I needed her the most. Even before that, it's like she'd left me emotionally."

Maddie had already figured out that Kendra could go from playful and chipper one moment to somber the next. Not sure if she should ask questions or stay quiet, Maddie decided to let Kendra lead the conversation.

"Before I got sick, Bree and I had pretty much emotionally gone our separate ways. She'd changed a lot since we first got together, but I stayed the same for the most part."

Maddie nodded in understanding. "It's amazing how

people can change so drastically, sometimes in good ways but often in bad ways. I'm definitely way different now than I was in my twenties when I carried on as if Drew and I had a normal heterosexual marriage. Even when I was with Ally, I was still pretty innocent when it came to being with a woman. Fortunately, I'm much surer of my sexuality now than I was back then."

Kendra clasped Maddie's arm and breathed out a soft laugh. "At least your change was positive. With Bree, it's as if she turned into a different person, someone I didn't like. I was young and naïve when I got married, only twenty-three. We separated seven years later."

Maddie liked the feel of Kendra's hand on her arm. The gentle way she touched her sent shivers through her body. "I'd say seven years is a pretty good stretch these days."

"Not if more than half those years were like living with a roommate. I was foolish to believe I'd be married to Bree till death do us part. More reason for me to believe 'happily ever after' only exists in rom-com movies and romance books. I can't imagine settling down with someone ever again. If I ever get sick again, I'd rather go through it alone." Kendra removed her hand from Maddie's arm.

Struck by Kendra's negative tone, Maddie considered the honesty of her words and thought about her own situation. More people had gathered around the fire, but everyone spoke in hushed voices. Maddie caught a whiff of weed. A few people clomped across the deck. Others sat by themselves and wrote in notebooks or on laptops. Maddie hadn't done much writing since she arrived yesterday except for the short exercises she did in the workshops. At the moment, she had no intentions of writing a new essay or poem, but the time here tonight with a romance novelist made her feel connected to one other writer.

Kendra let out a loud sigh. "Funny, but when I married Bree, I figured she'd not only be a great provider but also a deep, loving woman since she was so much older."

"How much older?" Intrigued by all these details, Maddie had so many more things she wanted to ask, but she would keep the questions to a minimum.

"Around twelve years. She was so together when it came to her career and money, but emotionally, she was pretty unevolved. Her bank account was way bigger than her heart could ever be. About midway through our marriage, I got used to doing things on my own. I didn't feel I had a partner." Kendra looked at Maddie and nudged her shoulder. "You're probably learning way more about me than you ever wanted to know."

"Well, we already bonded over cancer this morning at breakfast. I don't just tell anyone about my bouts of diarrhea and swollen ankles. I'd say at this point, no topic is off-limits."

"Good to know." Kendra shifted her body then straddled her legs around the bench and faced Maddie. "Don't know about you, but sometimes I'm grateful for the cancer."

"Grateful?" Maddie asked, her tone bitter. There was nothing about cancer that made her feel grateful. Cancer hadn't made her a better person. It'd made her scarred, jaded, and terrified.

"I just mean it's taught me to live in the moment and not fret about much. I've lived beyond the original prognosis. I'm in remission, a word any cancer patient longs to hear. Cancer gave me a whole new outlook on life, especially after Bree left me."

Maddie knew she'd likely never hear the word remission. At most, patients with her type of cancer extended their prognosis by months or maybe a few years if they were lucky. For tonight, Maddie would try to force the negative thoughts out of her head. Here she sat with a gorgeous woman by a warm fire under the moonlit sky, and she would do her best to stay in the moment and enjoy Kendra's presence.

"It's good you're not with an emotionally shallow person anymore," Maddie said, her brow furrowed. "Life's too short to be wasted on people like that, but it's during tragedies, traumas, and illnesses that one's partner should be there, no matter what." Since the fire was now too hot on her face, Maddie stood and sat back down with her legs on each side of the bench, facing Kendra.

Kendra hunched forward and clenched her hands around her arms. "Like I said, I'd gotten used to doing things solo and living life like I wasn't even married. Odd as this may sound, I'm now used to living this way, and it feels right to me. I guess I use my books to live vicariously through my characters. The whole 'happily ever after' just exists in the pages of my romance novels. It's a world I can control, not like my own love life, I guess."

Earlier, Maddie had put Kendra into the friend category, but now she realized they had something else in common besides cancer: they were both unattached. But Kendra had made it clear she had no interest in a relationship, no plans for a happily ever after with anyone ever again. This made Maddie relaxed and less awkward, more eager to enjoy tonight and not fret about tomorrow or next week or the following month.

"Have you...dated at all since your cancer treatment ended?" Maddie grimaced and hoped her question wasn't too forward.

"I wouldn't necessarily call it dating," Kendra said and smirked, her voice so playful. "I just can't imagine settling down with anyone ever again. Crazy as it sounds, my marriage with Bree got me in the habit of doing things on my own, but to others, we appeared to be fully committed to one another."

"Sounds like me and Drew. I guess in some ways, we still make decisions that a lot of married couples make, except he seems more like a cousin or a brother to me."

Someone put a couple more logs on the fire, which stirred up the flames and illuminated the area where they sat. Now that the fire was raging, Maddie had to squint from the brightness, but the coziness of the fire and the fresh ocean air made her open up even more. Feeling she might as well be up front with Kendra about having a pregnant teenage daughter, Maddie decided to admit she'd soon be a grandmother. "In a lot of ways, Drew and I still seem like a married couple, especially with how we raise our teenaged daughter. Well, our pregnant teenaged daughter."

Kendra's mouth flung open. "Pregnant? You hardly

seem old enough to be a grandma."

"I definitely don't feel old enough to be a grandma. Taylor's only sixteen. She's always been a good kid. The pregnancy is still so shocking to me. Haven't quite wrapped my head around being a grandmother in a few months."

"That baby will be lucky to have you as a grandma." Kendra nudged Maddie in the arm. "Always thought I'd have a kid by now, but that obviously didn't work out with me and Bree, and my ovaries are likely way too damaged from chemo for me to ever conceive a baby. But, I'm glad I finally realized that Bree leaving me was freeing, like I no longer had to pretend we were the perfect lesbian couple." Kendra's body went rigid, and a blank look washed over her face.

Bree had clearly left her with a lot of pain. Maddie gave her a warm smile. "Dating these days is so awkward and weird. Probably best to be alone."

"Yeah, probably so. Sometimes I miss those sweet moments shared between two people in love, but then I remind myself that one or both people end up falling out of love after a while. Just not worth the risk to me. But, I'm not living the life of a nun, if you know what I mean. I've definitely...um, tested the waters again. Just to make sure things still work, y'know?"

Usually so bashful when talking about sex, Maddie simply nodded, but she was intrigued by what Kendra said about testing the waters. She hadn't so much as kissed a woman since before she got sick. "So, do things...still work?"

"Oh, yes, very much so." Kendra looked at Maddie and grinned, the smile lighting up her whole face. Then she leaned in closer, her eyes trailing over Maddie's face, as if she was taking in every detail. "How'd you get that scar on your cheek? I bet there's a good story behind that."

Maddie rarely thought about how that scar got there—the mark on her face faint after all these years. "I was in a surfing accident when I was eighteen. When I wiped out, the fin from my board sliced my cheek."

"How scary!" Kendra reached across, set her hand on

Maddie's cheek, and gently ran her fingers over the scar.

A warmth flooded through Maddie's body, a sensation she hadn't experienced in a long time. Kendra removed her hand, leaving Maddie to awkwardly look away. "Yeah, it was very scary. I ended up not being able to surf for months after the accident. If it wasn't for Kai and a great physical therapist, I would have never gone on to win three surf competitions." Maddie gazed at the moonlit ocean but was certain Kendra hadn't taken her eyes off her. Kendra sat so close that Maddie could feel her breath on her neck. "Between lots of surfing scuffs, the birth of my daughter, and various surgeries, my body's got lots of scars."

"Every scar tells a story. They're part of our personal histories."

"That's for sure." Maddie let out a nervous laugh. "I don't know about you, but the fire's getting too hot for me. What was it you wanted to show me? When you asked if I was a rule breaker or follower?" Maddie met Kendra's eyes in anticipation of the answer.

"I'll show you what I have in mind." Kendra's tone was sultry, and there was a mischievous look in her eyes. She stood up, then slipped her hand in Maddie's and led her down the wooden steps and onto the gravelly path.

Maddie was nervous. Then scared. And then excited. She had no idea what Kendra had in mind for tonight, but for the first time in years, Maddie was ready to break some rules. With her hand clasped in Kendra's, Maddie placed a few tenuous steps on the damp lawn, uncertain of where Kendra was leading her but open to whatever might happen. Beyond the cliff, the moonlight cast strobes of light on the ocean. For tonight, Maddie would live like there really were many more tomorrows.

Chapter Six

Big Sur: October 2018

They were several steps beyond the lodge when Kendra slowed her pace and reached into her satchel. She fumbled around in the bag, then held both arms behind her back as if she was doing some sort of magic trick. Then, she held out two closed fists and grinned. "Pick one."

Why, Maddie didn't know, but she tapped Kendra's left hand. Totally sober now, Maddie looked at Kendra's opened hand to see a neatly rolled joint. Kendra had another one in her right hand. Not sure what to say, Maddie took the joint and glanced around to make sure no one saw they were about to smoke some weed. But this was Big Sur—a place where lots of people probably got high in public. It'd been a while since she smoked weed or consumed edibles to help get her through the side effects from chemo, but she always did like the way it made her feel. What'd be the harm in getting a little stoned tonight?

Maddie put the joint in the pocket of her hoodie, careful to make sure it wouldn't fall out while they traipsed across the grass. There was a hammock right on the edge of the bluff, a perfect location to get high, but Kendra seemed to have another destination in mind when she headed toward the gated pool area.

Kendra pushed open the squeaky metal gate and stepped to the edge of the pool. A couple paces behind, Maddie shut the gate slowly, mindful to not let it creak like it did when Kendra opened it. There was a wooden bench on the other side of the pool—an ideal spot to take a couple hits and chat with no one else around.

Only a dim lamp by the gate illuminated the pool area, but the moon cast silvery flecks of light on the water. Without saying anything, Kendra headed to the other side of the pool. Maddie followed, the slap of her flip-flops loud on the wooden deck, and she furtively looked around to make sure no one saw them here. The pool area was closed after dusk, and the last thing she wanted was to get reprimanded for being in a restricted area.

Kendra didn't waste any time in lighting the joint, taking a hit, and then handing it to Maddie. "Might as well share this one and save the other one for tomorrow...or for another day. I don't get high too often, but I've been saving this for a special occasion."

Maddie took the joint from Kendra. "What sort of special occasion? The last night at Monarch Bluffs before we return to reality next week?"

Maddie still had papers to grade and prep work to do for next week's classes, as well as an MRI to schedule, and an upcoming oncology appointment. As she tried to push those thoughts aside, Maddie took a hit but barely allowed it to stay in her lungs before exhaling. Since she didn't want to hog the joint, she handed it back to Kendra.

Kendra took a long drag as she gazed at the dark ocean, and then gave it back to Maddie. "I was waiting for the right person to share my special stash."

Not at all high yet, Maddie took another puff and held the smoke in her lungs for a few seconds until it made her cough. "I'm stoked you see me as the right person. I never got into weed when I was young, but it definitely got me through the side effects of chemo. I'm glad the harsh chemo is behind me. Well, hopefully it's behind me. Never know when I might be put back on it if the cancer returns."

Years ago, besides the marijuana easing the nausea from the chemo, Maddie also experienced another welcomed effect: It made her not care about how serious her type of cancer was. Back then, when she returned from treatment and took a couple hits from a joint or popped a couple edibles, she wouldn't fret about whether the chemotherapy was working. She would instead enjoy time with her family, read a book, or watch TV, all with a peaceful and clear mind.

Kendra took the joint from Maddie and inhaled one

more time. "As I always say, one day at a time. Today you're tumor free, right?"

"I don't know about today, but the MRI from several weeks ago showed no new tumor growth."

"Until you find out otherwise, you live like there's no new tumor growth," Kendra said, her voice calm and assuring.

Maddie considered Kendra's advice, but she had a hard time holding onto her optimism. "It's been a while since my last scan, so who knows what's going on as far as new tumor growth. Figures I'd get the type of tumor with microscopic tendrils that typically spread and infiltrate the brain." So far, the weed hadn't hit her at all. She needed more to help her forget about her fears—at least for tonight.

Kendra zipped up her sweatshirt and relaxed her body into Maddie's. "Until I hit the five-year mark, I had those same worries. I knew my type of breast cancer could come back with a vengeance, and I knew I couldn't stop it if it happened. I felt so powerless at fighting the cancer, even after I'd endured several rounds of chemo and did everything I could to live a healthy lifestyle."

That was how it was for Maddie—powerless at stopping the tumor from returning. Kendra handed her the joint, and Maddie took a long drag and held the smoke in her lungs for several seconds as she gazed at the moonlight reflected on the ocean. A couple minutes later, a soothing warmth flooded through her body. Her headache was gone, and her feet no longer ached. Relieved that the marijuana had finally hit her, she surrendered to the floaty sensation. Usually so resistant to using anything not prescribed by her oncologist or neurologist, tonight Maddie wanted more of this stuff. She wanted to float through the rest of the night feeling as if she wasn't being treated for brain cancer.

Maddie liked having Kendra's warm body next to hers. Maybe it was just the weed intensifying the wonderful sensation of a woman's touch, but Maddie felt more alive in this moment than she had in years. Resistant to give into this feeling, she knew that whatever happened tonight with Kendra would likely not go further than this weekend. Still, she enjoyed Kendra's hand gently resting on her leg.

They passed the joint back and forth a few more times as they talked about cancer treatments, how weed was better than benzos when it came to anxiety, and whether the pieces they'd written this weekend were worth expanding upon. Kendra made a joke about someone snoring like a grizzly bear in the last writing workshop, and Maddie let out a laugh that echoed around the pool. She clapped her hands over her mouth, which only made them both laugh more.

"I think your plan for tonight was perfect," Maddie said. "I had no idea I'd be getting stoned with a fellow cancer survivor tonight."

"That was only part of my plan." Kendra smiled as she ran her fingers through Maddie's hair. "The night's still young."

The feel of Kendra's hand in her hair sent shivers through Maddie's body. It was one in the morning, and she ought to get back to her room to let Dot know she was okay, but Maddie didn't want the night with Kendra to end. For once in a very long time, she was happy and relaxed. She wasn't Maddie-the-cancer-patient or Maddie-the-mom, or even Maddie-the-professor. She was just Maddie, being herself with a gorgeous woman by her side.

Kendra grabbed Maddie's hand and led her to the fence. Nearly too stoned to speak coherently, Maddie could only grin out at the dark ocean. Kendra retrieved two towels from the wooden bin next to the fence and handed one to Maddie. When Kendra removed her sweatshirt and crouched down to dip her fingers in the pool, it became obvious she wasn't here to just sit on a bench and get high under the moonlight.

Although overcome with an intense yearning for Kendra's body, Maddie didn't feel prepared for this—not at all ready to swim naked with a beautiful woman under the night sky. Her head always got in the way, blotting out any bit of arousal. Years ago, when she'd first ventured into a gay bar, she was nervous and awkward, but what finally helped her get up the nerve to dance with a woman were two pints of hard cider and lots of encouragement from the bartender. However, that was just one dance years ago in a gay club—far different than skinny dipping with an attractive woman under the moonlit sky.

Kendra peeled off her T-shirt and tossed it onto the bench. "You ever swum naked in the moonlight?" Kendra kept her gaze firmly on Maddie as she stepped out of her shoes and took off her pants.

"I surfed at night a few times when I was in my teens. Also surfed in Waikiki once late at night. The waves were lit up by the hotel high-rises on the beach. Plus, the area where I surfed had a huge strobe light focused on the water." Maddie smiled when she caught a glimpse of Kendra's black lacy bra and panties. She took another hit, but when she couldn't remember what she was talking about, she laughed. "What was I just saying?" This made her laugh even harder.

Kendra smiled in amusement. "Something about surfing at night in Waikiki?"

"Oh, right. With a strobe light on the water, it didn't really seem like I was surfing under moonlight. Looked more like unnatural light. So, no, I haven't actually swum under the light of the moon…not like this, not naked. But, isn't this pool closed at night? I mean, we really shouldn't even be sitting here by the pool right now." For Maddie, there was usually a point when too much weed made her overly chatty. Now that she'd passed the giggly stage, she couldn't keep her mouth shut.

"I think it's time to break some rules, don't you?" Kendra said, her voice quiet but playful. She smiled and unclasped her bra and stood there in only a pair of black lacy panties.

"Didn't we just break the rules by getting stoned in public?" Maddie let out a nervous laugh and took in Kendra's body: the smooth skin of her shoulders and arms, her perky breasts, her flat stomach, and those lacy black panties. Fully clothed, Maddie felt overdressed and even more awkward when she realized Kendra was about to get in the pool and wanted Maddie to join her. But how uncomfortable could this actually be? Kendra had already seen her naked body down at the baths.

Kendra removed her panties. "Oh, you should probably know that I don't know how to swim."

Maddie couldn't take her eyes off Kendra's gorgeous body. "You're a California girl who doesn't know how to swim?"

"I've always been afraid of the water, so I never actually learned to swim when I was a kid. Why don't you teach me, surfer girl?" Kendra's voice was so flirtatious, which caused Maddie to melt with desire. Kendra entered the water and walked down each step, then headed to the middle of the pool. She looked incredibly sexy in the moonlight—so perfect in every way. So what if tonight might only lead to a one-night stand?

Eager to join Kendra in the water, Maddie removed her hoodie, T-shirt, and pants. Then, she stripped off her undergarments and stepped into the pool. The warm water was soothing, nothing like the overwhelming heat of the baths. It enveloped her body, making her weightless. No matter if she swam in the ocean or a pool, water always made her feel free. And tonight, naked and stoned, the water made her totally uninhibited. She swam across the pool to where Kendra stood—in awe of how stunning she looked. Just imagining touching Kendra made her exhilarated and aroused.

Maddie stepped closer to Kendra, eager for skin-on-skin contact. "Ready for your lesson?"

"Been ready for a while." Kendra gazed at Maddie and smiled. Her eyes drifted from Maddie's face and then to her breasts and farther down her body.

That look only intensified Maddie's longing. "Okay, first things first, I need to get you on your back."

"Well, you don't waste any time." Kendra laughed softly.

"You'll soon discover that the best part of this lesson is that I'll have my hands on you at all times...to keep you safe in the water. But the most important thing right now is to get you used to floating in the water, like this." Maddie lay back on the surface, lifting her face to the cloudy sky. Weightless, she let the water cocoon her body as her fingers brushed against Kendra's arm. Then she lowered her legs to again stand next to Kendra and reached for her hand. "Now, your turn. I'll help guide you back in the water."

Although she looked a bit nervous, Kendra leaned back in the water. "You sure I won't sink and drown?"

Maddie marveled that Kendra, who'd been so confident earlier when they were chatting at the lodge, was unsure of herself. "You're not gonna drown. The entire pool is only four feet deep." Maddie steadied Kendra's body in the water. The feel of her hands on Kendra's skin was even more exciting than she imagined.

Kendra gazed at Maddie with fear in her eyes. "They say people can drown in only a few inches of water."

"I won't take my hands off you, and I'll help you stay afloat and keep you safe." Maddie set a palm on Kendra's lower back and placed her other hand under her head. Touched that Kendra was so trusting of her, Maddie stood very close and kept her hands secure under Kendra's body.

"You probably think it's silly that I never learned how to swim and that I'm afraid of water," Kendra said, her voice tinged with worry and apprehension.

"Not silly at all. There was a time right before I learned to surf that I was terrified of the water."

"Terrified?"

Maddie gave Kendra a reassuring smile. "I was just a teenager at the time, but if I hadn't broken the rules, I wouldn't have ended up being scared of the water. I was at a camp in Mississippi and ended up getting lost late one night with one of the counselors. We attempted to swim across the lake in the middle of the night but quickly became cold and exhausted. I'd always been a good swimmer, but I didn't have the energy to tread water, much less swim to the other side of the lake. It's kind of embarrassing to think about it now, but we had to be rescued by search and rescue."

"I can see why that'd make you scared of water. You're sure I'm safe in this pool?"

"Totally safe, especially with me here the entire time. Okay, now I'm gonna have you kick a couple times, just to let you feel how your legs can move you through the water." Maddie set her hand on Kendra's right hip and slid her hand down her thigh. "Kick from the hips, feeling the motion down your entire leg."

For a few moments, Maddie kept her hand on Kendra's hipbone and watched her kick through the water. Even in the dim light, it was hard to miss the dark mound between her legs. The urge to run her hands all over Kendra became more and more intense, and Maddie had to swallow before she could again speak. "Looks like you got the kicking figured out just fine. Now, let the water hold you for a moment. If you relax, you can float like this for a long time."

One of the only places where Maddie was totally confident was in the water. Here in the pool, with her hands under Kendra's body, she was in control and so alive. Heat radiated down her chest, through her abdomen, and settled between her legs.

When Kendra flailed her legs and arms, Maddie secured a hand on her upper back and another one under her hips to keep her safe. For a moment, she cradled Kendra's body in her arms to keep her afloat. A few seconds of this, and then she guided her back into a standing position.

In the shallow pool, their shoulders and chests were exposed. Maddie shivered from the cold air. She faced Kendra and gazed at her eyes and then at her lips. Still floaty from the weed, Maddie dipped under the water to warm herself but quickly emerged to see Kendra's beautiful face. Though the night was dark and foggy, Maddie clearly saw the eager look in Kendra's eyes—a look she hadn't seen from anyone in years.

Kendra stepped closer, setting her hand on Maddie's shoulder. As they looked deep into each other's eyes, Kendra placed her palm over Maddie's heart—right where the portacath was located just under the skin. A constant reminder of her battle with cancer, the port was usually so sensitive and painful to touch, but tonight, Maddie craved Kendra's hand on her skin.

Kendra ran her fingers over Maddie's port, her thumb brushing against her nipple. "They took out my portacath once I hit the two-year mark. I call the marks on my body battle scars."

"I remember you saying scars are sexy." Maddie smiled as she looked at Kendra's gorgeous body, so curvy and strong. Kendra ran her fingers down Maddie's chest, making her shudder with excitement.

"Definitely sexy, especially yours." Kendra kissed Maddie's scar, then ran her fingers over her chest and kissed her on the neck.

Shivers went up Maddie's spine, and she couldn't help letting out a moan. Kendra pulled back and guided Maddie's hand to her own chest. Though Maddie couldn't see the scar where the portacath had been removed, there was a slight hardness under the surface. The contrast with Kendra's soft skin only made Maddie want her even more.

Kendra gazed at Maddie under the moonlight. She ran her fingers over the scar on Maddie's face and kissed her gently on the cheek. "It was all I could do earlier up at the lodge to not kiss you right here, to get to know every inch of you, to taste you and feel you."

Maddie's arousal was higher than ever. It'd been years since anyone spoke to her this way, but because Kendra had admitted earlier that she wouldn't ever date again, Maddie retreated to that familiar place of hesitation. This couldn't possibly lead to anything more than a one-night stand or a weekend of intense passion, but when Kendra wrapped her arms around her, Maddie couldn't ignore her longing. Four years' worth of pent-up sexual energy spilled out of her as she ran her fingers through Kendra's wet hair and kissed her softly on the lips.

"My God, you're so beautiful." Once again, Kendra kissed Maddie but on the lips this time—the kisses soft, warm, and then intense. Kendra ran her fingers through Maddie's hair, caressing the bare spot on her scalp where the tumor had been removed.

"Maybe tomorrow morning I can teach you a couple swim strokes." Maddie ran her fingers over the scar above Kendra's left breast.

"Probably not a good idea to be in the pool together in broad daylight since I wouldn't be able to keep my hands off you, but...maybe you could show me those strokes tonight...in my room." Kendra kissed Maddie softly on the lips and slid her hands down her back.

Kendra's lips traveled to Maddie's neck and then down to her breasts. When her tongue flicked against Maddie's nipple, heat surged through her body. Maddie ran her hands through Kendra's hair and then set her hands on her face. Their kisses became more intense—Kendra's lips and tongue causing Maddie to whimper softly.

With a hunger she hadn't experienced in years, Maddie quickly pulled Kendra closer and kissed her passionately. The water slapped against their bodies, the sounds of the little splashes blending with their moans. Needing to feel and taste her, Maddie pressed her lips against Kendra's as her hand traveled between her legs. When Maddie ran her fingers through Kendra's soft hair and found their way to her clit, she could feel that Kendra was slick with desire. It was so tempting to go further, and to have Kendra reciprocate, but not here, not yet.

Maddie reluctantly removed her hand and instead slid both across Kendra's back, kissing her on the neck. The feel of skin against skin made Maddie shudder. "Mmm, I love the way you feel."

As the moon disappeared behind the clouds, Kendra's lips and tongue met Maddie's once again. "And I love the way your hands and lips feel on my skin. Can't wait to explore every inch of you. I'm glad I have that private cottage. You're gonna love waking up with a view of the ocean."

They kissed one more time, and then Maddie slipped her hand in Kendra's and led her out of the pool. Although she wanted to lose herself in Kendra's sexy body, Maddie knew what she wanted most tonight: to fall asleep after making love, to wake up in the morning, and feel safe and full of life. For once in a long time, with Kendra's hand clasped in hers, Maddie felt normal—as if she didn't have a terminal disease.

Chapter Seven

San Luis Obispo, California: October 2018

The ticking clock on the wall read thirty-five minutes past Maddie's scheduled appointment time. With no other seats available in the waiting room, there was no choice but to remain under the cold air conditioning vent until they finally called her for the MRI. She ran a finger over the koa wood bracelet, each bead highly polished after so many years of wear. Ever since Kai gave this to her years ago, she rarely removed it—except for when she had surgery or any sort of invasive medical procedure.

Maddie drummed her fingers on the plastic armrest and stared at the muted TV in the corner of the room. There was a travel show displayed on the screen, but her thoughts were focused on the long phone conversation she had last night with Kendra. At around nine o'clock, Kendra had called to ask more questions about Hawaii. They started talking about the best beaches in Hawaii and soon moved onto other subjects, including places they'd traveled to, first loves, favorite movies, and best restaurants in San Luis Obispo. Maddie talked about her surf competitions, and Kendra made a comment about Maddie looking great in a bikini. They were flirting the entire time. The next thing Maddie knew, it was well after midnight. This morning, she was still giddy with happiness and couldn't stop smiling.

Taylor sat next to Maddie and pored over her geography textbook while she sipped a ginger ale and nibbled on a cracker. Taylor placed tracing paper over a colorful map of Europe and began to outline each country.

"Is your tummy more settled now?" Maddie brushed her fingers through Taylor's hair and draped an arm around her shoulders.

Taylor shook her head and studied the map while she

popped another cracker in her mouth. By now, she had Wales, England, and Germany outlined, along with most of the major cities for each country penciled in—places Maddie would likely never visit again.

"I'm sorry your father or Dot couldn't take me today, but Dad has that rehearsal with his students this afternoon, and Dot's getting ready for the opening at a gallery in Monterey." Maddie glanced at the row of patients sitting nearby and lowered her voice. "Sweetie, the morning sickness shouldn't last too much longer. When I was pregnant with you, I used to get the queasiness all day long."

"Why do they call it morning sickness if it lasts all day?" Taylor said in an almost-whimper that made her still seem like Maddie's little girl, not a sixteen-year-old with a baby on the way.

"For me, after the fourth month, the nausea totally went away. When's your next appointment?"

"Next Friday afternoon. I made it for after your appointment with Doctor Cho."

"Dad can probably go with us. Can Braden make it to the appointment? Or does he have water polo practice?"

"He can go, but I don't want him there. We're not even a couple, so why does he have to be there?" Taylor focused on the map and furrowed her brow while she wrote in the names of more cities.

"Sweetie, if he wants to be there, you should let him." Maddie glimpsed at the other patients in the waiting room and hushed her voice. "Most guys his age would run the other way if they got a girl pregnant. As the father, he has every right to be a part of all of this. Regardless of whether you two are or aren't a couple, that baby needs a father."

Taylor didn't respond. She wrote "Frankfurt" toward the middle of the map of Germany, shut the textbook with the tracing paper wedged between the pages, and looked at Maddie. "I know Dad means well, but do you think he'd feel hurt if it's just you with me at the appointment? He's made it clear he's not happy about any of this."

"You know how much of a shock it was when you first told us," Maddie said quietly. "It's been hard on Dad and me."

Taylor sighed and opened her textbook again.

Maddie's phone buzzed in her lap with an email from the division office secretary at school. Excited that this could mean she'd been selected for an interview for the full-time position, she quickly tapped on the email.

The message consisted of only two lines:

The dean would like to meet with you regarding an important matter. Please email or call me as soon as possible to set up an appointment with Sharon on either Thursday or Friday of next week.

Maddie couldn't help rolling her eyes. It was probably another student complaining about their grade. Their refusal to incorporate her feedback or cite their sources was always somehow her problem. But, "an important matter" need not necessarily be anything negative. Maybe this meeting was regarding her recent work on the curriculum changes for the inmate education program. Even better, perhaps the dean wanted to prime her for the possibility of getting selected for an interview for the full-time teaching position. There were a few strong contenders, including Jamie Miller, who'd recently had a book published. It was Maddie, however, who had more useful experience, such as being a club advisor and member of a couple committees.

Without much more thought, she wrote a short response:

Friday morning works well for me to meet with Sharon—anything between early morning and noon.

Dot had a class on Friday morning and could give Maddie a ride. Whatever this important matter was would hopefully be settled with a short and informal meeting. Or maybe Maddie would be brave and drive herself to campus.

Maddie's phone buzzed again, this time with a text from Kendra. Although they'd texted a few times since last weekend, the messages were mostly brief and casual. While every text made Maddie smile, she kept her responses to a minimum since Kendra had been clear she didn't want to date. But this message was far different than the previous texts:

I loved that your voice was the last thing I heard before drifting off to sleep last night. Wish we were still in Big Sur. Can't stop thinking about you, especially those kisses and the way your body felt next to mine all night long.

Certain she was blushing, Maddie casually shielded the screen so Taylor couldn't see the message. As Maddie reread the text, her heartbeat sped up. She wasn't sure how to respond, so she slipped the phone into her purse and glanced again at the muted TV, quietly thrilled that Kendra couldn't stop thinking about her.

Taylor sniffled and wiped her eyes with her sleeves.

Maddie's attention snapped back to her daughter. "What's wrong?"

"I know me having a baby is probably the last thing you and Dad want to deal with right now." Taylor's eyes filled with tears.

Maddie wrapped her arm around Taylor and pulled her close. "Sweetie, we'll get through this. Look at all we've gone through with my surgery and chemo. Haven't you figured out by now that there's nothing this family can't handle?"

"Dad makes me feel like I'm a fuck-up, like I'm nothing but a big disappointment to him."

Maddie cringed, but she ignored the swearing for now since they had more important things to talk about. "Honey, you're not a disappointment to me or to Dad. He'll come around soon. You'll see. We both love you and will help you through this. Grandma said she'll come up after the baby's born to help as well."

A short, top-heavy woman in burgundy scrubs stood in the doorway and called out, "Madelyn Fong, we're ready for you."

Maddie didn't recognize this tech and already missed the peppy guy who normally did her MRIs. She grabbed her walking stick and purse but left her canvas tote bag with Taylor. "I'll be back in about an hour and a half." She gave her daughter a reassuring smile. "I've got string cheese in my bag and some sparkling water. A few sips of that and some protein might ease the nausea a bit."

Taylor's returning smile was weak but genuine. Maddie

therefore felt comfortable leaving her to follow the tech down the long corridor to the familiar exam room, which she'd first encountered four years ago. The tinny sound of country music filtered in from down the hall.

"Madelyn, I'm Gloria," the tech said, closing the door behind them. "Change into a gown, and then I'll do a quick blood draw."

"I go by Maddie. Is Freddie off today?"

"Sorry, hon, just reading the name on the order your doctor sent us. Freddie's on vacation. He and his husband are on a Hawaiian cruise. Lucky guys. Always did want to go to Hawaii. You ever been to any of the islands?"

Annoyed with Gloria's chattiness, Maddie offered a short response. "Went to Oahu a couple times, and to Maui and Molokai once."

"I so rarely make it out of California since my son and his wife had a baby recently. Is that your daughter in the waiting room?"

"Yes, that's Taylor. She only just started driving a few months ago, but she's been a godsend because some- times my hus—well, sometimes I can't always get a ride here."

"They grow up so fast, don't they? You two defi- nitely look related. Is she not feeling well?"

Perturbed by Gloria's probing questions, Maddie simply said, "Uh-huh." She opened the locker and pulled out the thin hospital gown.

Gloria furrowed her brow as she studied a sheet of paper. "Maddie, I understand that Doctor Hahn sedates you before we put you in the MRI machine."

"Yeah, she does. Can't get in that tube without some sedation. Maybe she's got something stronger for me this time? Might be nice to get in a little nap while you do the MRI." Maddie chuckled—partly out of nervousness but also due to not wanting to seem like she was drug-seek- ing.

"You feeling more nervous this time, hon?"

"A little," Maddie lied. For today's scan, she was extremely nervous—more than she had in the past few years of getting MRIs.

"I'll be right behind the glass, and you can talk to me

any time during the procedure. Truth be told, I'd wanna be totally knocked out if I had to put my entire body in that tube. I get claustrophobic on an elevator."

"Yup, me too. These never get any easier." Maddie smiled at Gloria. She wasn't as cool as Freddie, but her sweetness did alleviate some of Maddie's nervousness.

Gloria set her hand on Maddie's shoulder. "You can talk to Doctor Hahn about the anxiety. Put this gown on, and I'll meet you in the room around the corner. I'm sure you know where to go by now. I'll see you in a minute, hon."

Once she put on the gown and a pair of light blue non-slip socks, Maddie glanced again at Kendra's text and smiled. Blissful joy rushed through her body, just as it had when she'd woken up next to Kendra. Maddie wrote a quick reply:

I too wish we were still at Monarch Bluffs. I'm about to get my MRI. Pretty nervous about this one. To help distract me, I'll think about your lips on mine and your hands all over my body.

Maddie secured her phone and purse in the locker, then rounded the corner to the huge MRI machine. The procedure was so routine now. Maddie sat in a chair against the wall and waited for Gloria to come back to take some blood from her portacath. At the time of her first MRI, Maddie was told the blood draw had to do with monitoring kidney function due to the dye they injected for the second part of the MRI. But for the past few years, her bloodwork had come back fine each time.

This room, colder than the waiting room, looked the same as ever—the off-white walls, the giant MRI machine in the center, the glass windows separating this area from the office where the tech monitored the scans. The only difference today was the twangy country music playing from the speakers in the corners of the room. Used to Freddie's upbeat dance tunes, Maddie tried to tune out the country music as she rubbed her hands together to warm them up.

Down the hall, someone's shoes squeaked on the tile floor. When the steps got closer, Maddie's heartbeat sped up, and she clenched her hands into fists. Even though she'd had many of these MRIs and got a dose of sedative each time, she was still terrified when they moved her body into the narrow cylindrical tube. Her fear was always that she'd be caught inside the machine due to some sort of technical malfunction. When the door opened, Maddie glanced up to see Doctor's Hahn's beaming face peeking around the corner.

"Maddie, so nice to see you. Been awhile since I've been here to read your MRIs." Doctor Hahn leaned down to give Maddie a hug, then sat in the seat next to her.

"I'm so glad you're back from maternity leave." A huge smile washed over Maddie's face, temporarily easing the anxiety a bit. She'd developed a crush on Doctor Hahn from the first consult regarding the robotic radiotherapy. Maddie internally shook her head at herself for always falling for unavailable women but was thankful that this crush fizzled out and had become deep admiration. "I bet the twins have been keeping you busy."

"They're getting so big. I didn't think I'd end up having to take off two months before they were born and six weeks after, but it's good to be back. So, Gloria says you're more nervous this time. What's going on?"

"Maybe I'm just overly tired this time. Haven't been sleeping too well lately, and I've had chronic headaches. I'm sure you know what I'm worried about."

"I can see how that'd cause you to be more nervous today. Have you told your doctors about the headaches? How long have they been going on?"

"For a few weeks now. I haven't seen Doctor Lau in a while, and Doctor Cho doesn't know how bad or how frequent the headaches have been." Although the other doctors were compassionate and personable, Doctor Hahn's mellow demeanor made Maddie feel safer, no matter how scary the treatment or results could be.

"I'll be sure to get the results to them as soon as possible. Maybe your headaches are from grading too many papers?"

"Actually, not really. I went away last weekend and hardly did any grading. I'm pretty behind now, but the break was so worth it." Maddie giggled then dropped her gaze to her feet and continued to grin.

"Looks like you had a nice time, wherever you went...and with whoever joined you."

Gloria bustled into the room holding a syringe, an empty plastic vial, and an alcohol swab. She hummed to the song playing from the speakers.

"Gloria, I'll get her blood this time. Go ahead and set up the machine." Doctor Hahn held the empty vial in one hand and clasped her other hand on Maddie's arm.

Maddie tapped her foot to the steady beat of country music and checked to make sure Gloria was out of the room. "Gloria seems nice, but...I miss Freddie's dance tunes. Not quite the same to hear Garth Brooks as I go into the MRI tube. Freddie always has a way of distracting me with some sort of Rihanna remix or Madonna medley."

"I'll see if we can change the music once you're in the machine. So, you enjoyed a little getaway recently?" Doctor Hahn raised her brow and smiled, clearly eager to hear more details about Maddie's weekend.

"Yeah, I had an unexpectedly great time. I went to Big Sur for a writers' workshop. I expected to get back into my writing, maybe write a new poem or essay, but I ended up...well, not doing much writing but instead meeting a nice woman." Just saying those words caused Maddie to feel fluttery inside.

"Ah, so that's why you're glowing. You've got someone new in your life. So happy to hear that, Maddie." Doctor Hahn pulled down Maddie's gown a bit to reveal the location of the port. She quickly cleaned the area with alcohol, then poked a needle into the skin. The vial soon filled with blood.

"No, it's not what you think, but...it was nice feeling...well, alive again, if you know what I mean." Maddie couldn't even look Doctor Hahn in the eyes. Over the years, Maddie had opened up to Doctor Hahn about all sorts of things but never about her love life.

"Good for you, Maddie."

"Haven't felt that way in a long time. But, I certainly don't have any plans to go on a date or anything."

"Why not?" Doctor Hahn looked surprised and even a bit confused. "If you don't mind me saying so, I haven't seen you this happy in all the years you've been coming here for your scans."

"Doctor Hahn, there's no way I'd get involved with someone right now, not with the uncertainty of my health. Besides, Kendra made it very clear she's not into dating." Maddie held a cotton ball over the port and pulled the gown up close to her neck.

Gloria rounded the corner and took the vial from Doctor Hahn. "Doctor, I'll run the blood now and be back in a couple of minutes. Everything's all set for her MRI."

Doctor Hahn waited until Gloria was out of the room before responding. "Not into dating? Maybe she just hasn't met the right woman, but I bet the right woman could be you. Maybe you just need to convince her of that?"

"Oh, I don't know. She was so adamant about not ever wanting to settle down with someone. To be honest, I don't feel up for trying to convince someone that I could be right for them. Seems like a lot of work. I feel way too old for that. I walk with a cane, for God's sake."

Doctor Hahn leaned over to study the intricate design on the handle of Maddie's staff. "Looks more like a really cool walking stick than a cane."

"The thing is, lately I feel more like eighty than thirty-six."

"I don't tell a lot of my patients this, but do you realize I got pregnant at forty-five?"

"You look…really good for your mid-forties."

"Most days I don't feel like I'm in my mid-forties. For the longest time, I thought I'd just be married to my career and never fall in love."

"I can't imagine getting out there and dating in my condition. I've been so exhausted lately."

"Never say never. I'd nearly given up on love, marriage, a family, and all that other stuff. I didn't get married until I was forty-three. Now look at me. I'm a mom of twin baby girls. Thank God for a great fertility doctor, but I have so much joy in my life."

"You're lucky you found someone, but I'm not sure another marriage is in my future. Or even just a relationship. You know the odds when it comes to my type of cancer."

Doctor Hahn reached over and cupped her hand over Maddie's. "You've more than beat the odds. I'm confident the robotic radiotherapy removed every bit of new tumor growth two years ago. All your MRIs keep coming back clear. Depending on the results of this scan, I wouldn't be surprised if Doctor Cho suggests cutting back on the bevacizumab to every other week."

Maddie's chest heaved, and her eyes filled with tears. "I feel like it's just a matter of time until the tumor comes back."

Doctor Hahn handed Maddie a tissue and set her hand on her shoulder. "Then why not enjoy yourself and continue chasing after your dreams and goals? Why not convince Kendra she should date you? She'll spend time with you and quickly realize how amazing you are."

Maddie nodded and wiped the tears from her cheeks. The icy air coming from the vent overhead caused her to shiver. "I feel like my dreams were taken away when I first got diagnosed with cancer."

"Maybe don't look at this woman as part of any sort of goal or dream. Just go have fun." Doctor Hahn walked over to the cabinet to get a sheet and a blanket. Then she draped the sheet over the narrow gurney leading into the MRI machine and handed the blanket to Maddie.

Maddie set the blanket over her lap, tucked her hands underneath her legs, and grinned. "Kendra's a lot of fun. She's got beautiful blue eyes that kind of look deep into my soul, as corny as that sounds. She's funny, deep, intelligent. Would you believe she's also a cancer survivor?"

"There ya go, lots in common."

"But she made it clear she doesn't want to date."

"Then don't call it a date. Why not meet her for coffee? Or maybe go for a walk on the beach. Nothing wrong with a new friend."

That brought the phrase "friends with benefits" to mind, and Maddie laughed quietly as she recalled the moments with Kendra in the pool last weekend. Gloria returned to the room and handed Doctor Hahn the lab results. Maddie had seen so many of these—columns of words, numbers, and symbols showing the results of her complete blood count.

Doctor Hahn looked over the results. "Hmm," she said to herself, then took out a pen and circled something on the report.

A sick feeling traveled to the pit of Maddie's stomach. "Anything weird in my labs this time?" She'd never seen Doctor Hahn so much as pause after she checked her blood results.

"Not too weird, just different from your last few results. Your creatine level is slightly elevated, and your GFR is low. But, nothing to prevent you from getting a sedative or contrast for your MRI today. Probably wouldn't hurt to do a routine urinalysis, though. I'll give you a lab order for that before you leave today."

The GFR, or glomerular filtration rate, was the measurement to test kidney function. Months ago, Doctor Cho told Maddie that hers was a little low. Assuring her it wasn't anything to worry about, Doctor Cho said they'd keep a close eye on it each time Maddie got treatment. Doctors Cho and Hahn worked closely together with most of their patients, especially the ones needing imaging in addition to regular appointments with the oncologist.

Maddie glanced up to see Gloria smiling from behind the glass and giving them a thumbs up. She gave Gloria a thumbs up in response. "I guess it's time for me to be stuck inside that tube, huh? While I'm in there, I'll think about my ideal date with Kendra. But I might wait to find out the results of the MRI before I call her."

Doctor Hahn patted her on the arm. "Just remember this. I'd nearly closed myself off to what's become my greatest joy ever. Never thought I'd even be open to going on maternity leave for as long as I did."

"Yeah, which meant I had to see that old doctor for my last MRI. I don't even recall him talking to me when he gave me the sedative. He just put the meds in my IV and disappeared. I'm glad you're back now." Maddie walked over to the MRI machine and took her usual place atop the narrow gurney leading into the tube.

"That makes two of us. You ready for something to

relax you?" Doctor Hahn smiled and patted Maddie on the arm.

"Any chance you can make it a double?" Maddie grimaced and braced herself to be inside the machine for an hour and a half.

Doctor Hahn laughed as she efficiently started an IV in the back of Maddie's hand, and just as efficiently tucked the blanket around Maddie's legs and midsection.

Within seconds, a soothing warmth coursed through Maddie's body. Soon, the tension in her neck melted, the pain in her temples dissipated, and her body became heavy. Before she knew it, she was moved into the cylinder where she heard faint beeps and the drone of country music. Once again, she went to her happy place. Call it a dream or her vivid imagination, but this time her usual vision of being on a beach had the addition of a gorgeous woman with auburn hair and creamy skin.

Chapter Eight

Montaña de Oro: November 2018

Kai hiked a few paces ahead, and Maddie did her best to keep up. Still, she was winded after only a few minutes of trekking down the trail. The edema in her feet was a bit worse today, and her back and legs ached. Usually sore the day after she got an MRI, Maddie hoped the fresh air would revive her. The walking stick steadied her on the rough terrain, but she had to stop every few minutes to rest. Despite being bundled up in a fleece sweatshirt and a beanie, she was cold from the crisp fall air.

Kai wasn't fazed by the cold temps and was dressed in his usual T-shirt and board shorts. Although he was in his late sixties, Kai had the tan and muscular body of someone in his forties. He looked nearly the same as he did when Maddie and her mom met him over twenty years ago, although he was somewhat grey now. The tribal designs tattooed on his arms and broad shoulders always caught the attention of others, whether at the beach or when working at the surf shop he owned. Barefoot, Kai hiked over the dirt as they neared Hazard Canyon Reef.

From the high bluff, Maddie saw Morro Rock a few miles to the north. This was a good place to take a break and catch her breath. The musty scent of sagebrush was as strong as when she and Kai first discovered Hazard Canyon Reef. That was shortly after she and Drew moved to Morro Bay when Taylor was a baby. Ever since then, Kai visited her a few times a year to surf and spend time together.

Even though he'd made the drive up here last month, Kai insisted on visiting again this week. He told Maddie it was because the swell would be huge, but she knew that wasn't the real reason. After her MRI yesterday, Maddie chatted with Kai on the phone and expressed her fears to him. The next thing she knew, he said he was heading up to Morro Bay, muttering that he wanted to talk to her about something important. So far, he hadn't revealed what that was. Maybe he just wanted to help Maddie get her mind off things. Happy for the diversion, she looked forward to watching him surf while she enjoyed the fresh marine air.

Maddie and Kai followed the path through Hazard Canyon and soon reached the wooden boardwalk next to the creek. That meant they were almost to the beach. Without warning, Maddie's eyes filled with tears. She hadn't been to Hazard Canyon Reef in years, not since before her first seizure. Though she'd surfed at other beaches in Montaña de Oro, this surf break was the one that always gave her an intense workout. Between the undertow and the powerful waves, surfing here used to keep her in top shape. Now Maddie needed a cane just to walk down a path. She brushed a hand over her eyes, hoping Kai hadn't seen, and kept going.

At the entrance to the beach was a big white sign with bright red writing:

CONFIRMED SHARK SIGHTING. ENTER THE WATER AT YOUR OWN RISK. NO LIFEGUARD ON DUTY.

Above the warning was yesterday's date and an image of a great white shark. Although Maddie had surfed here many times, she'd never seen a shark, but over the years she'd chatted with surfers who'd seen great whites in this area. Drew knew the guy who'd survived a shark attack a few years ago at another surf spot in Montaña de Oro. Maddie had read about the attack while she was home recovering from brain surgery.

"You saw this sign, right?" Maddie tapped her finger on the image of the great white.

"The odds of getting attacked by a shark are pretty slim." Kai shrugged and plodded forward.

Maddie picked up her pace and caught up to Kai. "Yeah, but the shark sighting was only yesterday."

Kai stopped walking and looked at Maddie with such intensity in his eyes. "If we let fear stop us, we'll never truly experience life. Sharks are out there. I never let *maka'u* get in the way."

"I think there's a big difference between not letting fear get in the way and having common sense to not enter the water after a confirmed shark sighting."

"My buddies and I swam at a beach on Maui that was known for shark attacks, some of them fatal. In Hawaii, they have tiger sharks. Way more dangerous than great whites. Besides, the sign said there was a shark sighting, not an attack. Those great whites won't bother me. If they take a bite out of my leg, they'll quickly realize I don't taste good."

"If they take a bite out of your leg, your friends won't like having to run the shop until you recover."

Kai smirked, then trekked across the sand until they got closer to the water.

Maddie knew she couldn't convince Kai to stay out of the water, so she gave up trying to talk some sense into him. As a teenager, she'd mastered huge waves and wiped out in treacherous conditions, but once she moved to the Central California Coast, she knew better than to enter water where there'd been a confirmed shark sighting.

Maddie checked her phone hoping Kendra had texted her but was disappointed to find no cell signal. Maybe there would be one farther down the beach. After her chat with Doctor Hahn yesterday, Maddie felt brave enough to ask Kendra to get coffee with her this weekend.

Once they found a spot on the beach, Kai dragged a large piece of driftwood close to Maddie while she watched a few surfers ride the huge waves. Whenever a tumbler broke on shore, it created whitewash all along the coast. Kai continued to haul more waterlogged branches across the sand until he'd built a makeshift hut.

Kai set a few branches over the top. "This oughta block the wind."

"My own little fort." Maddie laughed and crawled into the shelter. "All we need is some hot cocoa and a bonfire."

Kai retrieved a thermos from his backpack, a huge grin washing over his face. "Or some of your mom's hot and sour soup." He poured some soup into a cup and handed it to Maddie.

Maddie savored a few slurps of Mom's soup and was finally less cold. "How'd you keep this hot since last night?"

"I had Taylor warm it up before we left the house. Your mom also packed some vegetarian spring rolls and tofu salad. For dessert, we've got sliced mango. Leave it to my Angie to pack fruit for dessert. Good thing I tossed a chocolate bar in my backpack." Kai pulled out a paper sack, set the items on a napkin, and poured himself some soup.

Kai was the only person who called Maddie's mom Angie. Even Popo called her Angela. Maddie always thought it was sweet that Kai spoke of Mom with such tenderness. Though Maddie didn't mind eating a vegetarian lunch, she knew it was unusual for Mom to hold back on meat and poultry when she cooked her most popular dishes at Royal Palace.

"Why is everything vegetarian? It's weird that Mom didn't pack some of her pork dumplings or chicken salad mixed with her yummy mayo and curry dressing."

"She's been on a health kick lately. She totally cut out red meat and pork at home, as well as desserts. Her diabetes is under control, but she seems to think I too shouldn't eat any sweets. Don't tell her I get a chocolate milkshake a couple times a week with my double-double cheeseburger and fries." Kai's cheeky grin made him seem like a naughty schoolboy instead of a guy in his sixties.

Maddie laughed, then crunched into a spring roll and poured more hot and sour soup into her cup. She wedged the thermos in the sand and lost herself in the breakers surging toward shore. Two surfers caught a huge wave, and one of them shot through the barrel. She closed her eyes for a moment and imagined gliding down the face of a wave.

Kai scooted closer to Maddie and cupped his hand over hers. "*Keiki,* I know the ocean continues to call to you. Maybe tomorrow we oughta come back here with your board."

Maddie didn't say anything right away. She instead

focused on Morro Rock in the distance. Horrible memories of that day flooded back. The numbness on the left side of her body. The awful sensation of getting caught inside. Her body tumbling through the whitewash. The results of her first MRI. Then the devastating news from the doctor.

Without looking at Kai, Maddie said, "The fatigue has been bad lately. I barely had enough strength to walk down that trail. I don't have the energy to paddle past the breaking waves. I'm just happy to sit on shore and watch you surf."

Kai pulled a fleece blanket from his backpack and draped it around Maddie's shoulders. For a few minutes, they sat close together and watched the waves. Way in the distance, whitecaps formed on the surface of the ocean. Rays of light reflected off the water. A layer of fog sat above the horizon.

"I'm glad you drove up here last night." Maddie set her head on Kai's shoulder.

"Me too." Kai wrapped his arm around Maddie and pulled her closer. "So, you probably wondered why I came up here without your mom. I wanted to talk to you about something."

Maddie dug her heels into the sand and hunched forward. As she shivered from the cold breeze, she wrapped the blanket tighter around her body. "If it's to talk about the results of my MRI, I don't think any amount of talking will diminish my fears."

"I didn't come here to talk about that. Besides, I know you well enough to know you'll worry, no matter how much I try to get you to realize the MRI will most likely reveal no new tumor growth. I came here to tell you I want to propose to your mom."

Maddie squealed in delight and sat up straight, her pain disappearing for the moment. "Oh, my God, that's exciting! But why now? You two have been happily partnered for over twenty years now."

"It just feels like it's time. Might as well make it legal and legit. You have to keep it a secret until I propose to her, but I wanted to tell you first."

"Are you asking me for my mom's hand in marriage?"

Maddie nudged Kai and laughed.

"No, but I'll need your help in picking out a ring. I'd like us to get married this summer when your mom is off for a couple months."

Maddie fell silent and gazed at the breaking waves. Would she be too sick to attend Mom and Kai's wedding? Would she even be alive this summer? Maddie took a deep breath and exhaled slowly. She refused to let panic take away from the happiness of this moment. "This is the best news I've heard in a long time. Maybe later today we can look at rings online."

Kai smiled and kissed Maddie on the cheek. *"Aloha wau iā 'oe."*

"Love you, too."

Kai gave her a quick hug and stood up. "Time for me to get in the water. You sure you'll be okay here?"

"I'm sure. But don't take too long. We need to shop for a ring!"

Kai smiled and headed over to his surfboard. He kneeled in the sand and rubbed wax on his board as he sang a song in Hawaiian—the same one he used to chant when Maddie was a teenager and they surfed together in Southern California.

"Ke ala nihi a'e lā...Ka 'uwea holuholu," Kai chanted softly.

And just like that, Maddie was transported back to when she was learning to surf. Kai would sing this song every time, although he only had to tell her the meaning once: The way is precarious, like a swaying tightrope.

Maddie closed her eyes and immersed herself in his soothing voice. Kai stopped singing to put on his wetsuit, and Maddie almost begged him to please start again. Instead, she only watched as he put on his booties and entered the cold water. Kai walked into the ocean until he was waist deep. For a moment, he stood there and sifted his hands through the water as the waves headed toward shore. Despite the lack of a hood and gloves, he didn't appear to feel the cold. He lay on his board, paddled through the whitewater, and soon reached the surf zone.

The sun peeked through the clouds, warming Maddie's face. Maybe surfing was out of the question, but there was no reason not to enjoy the water, at least a little. She took off her beanie and replaced it with a wide-brimmed straw hat. Her sneakers were easy to kick off, as were her socks, which she stuffed inside the shoes. Maddie left the hut and walked to the water's edge to get a better view of Kai as he surfed. She rolled her pantlegs up to her knees and stepped into the frigid ocean. Though in the mid-fifties, the water was refreshing. Years ago, she'd brave the frigid temps to surf the waves, but right now she was content just getting her feet wet.

She took a deep breath and inhaled the marine air, then glimpsed at her phone to see that she had no cell service. As she strolled along the shore, she stared intently at her phone and hoped for a signal. So far, nothing. Maddie continued to wander along the shore, and ten minutes later, she finally got a signal. Two full bars! But no new text from Kendra. Only a couple messages from Taylor. She walked down the beach a few yards, and her phone buzzed again with a text from Drew and a couple emails from Dot. But still nothing from Kendra.

Maddie's feet were now numb from the chilly water, so she returned to the dry sand and watched Kai catch a massive wave. He zipped down the ten-foot face and barreled through the rough surf. It'd been a while since she'd seen waves this big. Kai disappeared for a moment as he dove below a huge wall of water. When he appeared on the other side of the wave, his body looked tiny compared to the enormous breaker. Kai lived life with no fears. A recent shark sighting didn't even prevent him from doing what he loved most. Maybe one day she too would learn how to become fearless.

Chapter Nine

San Luis Obispo: November 2018

Maddie gazed out the window as she waited for the dean to arrive, the stunning view diminishing her irritation a bit. Hopefully this meeting wouldn't take long. Her last two meetings had been about students who complained about their grades, and the dean had sided with Maddie each time.

Mornings along the Central California Coast during autumn were often foggy and chilly, but right now, bright rays of sun filtered through the wispy clouds. Students flitted about on campus. Over the years, this campus had become so familiar to Maddie—a place where she'd often sit and find moments of peace before she taught class. From where she currently sat, she could see rows of eucalyptus trees. Each time she stepped onto campus, that scent reminded her of how much she loved teaching here and living in the area. Maddie smiled at both the view and the accomplishment of making the fifteen-minute drive to campus on her own this morning.

While she continued to wait, her phone vibrated with the arrival of a short email from the imaging center:

Doctor Hahn needs to see you in her office next week to talk about the results of your MRI. Please call us soon to set up an appointment.

Terror sat in the pit of Maddie's stomach, and she dropped her head in her hand. Why hadn't Doctor Hahn called her directly to tell her the results like she usually did? This email could only mean one thing: the MRI showed new tumor growth.

Since Doctor Lau upped her dose of anti-seizure medication, Maddie hadn't had any more seizures, but the headaches had gotten much worse. Maybe Doctor Hahn could do the robotic radiotherapy once again and eradicate the tumor like she did before. But maybe the

MRI showed only a tiny spot—something that could be treated with more chemo. That'd mean she'd lose her hair again and wouldn't be able to work due to how sick she'd get.

When she heard the dean's voice from down the hall, Maddie sat up straight and slowed her breathing. She had to get it together. As soon as the meeting with Sharon was over, she'd call to make an appointment with Doctor Hahn. For now, she'd do her best to be present during her meeting with the dean.

Sharon entered the office, and Maddie gave her a warm smile. "Good morning. So, which student is complaining about their grade this time? Is it one of the plagiarizers or someone who didn't like getting a D for writing a mediocre paper?"

"Give me a moment." Sharon's tone was cold, and she slapped a red folder on the desk.

The smile fell from Maddie's face. What was this about?

Sharon sat in her leather chair and rifled through the drawer until she found a red pen. She opened the folder and frowned at the contents, then looked back up. Sharon leaned forward, set her elbows on the desk, and regarded Maddie without a hint of friendliness in her face. "A few days ago, I got a call from HR. They said one of our part-time English instructors had violated federal privacy laws regarding students. I was surprised when HR told me it was you who they're investigating."

"I'm...being investigated?" Maddie gripped her cane. Surely, she'd heard wrong. The only federal privacy law Maddie knew about was FERPA. The federal law, more formally known as the Family Educational Rights and Privacy Act, meant professors couldn't reveal details about their students—be it their grade on an assignment or any other "identifiable information." Maddie became familiar with FERPA when she first got hired as a part-time professor years ago. Present at all of the pre-semester meetings and workshops, Maddie had listened attentively while administrators instilled fear in the instructors about what they could or couldn't reveal about their students.

Sharon slid the folder across the desk. "These are screenshots of your social media posts. Someone recently sent us images from your page. HR found these posts to be in violation of FERPA. Those screenshots are for you. HR has their own set of copies."

"Who took them? I don't even have any students added as friends." Maddie's free hand trembled as she peeked into the red folder. The familiar images of her Wall of Shame posts stared back at her, and the shock began to subside. So, that's what this was all about. Maddie should have this misunderstanding cleared up soon. "I think there's been some confusion. These kinds of private posts between professors are pretty common. Is it against the law to post students' errors?"

"It is when you include identifiable information."

"I never included identifiable information. Ever."

"We'll see. These are just some of your posts. HR is still investigating and continues to find more posts that violated FERPA."

Now Maddie was angry. "How are they able to see my posts? My page is set to private." Could it have been Diego who reported her? He often took students' sides and didn't seem to find Maddie's posts as funny.

Sharon tapped her pen on the desk and shrugged. "I'm sure they have their ways. They've hired lawyers and private investigators."

"Lawyers and private investigators?" Maddie stared at Sharon in astonishment. "For some private posts?" Any relief she'd felt vanished. This wasn't a meeting; it was a police interrogation. "But I never included the students' names with these posts. I only shared their errors and typos."

Sharon shrugged and sat back in her chair. "Like I said, we'll see."

"But a lot of English professors do this." Maddie was definitely going to contact her union rep after this meeting. She flipped through the printouts of her posts, including a screenshot of a works cited page that was full of errors. Nowhere on there was the student's name. But there were a lot of comments from fellow professors. "There are replies from Diego Estrada, Isaac Goldberg, and Jamie Miller. They're from the English Department. Why aren't they here?"

"That's not the point—"

"So many people from our college made comments on my posts." Maddie flailed her arm in the air. "Terri Smith, Miryam Abdullah, and Jamie Miller replied to my post. Jamie made a comment about there being no excuse for students to not proofread. Why aren't they being pulled up in front of the dean? Why am I being singled out?"

"Because they didn't break the law!" Sharon leaned forward and glared at Maddie. "All they did was comment on your posts, which isn't a crime. Not to mention that Professor Miller's name doesn't appear on your posts. At least one of my faculty members has some sense."

Maddie reread the screenshot. Sharon was right. Jamie's name was nowhere to be found. Maddie had never even noticed his comments had been deleted. When had that happened? Had Jamie deleted his account? Even if he had, his comments would still be in her feed unless he'd gone through and deleted them individually.

"To me, it's pretty obvious you've violated FERPA," Sharon said. "You have to realize this is possible grounds for termination."

"I might be fired?" Maddie blinked away the sudden tears. If she lost this job, it would be even harder to pay for her health care, not to mention for Taylor and her baby. "But I don't understand how these posts revealed any identifiable information. Like this one. How is it in violation?" Maddie slid the screenshot of the student's works cited page across the desk.

"You included the student's name at the top." Sharon tapped the page with the red pen and smirked at Maddie as if she'd won some sort of victory.

Maddie gripped the edge of the desk. "That's not the student's name. It's the name of the author of the first source on the works cited page. You can see right here that I used a sheet of paper to cover up the student's name in the upper right-hand corner of the page." Maddie took a breath to control her frustration. Sharon was the dean of humanities! How could she not recognize that this was a works cited page listing the authors and sources used in a paper?

"We'll leave it up to HR to determine if this one was a violation of FERPA." Sharon moved the paper to the side of her keyboard, slapped a yellow stickie at the top, and wrote something that Maddie couldn't see. "Later today, I'll check the rosters from your classes to search for this name. If it shows up, you could be terminated."

"I assure you that name will not show up on my class roster—because it's the name of an author of one of those sources." Maddie relaxed a bit. This was all likely just a blown-up situation. HR had nothing on her. So far, her posts were clearly not in violation of FERPA.

"Regardless, you've posted identifiable information that clearly violates FERPA. You have to understand something. Any student who's been publicly identified can sue you."

The nervousness returned. "I might be sued? Who took these screenshots?" Somebody must be out to get Maddie—someone who pretended to be her friend but was looking for any chance to get her fired. But who?

"Maddie, you've essentially made fun of your students. What does that say about you as a professor? The person who reported all of this said it seems like you hate your students."

Maddie gaped at her. "Hate my students? Absolutely not! I'm strict, yes, but I want them to do well. These kinds of posts, we all make them. It's just venting. We get annoyed, that's all. You know how intense grading can be. After seeing so many essays with numerous errors and dealing with students who often don't follow directions, we need to let off steam." In no way did she hate her students, many of whom she now considered friends, people she genuinely cared about. "It's why I make sure my posts are set to private, so no one gets hurt."

"I know exactly how stressful grading can be. Yet I never felt the need to humiliate people like this." Sharon looked down her nose, as if Maddie was something distasteful. "The person who reported this to us said you—"

"Who reported this? You haven't told me. Was it a

faculty member? A student?" Maddie's voice rose in anger. She was gripping her cane so tightly that her fingers hurt. Who would go so far as to take screenshots of her posts? Was it someone vying for the full-time position? Someone who wanted to take Maddie out of the running?

"The person who called the school and sent us these screenshots requested that they remain anonymous, and I've made that promise. Maddie, you've violated FERPA."

"I certainly didn't mean to violate FERPA. You know how I follow protocol with the district's rules. I've always been a rule follower." With the exception of skinny-dipping after-hours in the pool with Kendra. She definitely broke the rules then. Despite everything, Maddie couldn't help laughing under her breath at the memory.

"I don't understand how you can find this situation humorous. You've violated the law. Do you comprehend the severity of this situation?"

Maddie straightened her face. "I do. I promise. But I didn't include any names when I posted these things. I was just trying to—"

"There's one post that includes the student's age. That's identifiable information. It's the one where you mention that the student is a reentry student, a seventy-six-year-old grandmother."

Oh no. "Phillis Nunley," Maddie said under her breath. That was indeed identifiable information. This couldn't be enough to get Maddie into real trouble. Could it? She met Sharon's eyes and spoke with sincerity. "That was a genuine mistake. I'll delete the post. In fact, I'll delete all of them."

Maddie's breath became short, and she leafed through the pages. Whoever took these screenshots had captured most of the student errors she posted so far this semester, but then she saw a couple screenshots she definitely did not post—including one that did include the student's name. The image was simply a screenshot of the first page from Phillis Nunley's graded paper—the one full of glaring grammatical errors. Maddie recognized her own handwriting and saw all the errors she'd circled and corrected. The paper was one of the worst essays Maddie had ever read. She handed the screenshot to Sharon. "I absolutely did not post this one."

Sharon looked distinctly unimpressed. "There are so many inappropriate posts here that I'm not at all surprised you don't remember making all of them."

"I have never posted a copy of someone's essay!"

"You've publicly humiliated this student by including identifiable information in this screenshot. Her name is right at the top of the paper." Sharon's face twisted in disapproval, and she drummed her nails on the desk. "I'm disappointed in you. I thought you had much more integrity than this."

And Maddie thought Sharon had more faith in her than this. "But that's just a photo of a page from a paper I graded. How can you prove I posted that on social media? The screenshot doesn't even show it came from my page."

"We'll leave it to HR and their attorneys to handle the investigation. For now, you'll be on probation until HR further investigates the charges. There's a form I need you to sign to show that you're aware of the potential charges."

Sharon shuffled through stacks of papers. Maddie was sick to her stomach. Teaching was one thing that kept her going and gave her purpose. Never in her life had she been put on probation or been accused of breaking the law. She was certain someone was out to get her and had made it seem as if the page from Phillis Nunley's paper was something Maddie had shared. But she couldn't deny that she did make all of the other posts—including the one revealing Phillis's age. Was Phillis behind this? Was she getting revenge for what Maddie said about her? But how was it possible, when all the posts were private?

"I'll have to see if one of the secretaries has the form." Sharon stood, not bothering to look Maddie in the eye. "Wait here while I see if they can find it." She stormed to the other room, closing the door behind her with a loud thud.

Maddie shuffled the printouts back into the folder and slumped in the chair. Reprimanded, in fear of losing her job, and she still had to deal with that email from the imaging center. The only other time the center had requested an appointment was a few years ago when Doctor Hahn saw the new spot on the scan. It must mean the recent MRI showed new tumor growth; there was no other explanation. Maddie started to tremble and cry. She hadn't had a chance to tell anyone about the email yet, not even Drew or Dot.

But there was one person she wanted to tell right away—someone who'd totally understand. Maddie scrolled through her texts to find the latest one from Kendra and tapped out a few words:

Rough day at work. Also got a concerning message from the imaging center. Any chance you could meet me later today? Maybe help me get my mind off things?

Maddie paused while thinking of where they could meet. She wanted it to be a special location, a place which meant so much to her years ago. But was she ready to return to that spot? Without much more thought, Maddie added one more line about the time and place where they could meet, assuming Kendra would be available. Since Maddie comfortably made the fifteen-minute drive to campus this morning, she'd be able to handle a few more minutes on the road. At this point, with the fears about the MRI results and the possibility of getting fired, all Maddie wanted to do was be with Kendra.

When Sharon's heels clicked on the tile floor just outside the office, Maddie hit send and hoped Kendra saw the message right away. The only thing that could comfort her would be Kendra's hand in hers. So what if Kendra would only ever be a friend with benefits? For now, that had to be enough.

Chapter Ten

Morro Bay: November 2018

Maddie and Kendra sat on a wooden bench under the shadow of Morro Rock. Behind them was an empty lifeguard tower where one lone seagull perched atop the railing. Maddie shivered from the chilly breeze and snuggled closer to Kendra. The curves of Kendra's body, especially pressed tightly next to hers, were oddly familiar—as if they'd been in this position many times.

Although the fears continued to circulate in her head, Maddie wanted a few hours to not think about being sick, to not compare cancer stories or share her concerns about her upcoming appointment. For this afternoon, she wanted to live as if she didn't have glioblastoma, to not be fearful of more aggressive treatment in the near future. At this point, the possibility of losing her job seemed insignificant compared to more chemo and radiation.

The sun was low in the sky, but several surfers remained in the water. The waves peaked at three to five feet—perfect for a longboard. When Maddie used to surf at this break, she'd ride as many waves as possible before it became too dark to see.

A female surfer dipped into a cresting wave and rode it all the way to shore, bringing with it a tsunami of despair. Maddie could no longer surf and never would again. The next few months would be characterized by lethargy and a weakened immune system. She'd be lucky to perform routine daily activities without feeling winded.

But when Kendra kissed her softly on the lips, the despair vanished, and everything felt right. Maddie couldn't take her eyes off Kendra's face. Struck by how stunning she looked, Maddie's heart was full and happy. She gazed deep into Kendra's eyes and reached over to hold her hand. With their fingers interlaced, things were normal, at least for now.

Only a few vehicles remained in the parking area—the same dirt lot where she was taken away by ambulance four years ago. How different this place looked now compared to then. Being autumn, no lifeguards remained on duty at this hour. Fewer people rode the waves today compared to the numerous surfers who crowded the surf zone during summer when the evening air was warm. A cold breeze blew through the slats of the bench, causing Maddie to shiver again. The ridge above the sand was secluded—a perfect location to enjoy the sunset with Kendra.

Kendra wrapped her arm around Maddie and kissed her gently on the forehead. "It's probably getting too cold to stay outside. How about we get some take-out and head to my place? There's a great Thai food restaurant by my house that makes the best curry."

Maddie grinned. "I love curry. The hotter, the better."

Kendra gave Maddie a cheeky grin. "I like it really hot. I've got a chilled bottle of Chardonnay in the fridge...and French-roast coffee for the morning. How do cheesy grits and toasted bagels sound for breakfast?"

Doubtful that a California girl knew how to make grits, Maddie playfully narrowed her eyes. "You know how to make cheesy grits?"

"They might not be like your mom's cheesy grits, but I've been practicing ever since I heard you say how much you love Southern grits when we were at Monarch Bluffs."

Many things had surprised Maddie today, but none of them made her heart soar like this revelation. It was impossible to keep the broad smile off her face. "You have?"

"Of course!" Kendra gave her a mischievous smile in return. "As a romance writer, I know very well that the way to a woman's heart is through her taste buds."

"You got that right." None of Maddie's partners had ever learned to cook for her. This was a first, and she couldn't wait to enjoy the meal. "It all sounds perfect, but I want to stay here until the sun disappears, to savor every last moment before it's dark." Maddie set her head on Kendra's shoulder and closed her eyes for a few seconds, locking this moment into her memory for when she might be too frail or too sick to make it back here.

It was impossible to not let the fears about the MRI results ruin the moment, though. Maddie couldn't completely forget she could be facing a rough road ahead with more chemo. Though she hadn't expressed this to anyone, Maddie had one thought she couldn't get out of her mind—that she could simply refuse more treatment and let the cancer run its course.

"Been a while since I watched the sunset at the beach." Kendra pulled Maddie even closer. "And a really long time since I did this with a beautiful woman at my side."

Not used to anyone complimenting her appearance, Maddie felt awkward and wasn't sure how to respond. At a loss for words, she sat up and pressed her lips against Kendra's—the kiss so tender and perfect. The women Maddie had been with in the past rarely showed affection in public, saying that sort of thing should be saved for the bedroom. Maddie loved how uninhibited Kendra was with her kisses and the way she held her hand or pulled her body close to hers—even here in Morro Bay, where surfers exited the water and beachgoers walked along the shore.

Maddie focused on the orange orb sinking lower in the sky. Years ago, surfing at sunset was her favorite time to be in the ocean. "I hate how early the sun sets in mid-autumn. Back when I lived in San Clemente, Kai and I would surf until dark during the summer months. When I was a kid, summers used to feel endless. After I moved up here, I'd come here late in the day during summer and surf until sunset. It'd be after eight o'clock when I'd be packing up my gear and driving home."

"Sounds like a perfect way to end the day." Kendra ran her fingers through Maddie's hair—her touch so tender, as if they'd been together for years.

"Not as perfect as ending the day this way." Maddie set her hand on Kendra's face and kissed her, their lips so eager for each other. Although they'd only known each other for less than a month and hadn't actually gone out, Maddie was so drawn to Kendra and couldn't get enough of her kisses.

Kendra gazed at Maddie and smiled. "I could get used to this."

"Me or sunsets on the beach?" Maddie laughed, although she knew her question wasn't all that funny.

"I never thought I'd say this after Bree, but...well, both."

Maddie drank in the way the golden rays of sunlight reflected on Kendra's face. "Might as well enjoy as many sunsets as we can, huh?"

"I forget how necessary it is to slow down and watch the sunset every now and then. Seems I'm always busy working on a book or researching my next one. Probably best to just take it one day at a time and not think too far ahead. Who knows what tomorrow will bring?"

"Well, I know what Monday will bring, another appointment with Doctor Hahn."

Kendra slipped her hand in Maddie's. "I know how scary those appointments are."

"Right when I got diagnosed with cancer, I felt like I'd been thrown into uncharted waters and knew I'd have a rough road ahead. There were so many unknowns about whether the treatment would work, and here I am again, facing more uncertainty."

Kendra gave Maddie's hand a little squeeze. "Waiting for test results is scary."

Maddie blinked away the tears. "I always feel it's a matter of when, not if, as far as the cancer returning. I mean, look at my odds with this type of cancer."

Kendra leaned closer so that their arms and shoulders were touching. "If you've made it this far, don't you think you might actually be beating this thing?"

"I thought that a few days ago, but now I don't know."

"It's hard to not stay in the moment when waiting for test results."

Maddie nodded slowly. "It used to be that the most important thing to me was surfing and competing. When I was a teenager, that was everything to me. I'd get so upset if I lost a competition or if I couldn't surf due to bad weather. Now, the most important things are the simple moments…like this."

"I have a feeling you'll surf again," Kendra said quietly.

Maddie's eyes filled with tears. Kendra sounded so confident. "When I first surfed years ago, I was hooked right away. I pretty much surfed every day and was determined to get stronger and better on the waves. Whenever I rode the last wave of the day, I told myself there'd always be more surfing the next day and the one after that. Or if I didn't have such a good session of surfing, I'd tell myself there's always another wave. I had no idea four years ago that I'd ride my last wave."

Kendra looked deep into Maddie's eyes and set her hand on her leg. "I'm sure that wasn't your last wave. Maybe one day you'll show me where you used to surf in Hawaii. It'd be fun to meet your *ohana* and travel to a couple of the islands with you."

"On your dad's jet?" Maddie laughed and wiped the tears from her face.

"No, on a regular airline, how most people travel."

"I'd love to go to Hawaii with you." A big smile had replaced the tears.

"We could start by going to Oahu, then Maui, and then Molokai. I researched that island after you told me it best represents old Hawaii. Molokai definitely seems like a great locale for my next novel."

"You'll love it there." Maddie set her hand atop Kendra's and found she wasn't wearing her ring. Her finger looked bare without the wedding band. "No wedding ring today?"

Kendra looked at her hand and smiled. "For today, I feel like I don't need to pretend I'm taken to avoid someone hitting on me. Right now, being here with you feels right, but I guess if I think too far ahead, then I freak myself out."

Maddie loved the way Kendra's eyes lit up when she smiled. She nudged Kendra. "Then don't think too far ahead. That whole one day at a time mentality is probably best for both of us right now."

"As long as one day at a time means time with you, then I like that sort of mentality. I also like how nice it feels with you next to me. Ever since I got cancer, I've learned to cherish the simple things in life. Moments like this with you."

"So, since you're not wearing that ring to fend off potential suitors, does this mean I can hit on you?" Maddie batted her lashes in an attempt to be flirty.

"Well, I was hoping." Kendra grinned and cupped her hands around Maddie's face.

The kisses quickly became more intense—Kendra's lips and tongue causing Maddie to crave more of her. She threw her arms around Kendra, pulling her closer, their lips meeting once again. When they broke for air, Maddie pulled back and giggled. She could wait until they were at Kendra's place. For now, she was satisfied with Kendra's hand in hers as they watched the sun disappear beyond the ocean and leave streaks of lavender and orange in the sky.

Chapter Eleven

San Luis Obispo: November 2018

Barely awake, Maddie rolled onto her side and opened her eyes. The golden light of morning filtered between sage green curtains into the bedroom. Matching sheets covered the soft mattress and fluffy pillows. Best of all, Kendra was snuggled close and sliding her hand across Maddie's hip. In the dim light of the room, Maddie couldn't read the clock on the nightstand and had no idea if it was seven o'clock or eleven. But with the silky sheets against her bare skin and Kendra's warm body pressed against hers, Maddie wanted to stay in bed for as long as possible.

Kendra gently ran her fingers across Maddie's abs, who in turn got so turned on that she gasped. The depth of arousal surprised her, yet in the past couple days, she'd moved way beyond initial attraction and lust. Maddie was starting to really fall for Kendra. How could she feel so passionate about someone this fast? She barely even knew Kendra. Surely this was just infatuation—a distraction as she tried to keep her mind off her upcoming appointment.

But, so what if this was a distraction? For now, she had the rest of today to lose herself in Kendra. Still sleepy, Maddie set her hand on Kendra's and savored having her nude body spooned behind hers. This moment with Kendra seemed so familiar, even though it'd been years since Maddie had woken up with a beautiful woman. Kendra kissed Maddie's shoulder and brushed her fingers once more against her abdomen. Intense heat surged through Maddie, her breathing getting heavier. Despite falling asleep so sated last night, she craved Kendra even more right now.

Kendra kissed Maddie on the neck and slid her hand even lower, almost between Maddie's legs. "I love how your skin feels against my hand."

Maddie moaned softly and pulled Kendra's arm tighter around her body. "And I love how your hand feels on my skin." She shivered. "And your lips on my neck. Such a perfect way to start the day."

Kendra gently rolled Maddie over and met her with a sultry smile. "I could definitely get used to this sort of thing." She'd said the same words yesterday at sunset and again last night after they made love.

"Mmm, me too." Even though she too could get used to mornings like this, Maddie was aware that these moments would soon be limited. Then she stopped herself. There would be none of that this weekend. She was going to enjoy her time with Kendra.

"You feel like going out tonight?" Kendra ran her hand over Maddie's abs once again and then up to her breasts.

Kendra's touch brought Maddie back to the here and now. "Tonight? Did we sleep that late?" She tried to sit up to look at the clock on the nightstand.

Kendra quickly pulled Maddie back into her arms. "Tonight is hours away, but I don't have any intentions of getting out of bed anytime soon."

"I like the way that sounds." With Kendra's hand cupped around her breast and their bodies snug against each other, Maddie didn't want this morning or the weekend to end.

"Since my sister's out of town, we've got the whole condo to ourselves, but I thought we could go out later this evening."

"So, a real date? Like, dinner and a movie?" Maddie laughed quietly and relaxed into Kendra's embrace. It'd been so long since she'd gone out with a woman that she forgot what lesbian couples did on a Saturday night. Then again, she and Kendra were a far cry from being a couple.

"Not quite that cliché. I was thinking dinner and drinks at a gay club in SLO that my friend manages. You like to dance? My friend says they've got a guest DJ tonight from New York who plays lots of good EDM mixes."

"I love to dance to electronic dance music, but I'm

not sure I've got the right clubbing attire."

"Babe, you'd look great in anything." Kendra nuzzled her face close to Maddie's neck and slid her hand down her leg.

Did she just say "babe"? How did they move from a couple nights of having sex to using sweet endearments? But as Kendra snuggled closer, Maddie smiled and relaxed into her warmth.

"I feel like I'm way beyond my clubbing years, but it'd be fun to go dancing with you, especially if you're wearing something cute." Maddie set her hand atop Kendra's. The thought of going out with such a hot woman by her side filled her with pride.

"Great, so then it's a non-cliché date, but I first want to savor more time with you here in bed."

Maddie looked deep into Kendra's eyes as she ran her fingers through her hair. The morning light through the window illuminated Kendra's creamy skin, inviting Maddie to explore every inch of Kendra's body. As Maddie slid her hands down Kendra's back, she pulled her closer and kissed her softly on the lips. Kendra's lips and tongue met Maddie's, the kisses quickly becoming more sensual.

Kendra's breasts against her own left Maddie hungry for more. As Maddie pressed her body against Kendra's, they both moaned softly. Maddie was so in tune to the way Kendra moved against her. She pulled back and admired Kendra's body. It was perfect to her. Maddie ran her fingers across Kendra's ribcage and then over the scars below her breasts but didn't linger there for very long.

"It's been so long since someone's touched me the way you do." Kendra guided Maddie's hand to her lower abs.

"Everything about you is incredibly sexy." Maddie slid her hand down to her hip.

"My God, you are so hot," Kendra whispered into Maddie's ear, moving her hand to Maddie's inner thigh and inching her way higher.

Maddie's craving intensified, and heat radiated through her body. She moaned and slid her knees apart.

Kendra slipped her hand between Maddie's legs until her fingers brushed against her wetness.

Maddie gasped. "I can't get enough of you," she said between breaths.

"That makes two of us." Kendra kissed Maddie softly on the lips.

Maddie moved her leg between Kendra's thighs, the movement causing Kendra to moan softly and kiss her harder. As their kisses became more passionate, their breaths intensified, and Kendra's body moved in rhythm to her own. Kendra's lips found their way to Maddie's neck and then to her breasts. When Kendra playfully flicked her tongue against Maddie's nipple, she shuddered in ecstasy. Kendra wrapped her lips around Maddie's hard nipple, immediately causing Maddie to get even more wet, and she dug her fingers into Kendra's back.

When Kendra pressed her hand against Maddie's slickness, the intensity was almost too much for her. Kendra's gentle and steady strokes brought her even closer to the edge.

Maddie moaned softly. "Don't stop. I want you inside me."

Kendra's fingers worked their magic. "I love the way you feel. Every inch of you is so beautiful."

As Kendra increased the pressure, heat and electricity surged through every fiber of Maddie's body—moving from deep inside her chest and down through her abdomen. As Kendra's fingers entered her and as the kisses became more passionate, Maddie moaned and pulled Kendra closer. She never wanted this morning to end. In this moment, Maddie felt so full of vitality and joy, the kisses turning her world upside down.

Chapter Twelve

San Luis Obispo: November 2018

Halfway up the stairs, Maddie's legs became weak. Last night's clubbing had taken a lot out of her. Kendra had offered to do the shopping on her own, but Maddie wanted to make sure they got all the right ingredients. In return, Kendra insisted on carrying all four bags of groceries to the second floor of the condo complex. Maddie gripped her hand on the railing and took her time going up each step. A gentle breeze washed over her—the air cool and refreshing against her face. About an hour before sunset, hints of pink and lavender seeped through the clouds.

Out of breath from the short jaunt across the parking lot and up the stairs, Maddie paused before going up the last step. "Are you sure you're fine not going out tonight?"

Kendra unlocked the door and gave her a mischievous smile. "I think I got my fill of clubbing last night. Staying in on a Sunday night and having a beautiful woman cook me dinner is way better than going to a crowded restaurant or a loud bar."

Despite her exhaustion, Maddie smiled. This weekend had been perfect. At the club last night, Kendra had kept hold of her the entire time. If she wasn't firmly grasping Maddie's hand, then she had an arm wrapped around her shoulders. The cheesy grits Kendra made this morning were nearly as good as Mom's. Best of all was that they still had this evening and tonight—and another morning of waking up together.

Maddie followed Kendra into the kitchen. "It's been a while since I've stayed out so late with such a hot woman, but my feet aren't used to all that dancing. The edema is bad again."

"You're definitely up for cooking dinner?" Kendra

emptied the bag of vegetables and pulled jars of sauces and spices from the other sack.

"I want nothing more than to do something any normal couple would do on a Sunday night." Maddie let out a nervous laugh. The reference to them being a couple sounded odd, as if they were in it for the long haul.

"Same here. And I'll help you, even though I'm not the best cook." Kendra surveyed the ingredients displayed on the counter. "When did you learn how to make pork dumplings and low mein?"

"My grandma taught me most of the basics after my mom and I moved to California. My mom showed me how to make more unique dishes, things she'd fix at home for me and Kai. Popo's getting up there in age, but she's still in charge of Royal Palace, where my mom works on the weekends." Maddie arranged the jars and bottles on the counter—the labels all looking familiar from when Popo taught her how to make lo mein and pork dumplings.

"You're lucky you had a grandmother and a mom who taught you to cook. My grandma died when I was young…from breast cancer. Don't remember much about her since I was only six when she died. My parents tended to order take-out or purchased pre-made meals from high-end markets, especially after the divorce."

"I'm sorry." Maddie gave her a sympathetic look and squeezed her arm. "That sounds lonely."

"It wasn't so bad." Kendra shrugged, then let out a little laugh. "It made clean-up in the kitchen pretty easy."

Maddie smiled in response. "There's nothing quite like a home-cooked dinner. As long as you help me chop the vegetables and pour me a glass of wine, I'm totally up for cooking this meal."

"So, I'll be your very own sous chef," Kendra said, her voice playful and sultry. She took a bottle of Chardonnay out of the fridge and retrieved two glasses from the cabinet.

Kendra uncorked the bottle, and Maddie's eyes widened when she recognized the label. It'd been years since she'd tasted this wine and even longer since she could afford it. How many times had Maddie craved its unique vanilla and pear flavor, only to regretfully put the bottle back on the shelf because it was impossible to justify the expense? Kendra handed her the glass, and Maddie admired the golden color of the liquid. She took a whiff of the Chardonnay before tasting it. The buttery aroma, so reminiscent of freshly baked shortbread, made her mouth water. They clinked their glasses together, and Maddie sipped the wine—the richness of the liquid reminding her of life prior to cancer when she didn't have to budget her money or limit her consumption of alcohol.

Kendra peeled the carrots while Maddie opened the package of tofu and let it drain in a colander. She then rinsed the bok choy, shitake mushrooms, snow peas, and garlic, and set them on the chopping board. It'd been so long since she'd cooked a meal for someone she was dating, especially someone she was so into. She wanted to savor every single moment—each sip, each morsel, each kiss. While they chopped the vegetables and sipped wine, Maddie's heart was full and happy. She was proud she remembered how to make the sauce for lo mein and how to prepare the mixture for pork dumplings. Everything Mom and Popo taught her years ago came back to her so clearly, as if she were standing next to them in the cramped kitchen at Royal Palace and preparing entrées for the customers.

"Make sure the carrots are sliced thinly." Maddie stepped closer to Kendra and grabbed a paring knife from the drawer. "Long and thin like this."

Maddie stood behind Kendra and demonstrated how to make the carrots the perfect shape—thin and almost feathery. She pressed her chest against Kendra's back, their bodies moving in rhythm with each slice of the vegetables.

When Kendra's breathing got heavy, Maddie set the knife on the counter and kissed her on the neck. Maddie pulled the top of Kendra's sweatshirt back, and her lips traveled down to her shoulder blade. The softness of Kendra's skin against Maddie's lips filled her with longing. She reached her arms around Kendra's body and breathed in the sweet scent of her skin. Everything about Kendra was all that Maddie had ever wanted in a woman.

Kendra turned to face Maddie, and then their lips met. The kisses quickly became more passionate, Kendra's tongue making Maddie want to forgo dinner and escape to the bedroom. But with plenty of hours left until morning, Maddie would cherish every moment with Kendra, including cooking this meal together.

"Just a little appetizer to whet your appetite," Maddie said between kisses.

Kendra pulled Maddie closer. "You better save room for dessert."

When Maddie pressed her pelvis against Kendra's, heat radiated through her body, settling between her legs. Kendra's breaths matched Maddie's, their bodies moving as if they'd been together for years. Kendra pulled back and gazed into Maddie's eyes—the look of desire getting her more aroused. In the past few days, Maddie's attraction for Kendra had magnified, but those blue eyes got her every time.

"I'll always have room for dessert." Maddie slid her hand between Kendra's thighs, the movement causing both of them to moan softly. She pulled back and gave Kendra a sly smile. "I'd better get back to cooking or else we'll be eating dinner at midnight."

"Anything else I can do?" Kendra asked.

"Hmm." Maddie examined the chopped vegetables sitting in various bowls as she quickly washed her hands. "Not right now."

"Okay. Let me know when you need me." Kendra hoisted her body onto the counter and took another sip of wine. "You've definitely made me good and hungry. I love watching you prepare this meal. Always been a fantasy of mine to have a woman cook for me."

Maddie laughed. "This is your idea of a fantasy? Wait'll you taste my food. Then you might need to modify your fantasy."

"Maybe I will." Kendra gave her a wicked smile. "I can imagine you in a cute outfit while—" Her phone rang, and she looked at the screen. "It's my dad. I'll take it outside." Kendra hopped off the counter and quickly walked through the door onto the deck.

Maddie pried open jars of sauces and spices. It was

always fun to line them up in order of use. Now it was time to start cooking.

She filled a pot with water and set it on the back burner. Next, she set a skillet on the front burner, added some sesame oil, and turned on the stove. Bits of Kendra's phone call filtered through while Maddie methodically cut each piece of tofu into one-inch cubes and placed them in a small mixing bowl. The conversation was getting heated, and Kendra paced from one end of the deck to the other as she flailed an arm. Behind her, the sun dipped lower into the horizon.

Aware that she couldn't intervene or urge Kendra to end the call, Maddie busied herself by preparing the main entrée: lo mein. In a medium-sized bowl, she mixed cornstarch and garlic powder until they were evenly blended. Then she dropped in the cubes of tofu and made sure each piece was fully coated. She added more oil to the skillet, along with a couple drops of dark soy sauce, turned up the heat, and added the tofu. As it sizzled in the pan, aromatic steam wafted onto her face. Maddie added a couple more drops of soy sauce and a dash of mirin, in the precise ratio Popo taught her years ago.

The only thing missing was appropriate dinner music, so Maddie scrolled through her playlists until she found the one titled "Chill Tunes." It'd been years since she listened to this playlist—the songs selected right after she got cancer when she knew she'd be facing a difficult journey as she fought to stay alive. A blend of mellow electronic tunes, the mix always helped to make her feel more relaxed and centered. Maddie tapped on the first song and took out two eggs from the fridge for the fried rice, setting them on the counter for now.

On the counter next to the refrigerator were a few framed photos. In one of them, Kendra stood next to a young teen, probably her niece or maybe a fellow cancer warrior. Completely bald, Kendra grinned and held up her middle finger. The young teen did the same. The two of them wore black T-shirts with "FXCK CANCER" on the front in bold pink letters, the X fashioned into a pink ribbon. How fierce Kendra looked in this photo—bald, brave, and brazen. Maddie wondered if she had it in her to be that brave in this next phase of her own cancer treatment.

Maddie took another sip of wine, then added bok choy to the skillet and poured a bit of sesame oil over the vegetables. As the sauce sizzled in the pan, she lowered the heat and added the ramen noodles to the pot of boiling water. She'd forgotten how much she missed cooking, how meal preparation was such a creative process.

When "Venice Beach" by Dinka came on, Maddie moved her body to the rhythm and turned up the volume. Immediately, she lost herself in the steady beat. This track always took her far away, to a place where she didn't have to think about radiation or chemo. The blend of percussion and electronic beats were like the steady rhythm of the waves churning toward shore. For a moment, she imagined riding the cusp of a breaker—her body becoming one with the wave.

While she continued to cook, she bopped her head to the music, but then a wave of dizziness washed over her. Not used to the higher alcohol content of this Chardonnay, Maddie knew she should slow down and wait to have more wine when they ate dinner. But the dizziness was nothing new. For the past couple days, she'd had brief episodes of wooziness, along with the usual bad headaches. This time, she was also hit with a bout of weakness, and Maddie knew she didn't have it in her to make the dumplings or fried rice. She'd need to alter the menu for tonight's dinner and only focus on the items cooking on the stove. Maddie set the makings for pork dumplings aside and checked the noodles and veggies simmering in the pans.

A door clicked shut, and Maddie looked up to see Kendra leaning against the doorway and smiling. But the smile seemed fake, as if she was covering up how she really felt.

Maddie lowered the heat on the burners and turned down the music. "You okay?"

"I'm fine. Couldn't be any better. I like that you're already so comfortable in my kitchen, and I love how your body moves to the music." Kendra kissed Maddie softly on the lips, then leaned against the counter and crossed her arms as she dropped her gaze to the tile floor.

Something wasn't right. The deep lines in Kendra's brow and the faraway look in her eyes conveyed to Maddie all was not fine. "I take it the call with your dad didn't go well?"

"Depends on how you look at it. I told him once and for all that I'll never take over his business. He didn't exactly take it well, but I told him he has no choice. I'll never be a vice president of his company or a chief executive officer. He told me I'd never make it on my own with my writing and editing jobs, said I was making a huge mistake by not becoming a hotel developer."

"I'm sorry. Could you have some sort of limited role? Maybe be part of the company but not be one of the vice presidents?"

"I've always been an all or nothing kind of person. Ever since I got cancer, the thought of running a hotel development company doesn't appeal to me. Not in the least. It's like we talked about on the beach. Having cancer really makes you shift your perspective. My dad doesn't understand that I want to get the most out of life and not spend time doing things that don't interest me."

"Can you tell him that?"

"I've tried a few times, but he just doesn't get it. I did appease him by agreeing to help him with his website and write some promotional materials. Just some easy writing and editing here and there. Even that was a stretch for me as far as my involvement with his company."

Maddie gave her a wry smile. "I guess he'll finally read something you've written."

Kendra stared at her for a moment and then burst into laughter. "You know how to see the positive in a situation, that's for sure."

"I do my best," Maddie said, secretly pleased she'd been able to make Kendra laugh. "So, you're fine with not using those business degrees you spent all that time earning?" Maddie added some sesame oil and mirin to the skillet and reduced the heat to the lowest setting.

"After so many years of not being sure I'd live past thirty, I want to do something much more meaningful with my life, like write books and travel to Hawaii with you." Kendra wrapped an arm around Maddie's waist and pulled her close. "And eat what'll probably be the best meal I've had in a long time."

Maddie kissed Kendra softly on the lips, but when another wave of dizziness washed over her, she gripped her hands on the sink and took a few deep breaths.

Kendra set her hand on Maddie's back. "What's going on?"

Maddie didn't want to ruin tonight by being sick, but she also knew she couldn't hide anything from Kendra. "The dizziness is bad again. I'm hoping it's just the wine. Unfortunately, I've had to alter the menu for tonight. I ran out of energy to make the pork dumplings and the fried rice. I'm sorry our dinner is going to be so simple."

"Babe, it's okay." Kendra wrapped her arms around Maddie and kissed her on the forehead. "Trust me when I say I understand. Let's sit down and enjoy this meal. We need to get you off your feet. This looks like plenty of food. We can always make the rice and dumplings tomorrow night or the next night. Maybe you can teach me how to make pork dumplings."

Could she? Tomorrow, she would get the news about the MRI. Everything would be different after that. Maddie's eyes filled with tears, but she relaxed into Kendra's embrace. They still had several hours until Maddie had to leave in the morning.

"I don't want tonight to end," Maddie said quietly as she choked back tears.

"Me neither." Kendra held her tighter. "I'm not leaving your side all night long."

Chapter Thirteen

San Luis Obispo: November 2018

It was Monday morning—the day Maddie had been dreading. The waiting room was crowded and stuffy, so she kept herself preoccupied by rereading the texts Kendra sent earlier:

Although I'm not with you at your appointment, know that I'm there with you in spirit. Nothing about cancer is easy, but I'm glad our paths crossed when they did. I don't think we would've connected so deeply had we not shared our cancer stories. And for that I'm grateful. Cancer sucks, but it led me to you. If you haven't figured it out by now, I kinda like you. I think about you all the time and count the hours to when we can be together again. Looking forward to learning how to make pork dumplings!

Maddie smiled at the last two sentences, but a tinge of sadness washed over her. Everything about the last three days had been perfect—as if Maddie and Kendra had already shared many weekends together and would share many more. Although she too liked Kendra, Maddie had a rough road ahead because of more chemo and extensive treatment. Even if the scan only revealed a minuscule dot of new tumor growth, that would still require harsh treatment, which would be a lot to put a new girlfriend through.

Angela, Maddie's mom, sat to her right and Taylor to her left. Taylor was in her fifth month of pregnancy and no longer had morning sickness, but the baby bump was more prominent. Although she wore baggy sweats and oversized sweatshirts, Taylor wouldn't be able to hide the pregnancy for much longer.

Kai and Drew stood by the entrance since there weren't enough seats in the waiting room. Drew ran a hand through his sandy blond hair. His shirt was untucked and wrinkled. Kai looked tired, which was concerning, but he'd insisted he was fine. Maddie had to admit his presence was a comfort, even though she knew why Mom and Kai were here. Everyone in her family feared the worst. Maddie started to tremble.

Angela put an arm around her. "Honey, no matter what the results are, we're going to get through this together."

"Thanks, Mom." Maddie lowered her head as she blinked back the tears and read Kendra's text once more, focusing on the words, "Nothing about cancer is easy." While the phrase resonated in her head, she looked up from her phone to find Kai looking at her and smiling warmly. In her mind, Maddie could almost hear him say, "*Keiki*, you got this." No matter if she faced a surf competition, brain surgery, or radiation and chemo, Kai always had a way of reducing Maddie's anxiety.

Right when Maddie started typing a response to Kendra, a guy's voice called out to her. "Professor Fong!" Maddie looked up to see a clean-cut young man waving at her from across the waiting room. It was a former student from a few years ago—from before Maddie got sick. The guy walked over and leaned in to give her a hug.

Too exhausted to stand, Maddie remained in her seat. "It's always nice to run into a former student. This is my daughter, Taylor, and my mom, Angela." Maddie searched her memory for the student's name. She knew it started with a J but couldn't remember it. Jared, Josh, Jake?

The young man stood in front of Maddie and gave her a friendly smile. "I stopped by campus recently to pick up my transcript and was hoping to run into you. I even walked past our old classroom to see if you were in there."

"I'm only on campus one afternoon a week now," Maddie said, still uncertain of his name. He'd taken her literature class a few years ago and was the vice president of the pride club, which she co-advised until she got sick. But what was his name? Worried the lapse in memory was due to new tumor growth affecting the part of her brain which stored information, Maddie's stomach churned in panic.

"When I was on campus last week, I looked for you at the pride club meeting, but they said you hadn't advised it in years."

"I had to give that up when I got sick a few years ago. I'm still teaching, but I couldn't take on too much more during my treatment."

Suddenly, it all came back to her. How could she have forgotten Jace's name? She'd come out to him and even accepted his friend requests on two of her social media platforms, which was a rarity for her to do considering he was a former student.

"I heard you got sick." Jace smiled and shoved his hands in his pockets. "But it sounds like you're doing pretty well now. I saw you posted about going to Big Sur for a writing conference."

Maddie grinned. Being at Monarch Bluffs with Kendra had been so much fun. "It was a weekend retreat. Felt great to be around so many writers."

Jace folded his arms, and his face got serious. "I hope you're just here for routine tests. I'm here with my grandma. They found a spot on her liver, so now she needs more testing."

"Nothing about these tests is easy, so it's good you're here to support her." Maddie looked up to see a short older woman walking through the doorway.

"Oh, here's my grandma now," Jace said and smiled at her.

It was Phillis Nunley, the bitter old woman from class. Phillis was Jace's grandma? Phillis got closer, leaning on her cane and glaring at Maddie.

"Well, of all places to run into my English professor," Phillis said, her tone even more sarcastic than usual.

Maddie couldn't look her in the eye. "Jace, why didn't you tell me Phillis is your grandma? I had no idea you two were related."

"Yeah, imagine that. Me taking the same professor my grandson took." Phillis pursed her lips and looked out the window above Maddie's head.

Maddie saw gauze and tape on the back of Phillis's hand and figured she was given contrast for her MRI or

CT scan. Given that, she found it easier to meet her gaze. "I hope your procedure was quick and easy. I've had my own share of these sorts of tests over the years."

"Well, I try not to have a sour attitude about most things," Phillis said, her tone now more angry than sarcastic. "But what do I know? Apparently, I can't even write a coherent essay."

Maddie froze. Those words sounded familiar. Where had she heard them before?

Jace looked puzzled. "Of course you can. I've read your essays, and they're great. Right, Professor Fong?"

"Right." Maddie knew her smile was lukewarm, but what else could she say?

Jace stepped closer to the door. "Gram, we better get going."

"Nice to see you, Phillis. See you in class tomorrow," Maddie said, her tone polite but forced.

With an angry scowl on her face, Phillis looked out the window and sighed loudly. "No, you won't be seeing me in class. I decided to drop it and take Professor Miller's course instead. Fortunately, he's teaching one of those eight-week classes."

"Oh." That was unexpected. While professors were not allowed to add students so late in the semester to the standard sixteen-week classes, they did have discretion for eight-week classes. But Professor Miller didn't usually add students past the first week of those. Maddie wasn't sure how to respond to Phillis's harsh tone, but she was relieved to no longer have to deal with her sarcasm during class discussions.

"Oh," Phillis repeated mockingly. "And I'm supposed to be the incoherent one." She huffed and rolled her eyes.

"You're not incoherent." There was more than a hint of exasperation in Jace's voice. He mouthed, "Sorry," at Maddie and opened the door. "Gram, let's get you home. Nice to see you, Professor Fong. Good luck with your appointment."

"Hope Carmen treats you well," Phillis said quietly as she walked toward the exit.

"Who's Carmen?" Maddie asked, but by now Phillis

and Jace were outside.

"I think she said karma," Taylor said without looking up from her phone.

"What was all that about?" Angela asked, as Kai and Drew walked over.

"Just a student who didn't like me much," Maddie said.

"She didn't have to be such a bitch to you," Taylor said, putting her phone in her pocket.

"That's crazy," Kai said. "Who wouldn't like you?"

"Yeah, you're an awesome teacher," Drew said, patting her on the shoulder. "Your students love you."

"Thanks," Maddie said, trying to sound enthusiastic but failing. Her sluggish mind had finally pieced things together. If Jace saw the photos she'd posted of Big Sur, he must've seen the recent Wall of Shame posts. Could he have shown those posts to his grandmother? Maddie closed her eyes in mortification. She should never have posted the student errors! Of course Phillis was angry. The comments about her mistakes had been especially harsh. Maddie considered Jace somewhat of a friend—a sweet gay guy who was always kind to her. Would he be the type to report those posts to the dean? Or had Phillis done that on her own?

Maddie forced herself to draw in a deep breath. She was beyond frazzled at this point, and it was important to calm down before seeing the doctor. Now that she thought about it, maybe she was being too paranoid. It was more likely that another professor sent those screenshots to the dean. Probably Phillis's reference to karma simply meant she hoped Maddie's test results came back fine.

Another text from Kendra popped up on Maddie's phone, which immediately boosted her mood. But before she had a chance to read it, she got called to Doctor Hahn's office.

The good mood vanished. Maddie was again nervous and sick to her stomach. With her entire family by her side, she reluctantly made her way to the doctor's office. Kai pulled her into a tight sideways hug as they walked.

"No matter what, your mom and I will help you

through this." Kai held Maddie tighter. His embraces were always full of so much love. "I'll stay up here for as long as necessary."

Maddie fought back the tears. "What about the surf shop? I'm sure you've already got a wait list for your fall surf classes."

Kai stopped walking and turned to face Maddie. He placed his hands on her shoulders and gave her one of his intense looks. "*Keiki*, nothing matters now but you. Someone else can cover the classes."

"But you're the best teacher." Maddie's voice broke. Kai had taught so many over the years, including Maddie, and everyone agreed there was no better person to have by your side while learning how to master the big waves.

"Only because you were the best kid I ever taught to surf." Kai grinned, and his eyes lit up. "I saw how you overcame your apprehensions when you first learned how to surf. This isn't that different. It's a matter of facing your fear, just like how you conquered the big waves when you were a teenager."

Kai's smile made Maddie feel a bit calmer. He wrapped his arm around her and guided her down the corridor toward Doctor Hahn's office, the rest of the family close behind.

Kai had been there through the roughest times of Maddie's life—the surfing accident, her unplanned pregnancy, brain surgery, chemo, radiation. And now this. As tears filled her eyes, she tried to breathe slowly and calm down before hearing the results of her MRI.

Any attempts at calming down vanished when Maddie entered the office because she was confronted with the unexpected sight of Doctor Cho standing behind the desk next to Doctor Hahn. This must be horrible news if her oncologist was here to go over the results of the scan. Weakness overcame her, and only Kai's strong arms kept her upright. He guided her to the cushioned chair directly in front of the desk. Mom took the seat to the right of her, and Taylor sat on the left. Behind her sat Kai and Drew.

Doctor Hahn looked at Maddie and smiled. "Maddie, nice to see you and your family. So, we'll get right to why we needed to see you today. As you know, I've reviewed your MRI and had another radiologist read it as well."

"I knew this day would come eventually. How big is the new spot?" Maddie started to tremble, and Drew clasped his hand on her shoulder.

"The issue isn't actually with your brain this time," Doctor Hahn said. "The good news is there are no changes in the brain from the last MRI."

Maddie blinked. "No changes? At all?"

"Not a bit," Doctor Hahn said.

"So, no tumor growth? Nothing?" Maddie had to make sure.

"Nothing," Doctor Hahn said with a smile.

Around her, Maddie's family erupted into exclamations of relief. Her mom hugged her, and Taylor held up her palm for a high five. Kai rubbed Maddie's shoulder.

Drew was the exception. He was angry. "You had my wife terrified that the cancer had returned. Why did you call her in here to tell her there's no new growth? Why couldn't you have told her that over the phone?"

Doctor Hahn looked directly at Maddie. "I apologize for getting you all worried. The results of the MRI are rather complicated this time. For a patient with a history of glioblastoma, we look closely at the MRI to search for any changes. The scans show clear images of the brain, but at most they might show the C-1 and C-2 vertebrae. For your MRIs, normally we have the tech focus on the brain since we're looking for new tumor growth, but this time—"

"What are you trying to say? Did the cancer spread?" Fearful that the MRI revealed a tumor on her spine, Maddie couldn't stop her body from shaking.

"All is fine as far as the glioblastoma. But what happened when you had your recent scan is that we had a tech here who normally doesn't do your MRIs. This time, she got a full view of all the cervical vertebrae, which is where I noticed—"

"What are you trying to say?" Drew asked, his voice loud and intense.

Doctor Hahn continued. "I believe you're experiencing cervicogenic headaches."

Barely over the surprise of hearing that the tumor had not returned, Maddie couldn't comprehend what Doctor Hahn told her. Over the years, she'd learned a lot of medical jargon, but she'd never heard the word "cervicogenic." Was this treatable? Was it a direct result of the treatment she'd received these past four years?

Doctor Hahn shuffled through some papers, and then she glanced at a handwritten note. "Cervicogenic headaches are caused by damage to one or more vertebrae. Your MRI shows degeneration of the facet joints and significant damage right at the C-6 and C-7 vertebrae. The type of damage is rather extensive for someone your age. Two bulging disks, severe arthritis, and lots of degeneration. But to put it simply, your headaches are likely caused by referred pain from the cervical spine damage."

Maddie hadn't stopped trembling since she entered the office. "Why hadn't you noticed this before with my MRIs?"

"As I mentioned, normally we don't get a full view of all the cervical vertebrae. Gloria inadvertently did more views than necessary, but that's probably not a bad thing. Have you ever had a past neck injury?"

Drew leaned forward. "She broke her neck when she was eighteen."

"You broke your neck? Why isn't this in your medical chart?" Doctor Cho's tone was more alarmed than caring.

"Because I'd long since healed, and because having glioblastoma meant you'd be focusing on my brain, not my neck," Maddie said. "Who'd think a surfing accident from years ago would come back to haunt me?"

"It was only a hairline fracture," Angela said, her voice soft. As she shifted in her seat, she wrung her hands. "She healed fast, way faster than any of the doctors and physical therapists predicted."

Kai draped his arm around Maddie's shoulders. "She was surfing within only four months of the injury, even though her doctors wanted her to wait six months. Do you think she wasn't fully healed? Maybe we got you in the water too soon, and it caused more damage. I shouldn't have pushed you so hard to compete so soon after the accident."

With her usual caring demeanor, Doctor Hahn looked at Maddie and smiled. "Maddie, a broken neck like the one you experienced can heal, especially in a young person like you when it happened, but it can cause problems later in life because the anatomy of the spine has been changed from the injury. Cervicogenic headaches are often described as migraine-like and can be quite debilitating."

Maddie sagged back against the seat, the trembling finally subsiding. The MRI only showed damage in her neck from the surfing accident, no new tumor growth. She could handle arthritis and bulging disks—definitely treatable and not terminal like brain cancer.

Doctor Hahn shuffled a stack of papers into a manila envelope and jotted something on the front. "The good news is we can provide you with some relief. We'll make a referral for you to see an orthopedic specialist. They'll evaluate your condition and likely give you some physical therapy for your neck and possibly give you a nerve block like a cervical epidural."

"Sounds pretty straightforward," Maddie said, "but wouldn't an epidural cause potential bleeding? I've been told I shouldn't even get routine dental cleanings because of the bleeding risk due to B-vac."

"We'll talk about that in a moment," Doctor Cho said without making eye contact with Maddie.

Mom squeezed Maddie's arm. Taylor couldn't stop smiling, and Kai patted Maddie on the shoulder again. But Drew was angry.

"Will you talk about how you had us thinking the scan showed the cancer was back?" Drew spat out. "To call Maddie into your office without first letting her know that the MRI didn't reveal new tumor growth had us all freaked out."

Maddie turned around and patted Drew's arm. "Drew, it's fine. Let's celebrate the good news of no new tumor growth."

"It's not fine," Drew said.

"You're right, it's not," Doctor Hahn said gently and with compassion. "We'll make sure something like that doesn't happen again. But that's not the only reason we asked Maddie to come to the office." Doctor Hahn looked at Maddie and then at Doctor Cho.

"I'm concerned about your urinalysis and blood test results." Doctor Cho handed a sheet of paper to Maddie. "Both indicate kidney damage. B-vac has some potentially serious side effects, including kidney damage."

Maddie scanned the results. "So, I've got kidney damage from the drug that's preventing the cancer from returning. What exactly does this mean as far as my treatment?"

Doctor Hahn clasped her hands together on the desk. "The first step is to stop the drug. Doctor Cho and I are fairly certain that it may be causing kidney damage."

"Today we'll do more blood work to determine how damaged the kidneys actually are," Doctor Cho said. "But these preliminary tests indicate your kidneys are not functioning well."

Despite the whiplash of emotions, the reality of this news sunk in fast. "But it's what's keeping me alive." Maddie gripped the chair's armrests. "If we stop it, the cancer will return."

Doctor Hahn leaned forward. "We don't know that for sure. The robotic radiotherapy could've completely removed any trace of new tumor growth, but you have to understand that any more damage to your kidneys could result in kidney failure."

"Kidney failure?" Angela asked, her voice breaking. "That sounds serious."

Rather than feeling sad or scared, Maddie was angry. "We all know that glioblastoma doesn't go away entirely." Maddie couldn't stop herself from raising her voice. "It's hiding somewhere and will reappear later. We can't stop the only medicine that works."

"Maddie, I've never had a patient live this long with GBM," Doctor Cho said. "And because of that, we have to consider that the long-term use of B-vac led to the kidney damage. If the damage progresses, it could result in kidney failure, which would require dialysis and possibly a kidney transplant."

"So, the drug that's preventing the cancer from

returning is killing me." When her mom gasped, Maddie reached over to hold her hand. "Once it's out of my system, how long until the cancer returns?"

Doctor Cho opened a manila folder and pulled out a thick stack of papers. "At this point, we can't predict when...or if there will be a reoccurrence of cancer."

"For God's sake, we know all of this," Drew said, his voice loud and intense. "The median survival rate for glioblastoma is a little over a year."

"Drew, she's far exceeded those odds." Kai cupped his hand over Maddie's. "She's lived well beyond the original prognosis. Maddie is a fighter."

Doctor Cho handed the article to Maddie. "There's been promising research on mice in stem cell treatment for GBM, and clinical trials on humans are due to start very soon."

Maddie peered at the first page of the article and became overwhelmed at what she read. None of this made sense. How would she survive both kidney damage and a likely reoccurrence of brain cancer?

Doctor Cho leaned on the desk and looked at Maddie. "If we resolve the kidney issue, we can explore the stem cell option. You have to understand your kidney damage could improve over time."

"But I wouldn't be able to go back on the anti-cancer drug, would I?" Maddie asked, her voice quivering.

"It may turn out that you can go back on some sort of maintenance dose," Doctor Cho said, "but right now, we must stop it altogether."

"If we stop it, the cancer's gonna return." Maddie's breathing became unsteady, and she couldn't stop her body from trembling.

Doctor Hahn cleared her throat and looked at Maddie and then at her family. "Without any sort of treatment for the glioblastoma, yes, there's certainly a possibility that we'll see new tumor growth."

"So, then I'll die." Maddie's jaw went rigid as she tried to process all of this information. For four years, she'd beaten the odds, but she always knew it was just a matter of time until the cancer returned.

"Mom, don't talk that way," Taylor said, her voice

breaking.

Doctor Cho offered a forced smile. "At this point, you need to be aware that under normal circumstances, someone with that much damage to both kidneys might eventually need a kidney transplant."

Drew stood up and paced behind the chairs. "What do you mean, normal circumstances?"

Doctor Cho sat on a stool next to the desk and reached for a pen and a pad of paper. "Normal protocol for kidney transplants is that the patient must be in good health. For someone like Maddie, she'd need to be cancer-free for five years. But, exceptions are sometimes made, especially if there's a living donor transplant from a family member."

Taylor gripped Maddie's hand. "I'll give her one of my kidneys."

The tears brimmed at Maddie's eyes, but she tried to hold it together—at least for the sake of keeping Mom and Taylor calm. "Honey, you're in no condition to donate a kidney."

"Actually, the best match is usually a sibling," Doctor Cho said. "But really, we're jumping the gun here. We might not even need to consider a transplant. Let's hope the kidney damage improves simply by stopping the treatment."

"I don't have any brothers or sisters." Maddie glanced at her mom who suddenly looked agitated and very pale.

"What about a half-sibling?" Kai asked, his question so earnest.

Maddie laughed. "A half-sibling? Is there something Mom's not telling me?"

No one else laughed.

Doctor Cho gestured at Taylor. "If it comes down to you needing a kidney, then they can see if your daughter's a good match."

"Our daughter's pregnant," Drew said, his voice even angrier than before. "She's obviously not in any condition to donate a kidney. Had she not gotten pregnant, she would've probably been a perfect match."

"Drew, stop." Maddie clenched her hand in Taylor's,

who was now sobbing.

Doctor Hahn, usually so compassionate and under-standing, looked completely shocked at Drew's outburst. Although Maddie appreciated the support from her family, right now she wished it were just her and Doctor Hahn in the office.

"What about a parent?" Angela asked quietly.

"Mom, you're also not in any condition to donate a kidney."

Doctor Cho offered a kind smile. "If it comes down to you needing a kidney, your mom can be tested to see if she's a match. However, you should be aware that due to the usual prognosis for patients with glioblastoma, most surgeons won't do a kidney transplant. But, let's hope the kidney damage will reverse within the next few months."

Maddie sighed loudly and cursed under her breath. "Am I right that a diabetic can't donate a kidney?" She glanced at her mother, who looked away.

"That's right, someone with diabetes is not a possible donor. They can test your father to see if he's a match." Doctor Cho smiled at Kai.

"I'm not her biological father." Kai sounded defeated and sullen. "Angie, we should—"

Angela glared at him. "Not now, Kai. This isn't the place for that."

"Isn't the place for what?" Maddie couldn't under-stand why her mother was acting so strange. "Mom, what's going on?"

Angela ignored her. "How can you best help my daughter?" She stared at Doctor Cho and then at Doctor Hahn.

"I see you all care a great deal about Maddie and about the next phase of treatment for her," Doctor Cho said, "but at this point, let's just take it one step at a time. If she needs a kidney transplant, certainly a live donor from a close relative is her best option."

Angela trembled as she rocked back and forth in the chair.

"Mom, it's okay," Maddie said. "You heard Doctor Cho say we don't need to go there yet."

Angela dabbed her eyes with a tissue and looked

directly at Doctor Cho. "You mentioned dialysis. What exactly does that mean for Maddie?"

"We'll see what the blood tests and urinalysis reveal about her kidney function, but if she needs dialysis, she'll go three times a week, around four hours each time."

"I suspect the fatigue you've been having is due to the kidney damage," Doctor Hahn said. "Along with the edema in your feet and ankles. They're telltale signs of kidney damage, but the dialysis will likely make you feel much better."

"How long can I live on dialysis?" Maddie asked, her body trembling even more.

Kai set his hand on Maddie's shoulder. "*Keiki*, we'll get you through this. This is just a little speed bump along the way."

"Patients can live several years on dialysis," Doctor Cho said and paused for a moment. "If there are no other underlying medical problems. Of course, I have concerns that the cancer could return once we stop the bevacizumab, but it's imperative that we treat the kidney damage." Doctor Cho went on to describe how they'd do everything they could to keep Maddie healthy for as long as possible.

As everyone in the room continued to talk, all Maddie wanted to do was run out of here. She wanted to pretend she didn't have cancer or kidney damage, and find a quiet spot and forget about all of this. She tried to go to her happy place, like the beach in San Clemente where Kai first taught her to surf. She worked hard to take her imagination far from this office. When she closed her eyes, she envisioned strolling through London's Hyde Park on a warm day in June; she recalled seeing the Welsh coast for the first time; she imagined riding the cusp of a breaking wave and shooting out through the barrel; then she pictured herself sitting on the bluff in Big Sur with Kendra.

None of these happy places took her away from the horrid reality of what was happening right now. If kidney damage didn't kill her, then a reoccurrence of cancer would.

As the doctors talked about some specialists and other possible medical tests, Maddie looked at her phone and saw another text from Kendra:

This morning I came across a Woolf quote that reminded me of you...and of us: "I see you everywhere, in the stars, in the river, to me you're everything that exists; the reality of everything."

The quote was from *Night and Day.* Maddie started to cry. Right when she'd likely experience new tumor growth due to going off the anti-cancer drug, she had someone who wanted to be an "us"? It would've been easier if Kendra remained adamant about not getting involved with anyone ever again. And it surely would've been simpler if they'd just had a one-night stand. After the news she just received, Maddie didn't have it in her for being an "us." She didn't want to put Kendra through any of this. She'd survived her own battle with breast cancer; she shouldn't also have to walk the same path with Maddie.

"Honey, we're all going to help you through this." Angela leaned over to put her arm around Maddie.

Doctor Hahn slid a box of tissue across the desk. "Maddie, I know how scary this all is, but you have a lot of support from your family, and from me and Doctor Cho. And much to be excited about, like a grandbaby on the way."

Through her tears, Maddie nodded and offered a feeble smile. They had no idea why she was crying. It wasn't the fear that the cancer would return; it wasn't the apprehensions she had about thrice-weekly dialysis appointments or about possibly needing a kidney transplant. Maddie sobbed because she knew in her heart that she shouldn't burden Kendra with her medical problems—the issues now way bigger than she ever imagined.

Chapter Fourteen

San Luis Obispo: December 2018

Maddie had resolved to not put Kendra through any part of this new phase of treatment, and she kept her promise. Last month, she gave Kendra an update on her situation and did respond to texts, since Maddie would never just ghost someone. But she kept subsequent replies brief, as well as refusing any invitations to meet up, saying she wanted to focus on her health. A couple weeks ago, Kendra stopped texting and calling. Maybe once Maddie got accustomed to dialysis appointments, she'd text Kendra to let her know how she was doing. But right now, it was better to remain single and unattached. If Maddie didn't hear Kendra's voice or read her texts, she wouldn't miss her.

Angela held the door to the dialysis clinic open with one hand, clutching a large satchel and small cooler loaded with healthy snacks in the other. Maddie gave her a grateful smile and entered the dialysis clinic. It was very similar to the infusion room where she had chemo. Rows of recliners faced TV monitors mounted on the wall; each seat had a fleece blanket draped over the armrest. Next to the recliners were huge hemodialysis machines that could be hooked up to the patients.

A petite young blonde in navy blue scrubs came up to them. "Hi, I'm Nicki, and I'll be taking care of you this afternoon. Our goal is to keep you as comfortable as possible while you're here."

"Is it okay if my mom stays with me?" Maddie felt awkward to be a woman in her mid-thirties asking if her mother could stay with her during dialysis, but doing this alone would be unbearable.

"Of course!" Nicki waved an arm behind her. "I just need to weigh you and take your vitals first. If you can step into this room?" Nicki quickly and efficiently took

Maddie's weight, temperature, and blood pressure. She kept up a chipper conversation with only Angela, since Maddie did not have it in her to be cheerful and chatty.

Three weeks ago, Maddie had minor surgery to have a special blood vessel, called a fistula, created in her forearm. It would make it easier to transfer Maddie's blood into the dialysis machine and then back into her body. Unfortunately, it hadn't healed yet and wasn't ready to be used for dialysis. That meant Maddie had to get the dialysis through the central venous catheter in her neck, which had been inserted two days ago. All of this was because the area around her portacath had become inflamed. Doctor Larsen, the nephrologist, was worried about the risk of infection and opted instead for the central venous catheter.

On top of all of that, she had physical therapy twice a week. It was all so utterly exhausting.

Finally, Nicki was finished with the pre-dialysis procedure and led Maddie and Angela to a machine at the far end of the main dialysis area, away from the three other patients undergoing their treatment. "We've got a pretty comfortable seat for you," Nicki said to Angela as she patted a thickly padded chair.

Angela hummed quietly as she sat down. "This is perfect. And I've got plenty to do for four hours. I'm about halfway through knitting a blanket for my great-granddaughter."

Nicki gave them both an apologetic look. "You're welcome to hang out here all afternoon if you'd like, but just to let you know, because we're doing the dialysis through a central venous catheter, it'll take around five hours."

"Five hours?" Maddie's face fell in dismay. "Doctor Larsen told me it'd be four!"

"Unfortunately, it takes longer with the catheter," Nicki said, still smiling and overly chipper, "but I'd imagine you'll only need dialysis through that for a few more weeks until the fistula in your arm is ready."

Maddie pressed her lips together and bit off the words she really wanted to say. First the doctors made her think the tumor was back; now the nephrologist gave her false information. She'd brought her laptop and charger, so she'd have plenty to do. But having to sit here for five whole hours? Fortunately, her headaches weren't as bad now that she'd had a month of physical therapy and an epidural shot in her neck. But between PT twice a week, dialysis three days a week, and various medical procedures, Maddie's days were filled with appointments. The only good thing to happen in these past few weeks was Taylor finding out the sex of her baby and deciding to name her Aria.

Maddie slid onto the bulky recliner of the machine. "Seems easier just to get a new kidney than have to come here fifteen hours a week for God knows how long." She scowled at a poster on the wall—a generic beach scene at sunset. Over the years, she'd found that medical facilities decorated the walls with tacky peaceful beach scenes or cheesy posters of cute animals. Realizing she'd have to see that same ocean sunset three days a week for however long only added to her irritation.

Nicki pressed a few buttons on the machine. "My guess is they'll remove the catheter in about four weeks. In time, you'll barely even have a scar there."

"Yet another scar on my body." She sighed. Kendra had said scars were sexy, especially Maddie's. That night at Monarch Bluffs seemed like a lifetime ago, but Maddie still smiled every time she recalled Kendra running her fingers over the scar on her chest when they were in the pool. The smile quickly fell away. If only Kendra could be with her now. But she couldn't, so there was no point dwelling on it.

"You ready to get started?" Nicki asked with that same huge grin.

Maddie only barely restrained the urge to snap at her. "Do I have a choice? I guess this is my life from here on out."

Angela gave her an understanding smile. "Honey, you may not always need dialysis. Remember how Doctor Cho said your kidney function could still improve the longer you're off the B-vac?"

"I've been off it for five weeks now, and my numbers are still the same."

"You'd be surprised at how kidney disease can be reversed," Nicki said, "even to the point of you not needing dialysis forever. It may turn out that you won't need dialysis for the rest of your life."

The word "forever" didn't mean the same thing to Maddie as it did for most people. Whenever someone made a reference to "the rest of your life," Maddie knew this could be a mere matter of months for her, or a year or two at most.

Nicki began hooking Maddie up to the dialysis machine, and Maddie took the time to watch her mother. Angela had been behaving strangely these past few weeks, so distracted and secretive. She and Kai held whispered conversations that would stop when Maddie entered the room. Sometimes Angela would stare off into space or look at Maddie as if she wanted to say something. If Maddie asked whether anything was wrong, Angela would say no, everything was fine, work was just stressful these days.

Right now, Angela was fussing over her, as she always did when her daughter went through any kind of medical procedure. She draped a fleece blanket over Maddie and tucked it around her legs. Angela next rifled through her canvas bag to pull out a bag of almonds and a banana, and set them on the arm of Maddie's chair. Maddie felt both like a helpless child and immensely comforted that her mother was here today. Luckily, her first dialysis appointment happened during her mom's winter break. But it was also fortunate that Maddie was able to finish teaching her classes and submit grades before her first dialysis appointment.

Nicki was finally finished. With a perky reminder to call her the instant they needed anything, she finally left them alone. Maddie picked up her phone. First, she'd respond to some emails. Then she'd get out her laptop and binge watch a show.

Angela pulled out the blanket she'd been knitting for Aria, and that was yet another odd thing. She'd been working on the blanket for a long time but hadn't made any progress, ever since the appointment with Doctors Cho and Hahn. Angela would knit, stop, pull out the stitches, and start all over again. When asked why, she'd only mutter that it didn't look right.

Maddie watched her mother knit and count stitches under her breath, then took out her phone to see a text from Drew:

Hope your first dialysis session goes well. I hate that you have to go through this, but just know I'll always be there for you. I still care so much about you. I'm grateful that you and I have such a good relationship despite us not staying together. I'm glad you have Kendra to help you through this next phase of treatment. You seem really happy with her. Hopefully I can meet her soon. Let's double-date! We can go to dinner at that restaurant you like by Morro Rock. Love you!

Maddie furrowed her brow. For now, Drew didn't need to know about her decision to not see Kendra. She kept her response short:

Thank you for always being there for me. Love you, too!

Maddie hit send, then turned her attention to her email inbox. She paused at the email from HR a couple weeks ago, informing her she wasn't selected for an interview for the full-time position. It was disappointing but maybe for the best since she'd be so busy with dialysis appointments for who knew how long. Still certain Jace and or Phillis had something to do with her getting in trouble, Maddie had a hard time letting go of the resentment about her reputation on campus getting tainted.

What really upset her was the dean deciding Maddie shouldn't teach any regular classes on campus until the social media fiasco got resolved with HR. It didn't matter that she'd taken down all the Wall of Shame posts and deleted her comments on similar posts made by other professors. Being on probation meant no teaching on campus. Thankfully, she was able to teach two classes at the men's penitentiary in SLO. No one there cared about the slight on her reputation, and she'd been told the inmates were looking forward to her classes, including a poetry workshop and one on autobiographical writing. Working with incarcerated individuals gave her purpose.

A person's past should not define their future. These guys opened up in their narrative pieces, proving that words were powerful.

Maddie took a deep breath and moved onto the email from Matt, the pre-med student she'd met at Monarch Bluffs. He'd reached out to her right before she had her MRI to tell her he'd moved back to Southern California and would soon start med school. Maddie typed out a short update about her health, including the kidney damage, and invited him to keep in touch via email and social media. She also wrote a quick text to Dot, congratulating her on her new art show in Monterey.

There were more emails that needed a response, but Maddie felt like watching a show. "Mom, you don't have to sit here with me the entire time. I've got a full season of *Orange Is the New Black* to watch. If you want to go back to the house for a bit, I'll be okay here."

Angela stopped knitting. "I'm not about to leave you here by yourself all afternoon." She set her hand on Maddie's arm.

While Maddie looked at yet another sunset photo on the wall in front of her, she braced herself for having to sit here for another four hours and fifty minutes. "I can't believe I have to endure these long dialysis appointments three times a week for who knows how long. Seems easier to just call it quits."

Angela leaned over to pull the fleece blanket up closer to Maddie's midsection. "Now, don't go talking that way." Her brow furrowed, and her lips pursed—the expression that always conveyed disapproval.

"Sometimes it just doesn't seem worth it to go through all of this."

Angela shook her head, that displeased look again on her face. "You're just as bad as Kai when it comes to medical procedures. He's been putting off his stress test for weeks now."

"Stress test?" Maddie jerked her body toward her mother, the motion causing the tube to pull slightly from the catheter, making her wince in pain.

Angela set the unfinished blanket and ball of yarn on her lap. "It's nothing to be worried about. You know he's had high blood pressure for a while now. It's mostly under control with meds."

"Mostly under control?" Maddie swallowed, trying not to panic. "Then why would he need a stress test?"

"Last month, he had chest pain after he'd been surfing for a couple hours, but it didn't last long. I took him to the ER just in case. The EKG came back normal, but they gave him a referral to a cardiologist."

"He went to the ER for chest pain?" Maddie's voice rose, enough for Nicki to poke her head out of her office. She lowered her voice. "Mom, this could be serious. How could you not tell me? Why aren't you with him back home? You should make the appointment yourself and get him in to be tested."

"We didn't want to worry you."

"You worry me more when you don't tell me things!"

"Hopefully he'll get the stress test soon, and it'll reveal everything is fine. I think he's been working too hard and stressing about our wedding. You know how he is. He wants it to be perfect. But what I'm saying is that you two are so alike when it comes to how stubborn you are. I know you hate the idea of getting dialysis three days a week for five hours each day, but right now that's what you need to do until…well, until you can get a kidney transplant."

"A kidney transplant?" Maddie said, her words again louder than she'd intended. She glanced around the room and hushed her voice. "Hopefully the kidney damage will reverse, but if I do need a kidney transplant, who'd agree to doing it on someone with a history of glioblastoma?"

"Your doctor said they might make an exception for someone like you who's far exceeded the original prognosis."

"Yeah, but are you forgetting the most ideal option for someone in my condition would be a close relative? It's not like I'd be pushed to the top of the organ waiting list to get a kidney from some random donor."

Angela got quiet and dropped her eyes to the yarn in her lap, twisting it around her fingers in a knotted mess. "Maybe you won't need a kidney from a random donor."

Angela said those words so softly that Maddie wasn't

sure she heard her correctly. "Mom, we already talked about how you can't donate a kidney, nor can Taylor. I know she doesn't have much longer until Aria is born, but I wouldn't want to put her through giving up a kidney right after she has a baby."

"I don't mean me or Taylor." Angela fumbled with the yarn. "There might be someone out there who could donate a kidney to you."

Maddie shifted in her seat, but the red tube dangling across her chest made it hard for her to get comfortable. "I appreciate your optimism, but I'm not exactly a prime candidate for being pushed to the top of the waiting list to get a kidney."

Angela returned the knitting needles and yarn to her satchel and leaned closer to Maddie. "There might be a way for you to get a kidney from a living donor, from a family member. I never thought there'd be a need for me to reveal any of this to you, but seeing as—"

"Reveal what to me? What are you trying to tell me?"

Angela smiled, but it looked like she was going to cry. "When I found out I was pregnant, I was terrified. Didn't know how I'd handle being a single mom."

"Mom, you did well raising me on your own. You were an amazing mother when I was a kid, and still are." Angela had always appeared confident and certain. It never occurred to Maddie that her mother had also shared the same fears about being a single parent.

Angela gave her a tremulous smile. "When I found out I was pregnant, I wasn't sure I wanted to have the baby. For a couple weeks, I even thought about…ending the pregnancy. I was young at the time and scared."

That made no sense. "Ending your pregnancy? But you and my father were in love. I know it was probably hard to be pregnant with him away at war, but at least he knew he had a daughter before he got killed in Beirut."

Angela's eyes filled with tears, and she rocked back and forth as she focused on her hands clenched in her lap. "When you and I left Mississippi, it wasn't just to move to California to help Popo. I needed to leave Ellisville to get away from someone, a horrible man who could've ruined my life…and yours, too."

Out of nowhere, a memory surfaced of their move to California when Maddie was fourteen. They'd been stuck in a traffic jam and were arguing, and Angela had said there were "bad things" in Mississippi they had to get away from. She'd never elaborated, and Maddie had never asked. Maybe she should have. "Mom, who were you getting away from?"

Angela kept staring at her hands. "For months, I was horrified that I had his child inside me, that part of him would forever be a part of me." Angela dabbed her eyes with a tissue and didn't look at Maddie.

Maddie wanted to look away, wanted to pull the tubes from the machine and get out of here. She and her mother were on the edge of a precipice, and every instinct was screaming at Maddie to stop asking questions and run. Instead, she spoke in a soft yet determined voice. "But you said my dad was a sweet and honorable man. Was he not good to you?"

"Honey, the man you've always known as your father, the man in that photo, is nothing more than a friend from high school who joined the military."

Was that all? The man who was her father had just been a friend? Maddie had looked at the photo of her father so many times that the edges were frayed, but over the years she'd memorized Ben Rudolph's face. "So, you and Ben were never in love? Was it some sort of fling?"

"The man in that photo is not your father." Angela spoke without any bit of emotion, her voice flat and monotone.

Maddie's body tensed, and a strange sense of dread flooded through her. "The guy in the uniform is not my dad? Why would you have me believing he was my father all these years?"

Angela continued to stare so hard at her hands, it was as if she was talking directly to them. "I never wanted you to know anything about your real father. He was a very bad man."

"My real father?" Maddie became light-headed and overcome with a sense of unreality. "What are you saying?"

Angela set a trembling hand over her mouth and

closed her eyes. "I met your father in a bar."

"A bar? You don't even drink. Weren't you too young to even buy alcohol?" This was so hard to believe. Mom hardly ever drank alcohol as an adult. Yet she was going to bars as a teen?

"Back then, the drinking age was eighteen in Mississippi. There was a short time when I had a wild streak and ran with the wrong crowd."

"How'd you hide that from Aunt Nancy and Uncle Tim?" Maddie's mom had lived with them for a short time after her parents moved to California, and they were very strict.

"They figured I was babysitting or over at a friend's house. They were always so trusting of me since I never got in trouble. Years prior, when my brother and his wife moved to California to open a restaurant and took my parents with them, I should've gone with them, but I wanted to be on my own, so I got my own apartment when I was eighteen. Aunt Nancy and Uncle Tim often had no idea where I was or what I was doing."

Although she knew her mother was allowed to stay in Mississippi after her parents moved to California, Maddie never understood how she'd made it on her own at such a young age. "Drew and I couldn't even afford our own place had you, Kai, and Drew's parents not helped us out for a while. How could you have lived on your own at only eighteen years old?"

"Rent was dirt cheap back then. I was excited to no longer have to follow anyone's rules, so I found an apartment to share with a couple friends from high school. But had I not stayed in Mississippi, I would've never met a scumbag in a bar and got pregnant."

"Are you saying my father is some guy you hooked up with from a bar? Did you get pregnant from a one-night stand?" Maddie couldn't stop the questions, even as part of her silently begged her mom to stop talking.

"No, we dated for a while. Well, dated is probably an exaggeration. I hung out with him for a few weeks. Johnny was handsome, charismatic, even romantic in a rugged kind of way." Angela still hadn't looked at Maddie.

In contrast, Maddie couldn't look away. Her practical, kind, no-nonsense mother had lied about Maddie's father. "Why would you have me believe that my father was a soldier and then tell me he got killed in a war? For over thirty years, I've known Ben Rudolph as my father, and now you're saying that some guy you met in a bar is my dad?"

Angela took in a deep breath and let it out, then breathed in again. "I never told you any of this because your father was a horrible man and at times was very unkind to me. Johnny did some awful things and got arrested a few times. I wanted you to grow up thinking your father was a good man, but your real father was nothing but scum."

The combination of "your real father" and the details of his criminal background sounded so peculiar. "Why are you saying he was a horrible man? What did he do?"

"He boasted to me about robbing liquor stores and gas stations, but for some foolish reason I thought he was just some young rebel. I knew he'd had a rough childhood. He told me how his father would get drunk and beat him. Guess I felt sorry for him."

"You don't have to be ashamed of getting pregnant with this guy. Lots of people make mistakes, but I don't understand why you lied to me all these years."

Angela shook her head. She pressed her lips together and inhaled deeply. "Right after I got pregnant, I found out Johnny had been accused of assaulting a teenager."

Maddie gasped. Words refused to form. She could only stare.

"Evidently, they didn't have enough evidence to arrest him, but I knew in my heart it was him. I noticed the hate in his eyes on more than one occasion."

Maddie thought she was going to throw up. This couldn't be true. The details were something she'd see on a TV show. They didn't actually happen in real life. She was frightened to ask the next question, but she needed to know. "What did Johnny do to you? Did he hurt you? Am I...the product of rape?"

Angela's head whipped up, and she shook it emphatically. "No." Her gaze was open and honest. "Johnny was my first steady boyfriend, but everything we did was consensual. He was older than me, and at first it was all so exciting to be with him. I'd been so sheltered growing up, but Johnny showed me a part of life I never knew was out there. But after a while, he started to get mean. Then he got rough with me. When it got really bad, I finally called the police, but there wasn't enough proof of what he did to me to arrest him." As if saying this took all the energy out of her, Angela's shoulders slumped, and she looked away.

Appalled that her mother had been in an abusive relationship, Maddie didn't know if she should console her or remain quiet. She reached out a hand and patted her mother on the arm. "I'm sorry." It was all she could say. None of this made sense, and yet it was true.

Angela hung her head low and sighed loudly. "When I heard about the assault charges, I ran the other way. I'm glad I never told him about being pregnant with his baby. I wanted nothing to do with him being your father, so for a while I stayed with a friend, just so Johnny wouldn't know where I lived."

"Did he ever find you? Or find us?" For a moment, Maddie wondered if she'd ever set eyes on this awful man when she and her mom still lived in Mississippi.

Angela rummaged in her satchel. "According to my former roommates, he did go to my old apartment looking for me. For years, I always looked over my shoulder, fearful he'd find us." She pulled out a tissue and dabbed at her eyes.

This was almost too much to process, but there was one question her mother hadn't answered. "Why did you keep this all from me?" Maddie again asked. "I feel like much of my childhood was a lie."

"Honey, you grew up without a father. Well, until Kai came along. But I wanted you to grow up not knowing anything about Johnny. Imagine how different your childhood would've been if you knew your father was evil."

Would her childhood have been that different? Maddie's immediate thought was no, but she just as quickly realized she was wrong. It would have been very different.

Maddie had at least been able to tell her friends that her father was a war hero. When she'd struggled, she'd at least been proud to have a valiant lineage from a guy named Ben Rudolph. That had helped her get through. What would it have been like if she'd known her real father was evil and possibly still living in the South somewhere? Would she have ever felt pride? Or only shame?

Angela reached for another tissue, but she only held it in her hands. "After a year or so, when you were just a baby, I enrolled in college and eventually got a degree, then started teaching. All along, I'd worked at a market to make ends meet. Once I started teaching, I figured Johnny had moved out of state or been put in jail, so I relaxed and moved on with my life as a single mom.

"Years later, I'd heard that Johnny stopped at the market where I used to work. A former co-worker, unaware of my situation, told him where I taught. One day, he showed up as the school day was just ending. I never told him about you. You must've been around eight at the time. Thought it best he didn't know he had a child."

Maddie gasped and again reached for her mother's arm. "Did he...bother you at school or threaten you?"

"He started to show up a couple days a week and waited for me in the parking lot. School officials knew a bit about the situation and urged me to call the police. I finally did call the police, and they talked to him and warned him to stay away from me, but he'd still show up at school. Johnny never hurt me again, but I always feared he'd follow me home and see that I had a young child."

Maddie shook her head, tears coming to her eyes. "I had no idea you lived in fear all those years when we lived in Mississippi."

"I always wanted to protect you, which meant you not knowing that this man was out there. The police told me he'd been arrested the year before for assaulting a thirteen-year-old as she was walking home from school." Angela's tone became vehement. "That man is evil. I didn't want him knowing about you and hurting you in any way, so I filed a restraining order against him. With his criminal record, the court had no hesitations in granting the restraining order. The state of Mississippi still keeps me updated on his whereabouts. Last I heard, he's serving time for murder."

"Murder? My God, he's a monster." Maddie couldn't breathe. While the dialysis machine pumped the blood from her body and back into it, Maddie was locked to this recliner. Her father was a rapist...and a murderer. All she wanted to do was run out of here and get some fresh air.

Angela slumped in the chair and began crying in earnest. "I don't know the details of the crime, but I know he's serving a life sentence. Knowing he's locked up for life makes me feel better that he won't hurt anyone ever again. I was a fool to have ever gotten involved with him."

Maddie tried to take a deep breath, but her chest felt heavy. She caught sight of Nicki and waved her over.

When Angela finally looked at Maddie, she sobbed even harder. "I never intended to tell you any of this, but since you might need a kidney, I thought you should know that Johnny has another child, a couple years older than you." Tears streamed down her cheeks, and she scrubbed at them. "He might even have more kids. You heard Doctor Cho say that a half-sibling is sometimes a good match. Maybe Johnny would be a match."

Maddie would rather die. She wanted to rip the tubing out of her catheter and run out of here. When Nicki headed her way, Maddie kicked the blanket away from her legs.

"How are you doing, Maddie?" Nicki glanced at Angela, who ducked her head away and wiped her face with a tissue.

"Could you stop the dialysis?" Maddie asked, her voice quivering. "Could you unhook me now? I need to get out of here."

Nicki checked the machine and then bent over and set her hand on Maddie's arm and spoke to her quietly, her voice direct but soothing. "Sweetie, if we stop now, you won't finish the full dialysis session. You've still got three and a half hours to go, but it's important that you stay for the full duration or else it won't work."

"I don't care. I need to stop. Please, I can't tolerate this right now." Maddie's entire body shook, and it was impossible to make it stop.

"You're probably having a panic attack. It can happen during dialysis, especially the first time. Are you in pain or feeling nauseous?"

"I feel like I can't breathe." Maddie closed her eyes and tried to take in a full breath, but it only made her panic even more. "I feel lightheaded and really sick to my stomach."

Nicki pulled the blanket up to Maddie's chest and tucked it around her legs. "Sweetie, you're having a panic attack. I'll stay with you until you feel better. Being hooked up to this machine can sometimes feel claustrophobic."

Bothered that someone so young would call her sweetie, Maddie wanted to yank the tube out of her catheter and run out of here—far from what her mom just told her.

Angela opened the cooler. "Honey, how about some grapes? I've also got some pita chips. The salt might help settle your tummy."

"Mom, just put that away." Angela looked hurt, and Maddie regretted her tone, but she couldn't deal with that now. Her real father was a rapist and murderer, and this machine wouldn't stop drawing her blood.

Nicki pulled out a pen and a stickie pad from her pocket and jotted something down. "I can check your chart to see if Doctor Larsen has written an order for some anti-nausea meds, but if not, I can assure you the nausea will pass. The first dialysis appointment can be a little scary. The anxiety is pretty normal."

"What about meds for anxiety? I've got some benzos in my bag." Maddie's breath came in gasps. "Can I take them?"

"They should be okay." Nicki rubbed small circles on Maddie's back in what she probably thought was a calming manner. "Let me take a look first, though."

"Mom, could you get them out of my purse? They're in a clear pouch."

Angela rifled through the bag and pulled out a small

bottle. "These okay?"

Nicki checked the label and gave them a bright smile. "They're totally fine. Go ahead and take them."

Angela twisted the cap off and tapped an orange tablet into Maddie's palm. She then handed over a bottle of water and a baggie of pita chips.

Maddie popped the oval tablet in her mouth and took a sip of water. Relief flooded through her, even though the medication wouldn't kick in for a few minutes. Just having taken it was enough to calm her a little. "I'll be okay now. I'll holler if I need you. Thanks, Nicki."

"Are you sure?" Nicki looked doubtfully between them, as if noting Angela's red eyes and Maddie's inability to meet them.

"Yeah." Maddie tried to give her a smile. "Panic attack, just like you said. I'll be fine."

"Okay. I'm just a call away if you need me." With a small wave, Nicki walked back to her office.

The anxiety medication wouldn't erase what her mother told her, but Maddie hoped it would dull the reality a bit. For a few minutes, she closed her eyes and tried to process the news about her real father, but right now it was too much to absorb.

The intense anxiety subsided into manageable unease. Maddie looked at her mother, who sat there hunched over and dabbing her eyes with a tissue. Although still shocked about what she'd learned, Maddie felt so sorry for her mom. The last of the panic melted away, leaving only sympathy and gratitude. Her mother had taken them away from what could've been an awful childhood living in the same state as that horrible man, someone who could've hurt both Maddie and her mom.

Maddie pulled her arm out of the blanket and reached over to slip her hand in her mom's. "Let's hope I don't need a kidney transplant...from Johnny or any of his offspring. Maybe the dialysis will work, or maybe the kidney damage will reverse. What you told me feels...well, it feels unreal to me and probably will for a while, but I'm sad you kept this all to yourself for so many years."

"I always thought it was best you didn't know the truth about your father. I never intended to tell you about

Johnny," Angela said, her voice shaky. "Not until your doctors said you might need a close relative to donate a kidney. Even now after telling you about him, I realize it'd be unlikely for someone like him to give you a kidney or tell you the whereabouts of his children."

Since the benzos made her senses subdued and her muscles weak, Maddie was much calmer. "Mom, I know you meant well to tell me about Johnny. You've always done everything you could to protect me and take care of me when I was a child. And for the past few years, you've done so much to help me get through surgery, chemo, and now dialysis."

"Honey, you mean the world to me." Angela started to cry again. "When you got sick, I was devastated at the thought of losing you, but you quickly proved that you've always been a fighter."

While tears streamed down her own face, Maddie clenched her hand in her mom's and definitively decided she needed to continue to do everything she could to beat cancer and kidney damage. "You're the one who taught me to be strong. I guess if I got a kidney from a stranger, I'd have no idea if the person was a jerk or a nice person. It's just an organ, something to keep me alive."

Angela leaned over and set her hand on Maddie's face. "You've made it this long with brain cancer. I don't care what it takes to get you through this, even getting a kidney from a horrible person or one of his kids."

All her life, Maddie wondered what her father looked like beyond what she'd seen in that photo, what his voice and laugh sounded like, but now the haunting reality that her father was a monster sunk in with such horrid finality.

"It's weird to think I've got flesh and blood out there somewhere." Maddie stared at the framed poster of the ocean on the wall in front of her.

"I was so foolish back then." Angela shook her head. "I thought Johnny would change his ways…and be the sort of husband I'd always dreamed about, the type of man I wanted to help raise my little girl. When you were born, I even decided to honor him by naming you Madelyn Joan, your middle name being the closest female name to John. Part of me loved him, crazy as that sounds."

Repulsed that her middle name was the name of a rapist and a convicted murderer, Maddie again felt anxious and disgusted, despite having taken the pill. She'd always hated her middle name, but right now she despised it even more.

"When we left Mississippi," Angela said, "I erased that awful part of my life. I preferred to think that you didn't have a father, but then when I met Kai, we became a family. He's always loved you like his own daughter."

"His *hānai* daughter." Kai had tried to reveal all of this during the recent meeting with Doctor Hahn and Doctor Cho, but Maddie couldn't remember anything except Angela cutting him off. "So, Kai knows about Johnny being my real father?"

"Yes, I confided in him shortly after we became a couple. He never judged. He only loved me and you much more after I told him, but we agreed it was best you didn't know about Johnny."

Though hesitant to ask anything more, Maddie had one more question burning in her mind. Maddie was attached to her mom's last name, but she'd often wondered what sort of person contributed to the rest of her DNA—what type of ethnicity and background. Assuming the guy was white, Maddie still had to ask. "I know Johnny doesn't know about me, but…what's his last name?"

"Patterson," Angela said quietly. "His full name is Jonathan Patterson, but he always went by Johnny."

That surname sounded ordinary enough but not as pleasing as the one she'd always associated with her father's last name. How peculiar it was that her father was still alive—albeit locked away for life in prison. With so much swirling in her mind and another three hours of dialysis, Maddie welcomed the sleepy effects of the anti-anxiety pill.

The framed beach scene on the wall was so much like the sunset she and Kendra watched last month at Morro Bay. As she recalled how content she'd been with Kendra's hand in hers, Maddie closed her eyes and held tight to this happy memory and drifted into a dreamy sleep.

Chapter Fifteen

San Luis Obispo: February 2019

"Mom, I'm scared," Taylor said, her voice shaky. "The pain's really bad."

"I know, honey." Maddie helped Taylor get into a gown, guided her onto the gurney, and tucked the covers around her. "You squeeze my hand as hard as you want when the contractions hit. They'll get closer together when the baby's ready to come out. I'm not leaving your side until Aria is born."

Raindrops pelted against the window. Even though Maddie and Taylor arrived here mid-morning, the sky was dark with grey rainclouds. Unrelenting storms had hit California in the past two weeks, causing flooding and mudslides. Maddie had contacted Drew, Mom, and Kai, letting them know they were at the hospital, and warning them it would take a while to travel here due to the submerged roads. One of the coldest and rainiest days of winter, today didn't seem like the best day for a baby to be born, but at least Aria would enter the world close to Valentine's Day.

An older, heavy-set woman in light blue scrubs stormed into the room and wrapped a blood pressure cuff around Taylor's arm without even introducing herself. Once the nurse finished taking Taylor's blood pressure, she pursed her lips and glared at Maddie. "I understand your daughter went into labor early?"

Maddie frowned. The nurse should be addressing her questions to the patient. "Yes, Taylor has." While Taylor was still a minor, she was the one in need of medical care. Maddie read the name on the nurse's badge and went into protective mom mode. "Donna, maybe you can give my daughter something for the pain? She's really uncomfortable."

Now preoccupied with Taylor's chart, Donna didn't

look up when she responded. "Your daughter's regular obstetrician isn't here today, so I have no idea what he's authorized as far as pain meds."

"Taylor's doctor is a woman, and she assured us she'd authorize pain meds if the contractions got really bad."

Donna stood at the foot of the bed and put her hands on her hips as she once again only spoke to Maddie. "Her contractions are still pretty far apart. That baby's not coming out for a while. She probably could've waited it out at home for a few more hours."

Maddie ignored the last part. "Can't you give her something for the pain? Maybe a low dose of opioid meds? I can tell you which drugs work well for me, and you can tell me which one would be a good option for her."

Donna glared at Maddie. "We don't automatically give opioids to all women...or young teens who are in labor, but I'll see what the doctor can give her. You're lucky you were given anything at all when you gave birth. Lots of doctors try to convince patients that an epidural should be enough. Easier on the baby, too."

How could Donna be so insensitive, and to a teenager? It wasn't easy, but Maddie did her best to not reveal her frustration. "Actually, I didn't need anything when Taylor was born because she came out so fast." She swallowed her irritation and managed to give Donna a smile. "They barely had time to give me an epidural and get me prepped for the delivery room. But I did get pain meds years ago when they put in my portacath and again recently when they put in a central venous catheter for my dialysis."

Donna's expression softened a bit. "A portacath placement can be pretty painful. Had one myself about ten years ago before I went through chemo. I was glad to get that damned thing removed once I was in remission."

"They said I'll probably always have mine." Maddie dropped her gaze to the tile floor next to the bed. "Never know when I'll have to go back on chemo if the cancer returns, but...I'll do whatever it takes to beat it if that happens."

Taylor reached for Maddie's hand and looked at Donna. "My mom's a walking miracle but won't admit it. Even her oncologist said that."

"She didn't say that exactly." Maddie always felt awkward when anyone referred to her as a miracle, even if she had beaten the odds for her type of brain cancer.

Taylor, in contrast, radiated only pride. "Mom, she said she's never had a patient with glioblastoma live as long as you have. To me, that sounds like you're a miracle." There was so much confidence in her voice, such elation that Maddie had far exceeded the original prognosis, that it even made Taylor's pain vanish from her face.

Donna stepped closer to the bed, her demeanor much softer now. "They're certainly making strides with the way they treat cancer these days, even with brain cancer. Stem cell therapy, immunotherapeutic vaccines, gene therapy. Amazing how far they've come since I had lymphoma ten years ago."

Taylor's response was to grimace in pain, this time with tears spilling from the corners of her eyes. Maddie wiped the tears from Taylor's cheeks and held her hand. "Sweetie, I'm sure they'll give you something for the pain soon. I know you're scared, but I'll be in the delivery room the whole time."

"I'll try to contact the doctor again to see about getting you something for the pain." Donna smiled and hurried out of the room.

Taylor continued to cry as she looked up at the ceiling. "Sorry you had to miss dialysis today. I didn't think I'd have the baby this early."

Maddie pulled the blanket up closer to Taylor's chest. "Believe me, I'd much rather see Aria be born than sit all morning getting dialysis."

Maddie would have to reschedule dialysis for tomorrow. Although her kidney function had improved to fourteen percent, Doctor Larsen said dialysis was still necessary and that a kidney transplant remained a possibility. Fortunately, the edema and fatigue had significantly decreased thanks to dialysis. Off the bevacizumab for a few months now, Maddie feared the tumor would come back, but the MRI from a couple weeks ago showed no new changes. Grateful for these little daily miracles, she'd become better about living in the moment and not thinking too far ahead.

Donna returned to the room, much friendlier than when she'd first entered, and actually addressed Taylor directly. "The doctor has authorized pain meds and should be in to see you in an hour or so." She efficiently but carefully started an IV in Taylor's hand, explaining what she was doing and why. Donna stepped back when she was done and smiled at them both. "Now that the IV is in, I can give you the medication. It'll kick in fast to decrease the pain, but you're probably gonna still feel some discomfort the closer you get to the time of birth." She picked up a syringe and injected the medicine into the IV. "There you go. It's gonna be a while till you're ready to deliver that baby. The contractions are still pretty far apart. I've got some other patients to check on, but you just call if you need me, okay?"

They thanked her together, but as soon as Donna left, Taylor teared up again. "I was thinking I could handle this all without any pain meds, but it hurts way worse than I thought it would."

"I remember that all too well." Maddie had been terrified when she'd gone into labor. Her mother and Drew didn't leave her side the whole time, distracting her from the pain and keeping her calm. Now it was Maddie's turn to do the same for her daughter. "You know, we still haven't decided what Aria is gonna call me."

"Not Grandma or Popo." Taylor winced in pain and squeezed Maddie's hand hard.

"Right, those names are taken. Besides, I don't feel old enough to be called Grandma."

"How about Nana?" Taylor suggested, sounding so earnest and sweet.

Maddie shook her head. "Nah, Nana would make me feel kinda old. When I think of a nana, I picture an old woman baking cookies and making scrapbooks. I'm too young for those things."

"Hmm." Taylor studied the view out of the window and squinted when a ray of light broke through the clouds. "Braden calls his grandma Oma, which is cool, but that's because that side of his family is German."

"Oma is sweet, but I'd imagine Braden's mom might be called that. Plus, as far as I know, I'm not German. I feel like we might need to come up with something unique for me, a name we haven't even considered yet."

Taylor's eyes started to get heavy. "What'd you call your other grandma? I mean, your dad's mom?"

Maddie hated to carry on the lie her mother started long ago, but this was not the time to tell Taylor about Johnny Patterson. "I never met my paternal grandparents."

"Did Grandma ever meet them?" Taylor asked through heavy-lidded eyes.

"She and my dad didn't have a chance to ever become a family, so she never met his parents." Since this was what Maddie had always believed growing up, she figured these details weren't too far from the truth.

"You never got curious to find out who Ben Rudolph's parents were? You can find just about anything online. I bet I could find lots of information with just a quick search."

"I grew up with amazing grandparents who gave me all the love I could ever need. It never felt weird only having one set of grandparents. Besides, I'd rather use what energy I have on the family I know and love." Although Taylor's questions were earnest, Maddie wanted to discourage her from searching for any information on Ben Rudolph or his parents. One day, she'd tell Taylor about Johnny Patterson. But not today. And probably not any time soon—unless it came down to her needing a kidney transplant.

"Maybe we're part English. Rudolph sounds like a British name, huh? Don't people in England call their grandmas Nan or Grams?" Taylor closed her eyes again and finally looked relaxed and out of pain.

"Seeing that I grew up in the U.S. and don't really know what my dad's ethnicity was, I say we oughta come up with something more fitting for me than Grams."

Taylor could be right about them possibly being part British. The name Patterson did sound English or Scottish. Could that be why she'd always been drawn to the

UK? Yet did her ethnic background matter at this point in her life? Once she stopped caring what the kids in school said about her being mixed race, she was proud of being Chinese-American. Then in her mid-teens, she forged a connection to Kai's Hawaiian roots and was honored that his *ohana* was also her family. Although still curious to know more about her biological father's heritage, Maddie didn't want to have any ties to that man.

Taylor shifted slightly to her side and smiled sleepily. "How about G-ma? Too trendy or weird?"

Maddie could tell the pain meds had totally kicked in and was relieved that her little girl was more comfortable. "You know, I think G-ma might work. Definitely better than Granny or Grams. G-ma sounds like a hip name for a grandma." Maddie smiled back, suffused with joy at becoming a grandmother.

Once Aria was born, there would be five generations of women in Maddie's family. Frail and unable to travel, Popo couldn't make it for the birth of Taylor's baby, but as soon as Aria was a couple months old, Taylor and Maddie would drive down to Southern California to introduce the baby to Popo. Then all five generations would be together. But Maddie would need to make arrangements to get dialysis while in Southern California. It was so frustrating to be tied down to that routine three days a week. Maybe it would be easier to get a kidney transplant.

When Taylor winced in pain again, Maddie glanced out the door to see if Donna was nearby. "Sweetie, I'll find the nurse and see if they can give you more meds."

"No, I'll be okay. That was just a bad one. I don't want you leaving my side until the baby's born."

"Don't worry, I won't." Maddie gently squeezed her hand, sending all her love through the touch. Although she never imagined Taylor having a baby at such a young age, Maddie was elated to still be around to experience this with her. More pelts of rain hit the window, and the sky looked even darker. Despite the annoyances of the medical professionals, Maddie had been right to get Taylor to the hospital way before necessary. They'd have been stuck at home otherwise, or worse, on a flooded road. Safe inside, they'd wait for Aria to enter the world. Not even noon yet, it looked like the sun had left the sky entirely. Winter this year had hit with a vengeance. Time had passed so fast. She'd started dialysis in December, yet here it was already February.

"Mom, what happened to that woman you met in Big Sur?" Taylor asked, her voice so curious and child-like. "She sounded cool. I thought you liked her."

Surprised by the sudden change in topic, Maddie blurted out, "How'd you know about Kendra?" She dropped her gaze to the floor, immediately regretting having said anything. It was so awkward for her daughter to ask about a woman she'd met months ago.

"Dad told me. He said you were way into her, but then you stopped seeing her."

Maddie couldn't help smiling to herself. Of course he did. Drew was now in a committed relationship with the French professor and wanted Maddie to also be with someone special. "It didn't work out with us. Kinda hard to date while going to dialysis three days a week and PT on the other days."

"You finished PT a while ago," Taylor mumbled, hardly able to keep her eyes open. "Plus, you have nothing on the weekends."

"Now that I'm about to become a G-ma, my weekends will be pretty full."

"Grandma Richards said she'll help with the baby, and Braden's mom wants to help, too. Well, and it's not like I'm clueless about how to take care of a newborn. Does Kendra even know you're about to become a grandma?"

For months, Maddie had put Kendra far out of her mind. All these questions were bringing her back and undoing Maddie's good work. Besides, it didn't even matter. Kendra had probably moved on to another fling by now. "Kendra knows you're expecting, but I haven't talked to her in a while."

"Why not?"

"It's complicated."

"Doesn't seem complicated to me. When you like someone and they like you, then you hang out. I never met Kendra, but I saw how happy you looked after you spent that weekend with her a while back."

Shocked that Taylor had noticed anything, Maddie felt even more awkward. Parents didn't need to discuss their romantic drama with their children. "Honey, I'm facing the possibility of needing a kidney transplant, and I'm still going through dialysis three days a week."

"You went through brain surgery, radiation, chemo, and a whole lot of other stuff to treat your cancer. What you're going through now doesn't seem all that complicated. Why don't you just text Kendra to tell her you're okay? Or call her after Aria is born to tell her you're a G-ma."

"Taylor, I think maybe the meds have kicked in. It's probably best you close your eyes and enjoy the break from the pain."

Eyes fully closed, Taylor started to slur her words. "I might be sixteen, but I'm grown up enough to know when my mom is interested in someone."

What Taylor said was true, but Maddie didn't want to continue this conversation much longer. "Okay, maybe I'll let her know how I'm doing, but right now, you're about to have a baby. Let's focus on that, okay?"

The rain had finally stopped, the dark clouds parting to reveal strobes of sunlight filtering into the room. Maddie welcomed these rays of winter sunshine. She stood at the side of the bed and gazed at Taylor—excited but apprehensive about how life would change once Aria entered the world. Pleased that Taylor chose such a beautiful name for the baby, Maddie hoped she'd still be alive to see Aria's first steps and hear her first words. When Taylor started to cry again, Maddie looked for a nurse to see about getting more pain meds, but none were in sight.

"Won't be much longer, sweetie." Maddie kissed Taylor on the forehead. "Pretty soon, your baby's gonna be in your arms, and all this pain will be behind you. I remember before you were born, I was so curious to see what you'd look like. When you first look at Aria, you'll see a little bit of you in her, some of Braden, and some of me and Dad."

"I hope you're not...disappointed in me," Taylor said

between sobs.

Maddie set her hand on Taylor's head and caressed her hair. "I'll never be disappointed in you. You're always gonna be my baby girl. I love you. Look at all you've managed to do while pregnant. You're only sixteen, but you're way ahead of most students with your independent studies. You'll probably graduate from high school even before the baby is a year old. I'm proud of you. Always have been."

Taylor looked away from her mother, and her shoulders tensed. "No, I mean disappointed that I got pregnant at such a young age."

Maddie gave her a hug. "Sweetie, we've talked about this before. I was a young mom, too. Believe me, I didn't expect to get pregnant when I was nineteen, but you being born was the best thing that ever happened in my life."

Taylor relaxed her shoulders and turned back to Maddie. She smiled. "I'm glad you're here with me for this."

"Honey, I'd never miss the birth of my first grandchild. I'm honored that I'm the only person you want in the delivery room besides the nurses and doctor."

Taylor's eyelids drooped again, and her speech started to slur even more. "No, I mean I'm glad...you're still alive to see me give birth."

Although Taylor's directness startled her, Maddie realized how much she'd managed to do in the past few years despite such a poor prognosis. "Next to you being born, I have a feeling this'll be the second-best day of my life." Maddie would always remember how she was filled with joy when the nurse first put Taylor in her arms.

"When we first found out about your cancer, and they only gave you...a few months to live, I thought about all the things you'd miss if you—"

"Honey, don't think about that right now." Maddie's eyes filled with tears, and she set her hand on Taylor's cheek.

"At first, I knew having a baby at such a young age would be a bad idea, but I realized I needed to do this. I mean, do it for you."

"What?" Maddie stared at Taylor in shock and dismay.

"You're saying the pregnancy wasn't an accident? Why would you do that? You're only sixteen."

"No, no." Taylor stifled a yawn. "It really was an accident. You told me your story, and I was so careful with the birth control. I was, I promise. But then it happened anyway, and I figured…I wanted you to be a grandma before you…before you passed. You'd exceeded the doctor's prognosis, but the more I read about your type of cancer, the more I realized…it'd only be a matter of time until it came back." Taylor got quiet and closed her eyes.

The shock vanished, but left in the silence were those words: until the cancer came back. Everything in Maddie's life centered around the likelihood that the tumor would return; after all, people with glioblastoma at most exceeded the life expectancy by only a couple of years. But here she was, about to become a grandma when a few years ago, she wasn't sure she'd be alive to watch the next season of *Orange Is the New Black*.

With what appeared to be great effort, Taylor opened her eyes. "After you got diagnosed, you said how you'd miss all the big events in my life—graduations, my wedding, my first child. I just wanted you to be a grandma before you died. I know I'll be a young mom, but at least Aria will meet her grandma."

Maddie had always been proud that Taylor could so openly use words like "died" when talking about the realistic possibility that brain cancer or kidney failure could be fatal. Many people dodged the subject of death when a family member had cancer, but Taylor had always bravely embraced the topic. But that bravery had come with a price. Taylor had made a well-meaning but unwise choice that altered the entire trajectory of her future. Maddie's life wasn't the only one irrevocably changed by the cancer.

Still, what was done was done, and there was nothing for it but to accept the current paths of their lives. "Honey, no one knows with certainty what'll happen tomorrow or next month or next year, but what I do know is that we have today. I can't say the road ahead will be easy for you or for me, but today I'm gonna be a G-ma, and you're gonna be a mother."

"That drug they put in my IV makes me feel weird." Glassy-eyed, Taylor reached a limp hand toward Maddie.

"Close your eyes, sweetie. You'll need all the rest you can before you give birth."

"'Kay." Taylor finally stopped fighting the medication, and her eyes shut. The big hospital pillow puffed up as she fully sank into it, her whole body lax and pain-free.

Maddie held Taylor's hand as she drifted off to sleep. Taylor's intentions about remaining pregnant at sixteen were heartfelt, albeit foolish and immature, but right now Maddie couldn't wait to welcome Aria into the world and hold her in her arms.

Maddie took a seat in the chair next to the bed and picked up her bag of books. Taylor had gone into labor right when Maddie was gathering snacks and reading material for her dialysis appointment, which meant she now had something to occupy her time while waiting to go to the delivery room. Maddie decided to reread Virginia Woolf's *Night and Day*, which she'd discovered when she was a freshman in college. She'd last read it only a few months before she became pregnant with Taylor, so it seemed fortuitous to reread now.

Maddie flipped through pages she'd bookmarked years ago in college. Written on tattered stickie notes were various words and phrases describing themes, motifs, and symbols to help write a paper for her literature class. One of the notes read "love and longing," and Maddie thought about how naïve she was at age eighteen. Now, this book meant much more to her—after she'd fallen in love a couple times and had her heart broken more than once.

Maddie gazed out the rain-speckled window. Kendra had once texted her a line from this book at a time when Maddie could not begin to handle the emotions evoked by both Woolf's words and Kendra herself. But there was more to the quote than what Kendra had included in the text. Compelled to find the rest of the passage, Maddie quickly skimmed the pages to where she vaguely remembered the relevant scene took place. There, midway through the book, she found the excerpt—the words underlined years ago when she'd first read them:

I see you everywhere, in the stars, in the river; to me you're everything that exists; the reality of everything. Life, I would tell you, would be impossible without you.

She fell back into the chair, barely registering the resulting thump. Taylor was right. Maddie laughed to herself. If her child and the father of her child were saying the same thing about Kendra, then she needed to listen to them. Maddie was being dumb about cutting things off with Kendra. There was no denying the happiness that suffused her being when they were together. The way her body and mind connected to Kendra's was unlike anything she'd ever experienced. Much more than bonding over cancer, Maddie understood that life really would be impossible without her—no matter how much more time either of them had.

In a burst of energy, Maddie flipped through *Night and Day* in search of a quote that could convey how she truly felt about Kendra. As if by magic, a line leapt off the page, and it was impossible to ignore:

She seemed a compound of the autumn leaves and the winter sunshine.

It was perfect. Hadn't she met Kendra in autumn and immediately wanted her to be part of her winter, too? And spring and summer as well.

But Maddie didn't need to cite Woolf quotes to speak from the heart. Without much more thought, she tapped out a few words to Kendra—to hopefully rekindle the embers that burned a few months ago.

I'm sorry I pushed you away. I was an idiot to cut things off, especially without much of an explanation. Today I was reading passages from Night and Day and came across the quote you sent me months ago. Though we haven't seen each other for a while, I too see you everywhere—in the wispy clouds after a winter storm, in the soft rays of sun at dusk, even in the grains of sand at the beach. I shouldn't have let so much time pass since I last texted or called you, but I'm finally taking your advice to live in the moment. I'm still tumor-free, and best of all, I'm about to become a grandma.

Maddie hit "send" and watched the raindrops trickle down the glass window pane. An intense longing washed over her—a desire to feel Kendra's hand in hers. With so much more to say, Maddie started to write another text. The words poured out of her, the longing for Kendra now so obvious.

I think about you every day and recall how right things felt when we watched the sunset that one evening: your hand in mine, my lips on yours. I only wish we—

Before she could finish the text, Kendra replied. As her heart thudded hard in anticipation, Maddie read the message:

This is Bree, Kendra's wife. Right now, Kendra's—

Her wife? A few months ago, Kendra told her she and Bree had divorced. Why would she lie to her about that? Kendra had been so passionate when they made love. Her desire had rivalled Maddie's own, and they both couldn't get enough of each other. Maddie stared at Bree's response. Kendra must've only seen their involvement this past autumn as a brief fling—an affair in all reality. A sadness washed over her as she read the rest of the text:

Right now, Kendra's getting a CT scan of her lungs and a biopsy. Last week she was in a car accident. Fortunately, there were only minor injuries, the worst of which is a fractured rib. But the x-ray showed a spot on her lung. They're worried it's cancer that's metastasized from the breast cancer years ago. If I remember correctly, you're the friend she met in Big Sur who's also a cancer survivor. I figured you'd want to know what's going on. I'll tell her you texted.

A friend? Was that all she'd been to Kendra? Just a friend with benefits? Maddie had been a fool to have gotten involved with a married woman again. Hardly enough time for them to fall in love, their few weeks together were fun but obviously nothing meaningful to Kendra. So be it. Though disappointed, she was not surprised. She was grateful for the brief interlude with Kendra—for the opportunity to feel flesh on flesh and soul to soul.

Given the potential severity of what Bree just wrote to her, Maddie should offer a few supportive words. She deleted the text she started to write and replaced it with two brief and friendly lines:

Thanks for letting me know. Hoping for the best with the biopsy results.

Already on borrowed time, Maddie knew her brief interlude with Kendra was more than she'd ever expected. Soon, Maddie would witness her granddaughter entering the world, which up until today she never imagined experiencing. Right now, life felt perfect. Maddie wouldn't look back and would only look forward from here on out.

Chapter Sixteen

Mississippi: March 2019

Along the drab stretch of Highway 61, there was nothing but flat land and sparse trees. It'd been over twenty years since Maddie was last in Mississippi. This state looked so unfamiliar that it might as well be another country. Maddie and Dot had been in the car since early this morning, but the map on the phone indicated they'd get to the Mississippi state prison in thirty minutes—which meant she'd meet Johnny Patterson within the hour.

As a child, Maddie had never seen the northern part of Mississippi, but being back in the state made her realize how much she loved living in California. Tired from the redeye she took last night, Maddie didn't speak and only gazed at the farmlands that blurred past. Grateful that Dot also remained quiet, Maddie was incredibly comforted at having a friend along for the ride. It wasn't as if she'd had any choice, though. Upon learning Maddie had decided to meet Johnny, Dot insisted on being there for moral support. "Besides, I could do with a break from the art world!" Dot had said with a laugh. "Those critics, let me tell you. Visiting a prison has to be more fun than dealing with them."

Years ago, one thing Maddie learned right away was that she shouldn't ever say no to Dot.

Maddie had requested a few days off from teaching at the men's prison in SLO in order to come to Mississippi. Her boss at the prison was incredibly accommodating and supportive, unlike her dean at the college. HR finished their investigation and did not have conclusive evidence that Maddie had violated any federal privacy laws. Although HR had only given her an informal reprimand for what she'd done and had offered her two classes at the college, she'd said no. The way they'd handled the situation was disappointing. No apology. Not even an acknowledgement that Jamie Miller's submission of a grievance regarding Maddie's lack of attendance at on-campus trainings was bogus. Everyone knew that Maddie had been given special permission a while back to do her professional development training online. The grievance had been quickly dismissed, but Jamie was not punished for wasting everyone's time. In fact, he'd been given the British literature class that Maddie used to teach. Maddie was now positive he was the one who'd told Phillis about the social media posts since he'd posted a photo with a group of students from his class, including Phillis smiling with her arm linked in his. Jamie wrote something about how his students were in better hands with him than any other English professor at the college. Such an arrogant jerk.

Maddie wanted nothing more to do with that school. Word had spread fast at area prisons and juvenile detention centers that Maddie's classes were greatly benefiting the inmates. If she wanted to teach more than a couple classes, she could easily reach full-time status in the inmate education program.

And here she was today, on her way to a prison to meet her biological father. The irony couldn't be ignored.

A sign indicated they were nearing their destination, and Maddie yet again privately affirmed her determination to go through with this. Now that Aria was six weeks old, Maddie would do whatever it took to stay alive, even if it meant getting a kidney from a man in prison for murder or from one of his offspring.

A couple weeks after Aria was born, Maddie told Taylor about Johnny Patterson, but she hadn't told Mom or Kai she was planning to meet him. Maddie got in touch with a Lieutenant Annie Wright who assisted her in setting up a meeting. Lieutenant Wright had warned her Johnny would likely say no and to not get her hopes up. To both of their surprise, he didn't reject her request. Maddie was extremely nervous about meeting him, but she knew this was necessary in order for her to have any chance of long-term survival. Although her doctors were pleased to see that kidney function had somewhat improved, Maddie still feared her kidneys could fail and wanted to get some options in place should she eventually need a transplant.

Chipper and alert, Dot hummed to a twangy country song on the radio while she sped down the highway. "Depending on how things go, I think we oughta find a roadside diner after you meet Johnny, preferably a place with a bar."

"Not a bad idea." The view from the windshield still only displayed grasslands on one side of the road and a few trees on the other. "You think they've got a gay bar around here?"

"Probably nothing but dive bars in this part of the state. We'd likely have better luck driving back to Memphis. Bet they'd have loads of gay bars there."

"Sure, if you like dancing to country music and drinking beer out of a bottle."

"Hon, that might be just what you need. Meet yourself a cute cowgirl, maybe do a little two-step with some young hottie in cowboy boots?"

"With my luck, I'd meet another married woman or a jerk. I should've trusted my gut and not gotten involved with Kendra."

Curious, and admittedly concerned, about Kendra's biopsy results, Maddie sometimes considered texting her again, but she was still hurt that she'd lied about not being married. Plus, since Kendra hadn't responded to her text weeks ago, Maddie figured Bree might've had something to do with the lack of contact.

Dot pursed her lips and shrugged. "At least you only went out a couple times. Nothing wrong with a quick fling. It's not like you fell in love with her."

Maddie could've easily fallen in love with Kendra. Probably already had to some extent. Sensual and deep, Kendra had awoken something in Maddie which had been dormant for way too long.

Dot turned down the radio. "While you're meeting Johnny, I'll search online to find us a bar. There's gotta be something around here."

"After I meet him, I might need something stronger than beer or wine." Maddie reached behind the seat to grab her backpack. In the side pouch was a bottle of anti-anxiety medication in case she needed something to calm her nerves. For the first time since she got stoned with Kendra in Big Sur, Maddie wished she had some edibles or a joint, but for now, half a pill would have to do.

Up ahead were the sprawling buildings of the state prison. Lieutenant Wright said she'd meet her in front of the visitor center. So different than where Maddie taught, this facility looked like it was in the middle of a desert. The visitor protocols were likely the same, though. Maddie would leave her walking stick and valuables in the car and only bring her ID, a pad of paper, and a pen into the prison.

Dot idled at the security booth, and a serious-looking guard inspected their IDs and the back of the rental car, then looked briefly at Maddie. He told Dot where the visitor center was located and motioned her into the parking lot.

The closer they got to the main buildings, the more Maddie trembled in anxiety. In addition to inquiring about Johnny or his offspring being a possible kidney donor, Maddie wanted to meet the man who contributed to her DNA. Although Kai filled the role of father, she needed to see the face of the man who was her biological father and hear his voice. She needed to look into his eyes to find out if blood was thicker than water, if there was any connection between the two of them despite never meeting until now.

Dot parked near the visitor center where Maddie would meet the lieutenant. Professional yet personable in her correspondence, Lieutenant Wright had responded to all of Maddie's emails and had been more than accommodating as far as setting up this meeting. Her warmth encouraged Maddie to share the details of her cancer and kidney treatment, which resulted in a long, supportive response. Although the lieutenant didn't work at the state prison, she had professional interest in Johnny and was therefore allowed to assist Maddie. Only aware of some of the particulars of Johnny's conviction, Maddie did her best to not think too much about what he'd done and to put all negative feelings aside when she met him.

Maddie unclasped her seatbelt and opened the car

door. "Since I won't have my phone with me, I won't be able to let you know when I'm heading back to the car. Might be a short visit or might be long. Depends on how receptive he is to me being here."

Dot lowered the window on her side. "Take all the time you need. I've got loads of things to do. I reckon I might even take a nap while you're in there. Plus, I can catch up on *Grace and Frankie* so long as my tablet battery lasts."

"I'm at nearly a hundred percent on my phone, so feel free to use it if need be." Maddie got out of the car and leaned against it. The nerves were making her sick to her stomach. Taking deep breaths helped, and the crisp air and warm sun felt good on her face, but she couldn't stop her body from trembling. It was only when a uniformed woman approached her that she was able to gather some strength.

Maddie gave the woman a small smile and stepped away from the rental car. "Lieutenant Wright? I'm Maddie Fong."

The lieutenant shook Maddie's hand and smiled in return. "Please, call me Annie. Don't let the uniform make you feel that you have to be overly formal. I've got this on today to hopefully expedite getting us through security and to the visiting area." Annie glanced into the car and ran a hand through her short salt-and-pepper hair. Tall and somewhat soft in the middle, Annie had a toughness about her that made Maddie feel safe.

"You don't think he'll change his mind about seeing me, do you?" Maddie asked.

"Not likely, given that he agreed to your request," Annie said. "For all he knows, a cousin came by to check up on him. I'm sure he's clueless about why you came here to see him. When did y'all get to Mississippi?"

Maddie waved an arm toward the car. "My friend, Dot, and I just got here. We took the redeye from California and landed in Memphis early this morning. I'd heard it was the quickest drive from the airport."

Dot gave Annie a smile and quick wave and returned to her tablet.

Annie smiled again, and her entire face lit up. "What

part of California are y'all from? I used to live in San Diego."

"San Diego's great," Maddie said. "I live in Morro Bay, a town in the Central California Coast area. I'm originally from Southern California. As I mentioned in one of my emails, I lived in Mississippi when I was a kid, but California feels more like home to me than this state."

"Can't beat Southern California. I'm fixin' to possibly move there once I retire. Well, seeing as visiting hours for maximum security prisoners are pretty limited, we oughta head in there." Annie set her hand on the small of Maddie's back and led her toward the visitor center.

Canes were not allowed inside the prison, which meant Maddie had to leave hers in the car. She moved slowly without it, and Annie graciously offered her arm for support. As they walked, Annie ran through the safety information she'd already shared in the email. When they reached the entrance, Annie stopped and lowered her voice. "Before we go in there, you should know there's no telling how he'll react to you saying you're his daughter, but rest assured there will be a barrier between you and him."

At those words, Maddie became queasy and light-headed. "Never imagined I'd be meeting my father in a prison. I'll probably be ready for a drink after this visit." Maddie laughed and averted her eyes from Annie's.

Annie smiled and glanced beyond the parking lot. "Not too many decent bars around here, but I'm sure there are lots of places off the 61 as you head back to Memphis." She patted Maddie's arm. "I'll be nearby the whole time, but if things get too uncomfortable, you let me know, and I'll escort you out of the prison. And if he gets too out of line, I'll talk to him. He probably won't want to see my face again, but I'll put him in his place if need be."

"Thank you. It's good to know I won't be alone." Maddie bit her lip. "I read a bit online about his conviction, about why he got a life sentence."

The warmth in Annie's face vanished and was replaced with a cold anger. "There's much more to it than what was public knowledge, but let's just say he's where he needs to be. A life sentence definitely fits, considering all he'd done over the years. Well, all the way back to when your mom met him."

It was still so surreal that a vile man like Johnny was her biological father. "I have no idea what to expect when I meet him."

"Patterson's a pretty hardened man, but who knows if a few years behind bars have softened him. From what I've witnessed, you never know what sort of evil will spew out of his mouth. Definitely best if he doesn't know I'm here." Annie rubbed her brow and glanced at the prison entrance as she shook her head. "We probably won't have much time to chat after you see him, but if you need to talk later today or in the next few days, feel free to call me. I know you have my direct line at the station, but here's my cell." Annie jotted her number on the back of her card and handed it to Maddie, who slipped it in her notebook.

They entered the building, signed the visitor's log, and were then screened through security. So far, the process was identical to when Maddie went to the penitentiary to teach the poetry and autobiography classes, except she wasn't even allowed to bring in her notebook and pen. They had to be placed in a locker. A guard would provide her with pencil and paper later on. From there, Maddie and Annie were ushered onto a bus with about ten other people and rode across the premises until they reached the visiting area for maximum security prisoners. No one on the bus uttered a word, or even met anyone's eyes, during the entire ride. The atmosphere was stifling and remained so even as Maddie followed Annie off the bus. Her mouth became dry, and she couldn't speak even if she wanted to. Thankfully, Annie did all the talking, and soon a muscular guard with a buzz cut was leading them down a long corridor and into a room with partitions and chairs next to a few small windows. Though Maddie had never visited a prisoner in this sort of setting, she'd spoken with men who'd committed horrific crimes, many of whom had totally changed their lives after doing time. Hoping Johnny would be receptive to her visit and wasn't as evil as Annie had implied, Maddie braced herself for whatever she'd encounter.

The guard handed Maddie a sheet of paper and a dull pencil, and told her to take a seat at the farthest cubicle. Maddie gripped Annie's arm to steady herself until she got to the last partition.

Annie helped Maddie into the chair and gave her a reassuring smile. "Don't worry, I'm right here," she whispered. Annie stepped away and stood by the doorway but was still in Maddie's line of sight.

Maddie had been trying hard to think of this as just meeting a stranger who could potentially save her life. It helped a lot to know Annie stood nearby and would assist her if need be.

On the opposite side of the thick, glass partition was an empty seat. The stark white walls were much like those of the hospitals Maddie had been in over the years, except the walls in the prison were made of cinderblock covered with thick white paint. Maddie's leg jittered in nervousness. Was Johnny even going to show up? Maybe he'd declined her visit after all. Maybe he somehow figured out who came to see him. But then, a guard escorted a tall, scrawny man to the chair behind the glass. The breath rushed out of her, but whether in relief or fear, she didn't know.

Johnny made eye contact with Maddie, and his brow furrowed as if trying to recall how he knew her. His eyes narrowed, and he reached for the phone without taking his sight off her.

Nervous to hear Johnny's voice, Maddie hesitated before lifting the receiver. She glanced at Annie, who nodded and smiled. Maddie put the phone to her ear and carefully studied this man who had a vague resemblance to her, at least in the eyes, lips, and forehead.

Johnny leaned forward and set his elbows on the ledge. "You Madelyn Richards? Them guards told me I had a relative wanting to see me. Don't know nobody named Madelyn."

"That's the name I had to put on the application. I go by Maddie. Do you get a lot of visitors?" Maddie asked, her voice hoarse.

Johnny threw his head back and laughed. He had dimples—the same ones she had when she smiled. But when his grin turned into a scowl, the anger in his eyes was visceral.

"Ain't nobody ever come see me here. Don't have no relatives who'd wanna visit me, especially someone who looks like you." Johnny leaned forward and breathed loudly into the receiver. "You one of my dad's cousins? If so, then you can get the fuck outta here. Don't want nothing to do with his side of the family. That man can rot in hell far as I'm concerned."

"No, I'm not a cousin." Not sure how best to converse with someone incarcerated for murder, Maddie became quiet and looked at him for a moment, studying the way he behaved when he talked.

Johnny's face twisted in rage. "Then who are you? You another one of those crime pod reporters or whatever? I got nothing to say. Already got life for what I done. Why you gotta be digging up all that?"

Alarmed that Johnny might leave before they'd started, Maddie spoke quickly. "No, no, I'm not here to talk about any of your crimes. I just have some questions to ask you about someone you met over thirty years ago. Do you remember a woman named Angela? Do you recall being involved with her back in the early eighties?" Maddie's heart thudded so hard she was sure everyone could hear it.

"The eighties? Don't remember where I was back then."

"You met her in a bar."

"You here to accuse me of raping her? If so, I'm not gonna—"

"I'm not here to accuse you of anything. Just wondering if you remember meeting a woman named Angela in the early eighties."

"Can't expect me to remember nobody from back then, especially a lady from a bar. Took a lot of ladies home or just fucked them out back behind the bar."

Maddie cringed at Johnny's choice of words. She glanced at Annie, who was leaning against the wall. Comforted by her presence, Maddie searched for the right words to tell Johnny that he was her father. "You and Angela went out for several weeks. She wasn't just a one-night stand."

Johnny screwed up his face, as if trying to think. "What's she look like? Like I says, I been with a lot of ladies."

"She looks somewhat like me. She's my mom. I have her skin tone and the same round face, but I'm much taller."

"She a Oriental lady?" Johnny smirked. "Really short? I think I remember her. Fine looking woman with little bitty titties and a tight ass. Went out for a coupla months. Had me some fun with her."

Although Maddie couldn't bear to look at Johnny after what he'd just said, she made herself respond to his questions. "My mom's Chinese, not even five foot. I obviously didn't get my height from her. I got it from my father. Same with my dimples. I got those from my father...from you."

Johnny glared at Maddie and grunted into the phone. "From me? Angela would've told me if we had a kid together. Like I says, I don't remember much from the eighties. How do I know you're not some stranger just wanting to say her daddy is a murderer?"

Maddie shook her head. "I saw how my mom reacted when she told me about you. She wouldn't lie to me about this."

"How'd you know how to find me?"

"You were pretty easy to find online. Actually, my mom first told me about you being in prison, and then we found out you're here."

"Why'd you wanna see me? Like I says, no one visits me."

Maddie glanced at the clock on the wall. Time was going by way too fast. She got to the point. "A few years ago, I was diagnosed with brain cancer. I was told I only had a few months to live."

"So, your dying wish was to meet your daddy?" Johnny shook his head and laughed, his face lighting up but quickly getting serious again.

"I didn't know about you until a few months ago. The

truth is that treatment for cancer is harsh, and the meds they use can cause kidney problems after a while. I've been on dialysis for a few months, but the doctors say I might need a kidney transplant, one preferably from a living relative, such as a parent or a sibling."

"A kidney transplant?" Johnny's brow rose in disbelief. "Thought you says you're dying of brain cancer?"

"I've somehow beaten the odds." Despite the situation, Maddie's lips curved in a small, genuine smile. "So far at least. My daughter says I'm a miracle. But one of the drugs I was on for a few years caused kidney damage."

"If you got a kid, that means I'm a granddaddy." Johnny shook his head and mumbled something that Maddie couldn't understand.

Maddie opened her mouth to tell him he was actually a great-grandfather but already regretted even telling him about Taylor. She did not want this man knowing about Aria. Maddie gave him a weak smile. "Yes. It's why I'm doing all I can to stay healthy and alive. If I can get a kidney transplant, the doctors say—"

"You saying you want one of my kidneys?" Anger washed over Johnny's face, and his eyes bored deep into Maddie's. "You think they'll let a man in prison for life donate a kidney? They shackle me even when I gotta see the doc here."

Maybe Maddie's plan was outlandish and impossible, but she kept trying. "I read online that in certain situations, a prisoner can donate a kidney to a family member. But the doctors say a kidney from a sibling is the best match, and that one from a half-sibling is sometimes a match. My mom mentioned you had a child, someone a couple years older than I am."

Johnny gazed through the glass and focused somewhere above Maddie's head. His eyes brightened momentarily, as if welling up with tears, but he quickly blinked and composed himself. That hardened look returned to his face. "Haven't talked to her in years. She don't even know where I'm at. Last I heard, she got married and moved to some big city in California. Probably wanted to get as far away from me as possible. My other kid calls me occasionally. Or used to anyway."

Two half-siblings? Maddie had even more family out there? She was overcome with the desire to know everything, but right now, she only needed the vital information. "So, you know where your other child lives?"

"He's in Tennessee where his mom's from. A while back, he had a run-in with the law, something drug-related, but he quit the drugs and alcohol once he did time behind bars. Haven't talked to him since before I got arrested. Probably best that he don't have much contact with me. I'm obviously not the best father. Never actually saw them grow up. Not one of them have my last name."

Maddie stared at the stranger on the other side of the glass. The faint resemblance in their faces wasn't enough to make Maddie feel any sort of link to him, but her mother must've felt something strong enough to get involved with him years ago. "My middle name was chosen because it's the closest thing to your name. I rarely use my middle name, but it's Joan. Guess my mom wanted me to have some sort of connection to you."

Johnny leaned forward and studied Maddie's face, his expression softening just a little. "You remind me of my first kid. Same eyes and tall like me."

As she thought about what Johnny had done, why he was serving a life sentence, Maddie wished she could go back to thinking her dad had died in a war, but she couldn't deny her curiosity about what else she'd inherited from Johnny besides her dimples and her height. "Always got teased as a kid for being tall for my age."

"Yeah, them kids in school used to tease me for being scrawny, but I showed them I wasn't about to let that go on for too long. Quickly became the kid others were afraid of. No one teased me after that. Well, my dad used to tease me. Beat the shit outta me whenever he got drunk, which when I was a kid was nearly every night." Johnny's eyes glazed over for a moment, but then he rubbed his face and looked back at Maddie without saying another word.

That lined up with what Angela had told her. "When I was a kid, I used to think not having a dad was one of the worst things ever. When I was fourteen, my mom met an amazing man who took me in like his own child. Couldn't have asked for a better dad."

"You're lucky you had a dad who took care of you. Like I says, probably best that none of my kids had much contact with me. You asking me to get them to give you a kidney? Cuz I don't got no contact with my firstborn."

"Any information you can give me would help. Since a half-sibling is sometimes a good match for a kidney, it'd be worth a try to see if they'd help. Or see if you'd be a viable match."

"What do I have to do to give you a kidney?"

"I'm guessing they'll take blood, run some tests, and go from there. If you're a match and if I do end up needing a kidney, I'm sure we'll have to go through a lot of red tape to get this to happen. Might depend on if you're a model prisoner and if—"

"Never broke no rules here. Always keep to myself. Not much to do in prison besides think about what I done."

That sounded promising, although Maddie kept her expression neutral as she nodded. "If you do donate a kidney, you'd be transported to a hospital where they'd remove your kidney. You'd likely stay in the hospital for a few days to recover."

"Probably get me some better food in a hospital than the shit they feed us here. Don't sound like such a bad thing to have them cut out my kidney."

"I'm sure you'd be able to eat nearly anything you'd like, but they'd need to monitor you for a while after the surgery to make sure you don't get an infection. You'd probably have to take it easy for a few weeks." Maddie took an audible breath. "I realize it's a lot to ask of you, especially since you never even knew you had another child."

"Ain't no one ever asked me for something this big. They might not let me do it because of what I'm in for."

Maddie's stomach dropped. Like her mother, she'd briefly felt sympathy for this man, but he was still a rapist and a killer. She was so grateful her mother had fled from Mississippi. How different their lives would've been had Johnny been in her life. The adrenaline that had brought her this far was fading, and exhaustion was starting to take its place. Maddie just wanted to obtain the necessary information and get back on the road.

Not willing to look at him, Maddie gathered her strength and said quietly, "My doctors say I'm jumping the gun by asking if you'd donate a kidney. I'd imagine it'd be more feasible for one of your offspring to be a more likely candidate...so long as I can find them."

"Bet you could find them if you searched online. Their names are Adam Castle and Danielle Hayes. Like I says, Adam's in Tennessee, and Danielle moved to California. Her last name might not be Hayes anymore since she got married. I still know Adam's phone number by heart. Might've even given him Danielle's cell phone number a while back. Bet he'd be able to get you in touch with her."

Maddie jotted down their names and the states of where they lived, along with Adam's number. The exhaustion momentarily disappeared as she found herself antsy to leave the prison and call him as soon as she got to the car.

The guard announced that the visiting hours were almost over, and Johnny became agitated. Instead of looking into Maddie's eyes as he'd done during most of this visit, he hung his head low and became sullen, although he didn't hang up the phone.

Maddie felt no compassion for him, no connection to the stranger who sat behind glass. But with a fierce will to fight to stay alive in order to see Aria grow up, Maddie hoped she'd inherited Johnny's blood type, that he'd be a match and could therefore donate a kidney. "I guess I'll be in touch should I actually need a kidney." Maddie scooted her chair back from the window.

Johnny turned around when the guard approached him but quickly turned back and spoke into the phone. "If you do get my kidney, will them doctors tell me if it worked? I mean, if it helped you stay alive?"

That was an unexpected question. The guard on Johnny's side raised his brow, and Maddie was sure he was shocked at what he heard. Maddie still felt no compassion for Johnny. That would never change. She'd spent the last few years wondering if surgery and chemo would keep her alive, and soon she might be relying on a kidney transplant to help her survive. Johnny likely faced a few more decades in prison before he'd die of old age, yet he seemed eager to help her—to give her the gift of life.

Maddie leaned forward and looked directly at him. "I could write to you after the surgery to let you know how I'm doing, but maybe I won't even need the kidney. Maybe like my daughter says, I'll continue to be a walking miracle and beat kidney damage like I beat brain cancer. But should I need your kidney, and if things...don't go well, I'm sure someone from my family could write to you...to let you know."

Johnny gave a quick nod in response, and the guard crossed his arms in impatience, so Maddie said an equally quick goodbye and hung up the phone. She watched as Johnny was led away. It would have been so nice to still think her father was someone who'd died in a war, and not a man who'd committed heinous crimes. But Maddie now knew the definitive truth. Blood was not thicker than water. There was no connection to Johnny, nothing to salvage or save. All she got from him were her dimples and height. He was not family. Besides Mom, Taylor, and Aria, Maddie's *ohana* consisted of people who weren't even her blood relatives. When Kai had come into her mom's life, he'd made their family complete. The closest Maddie had ever come to telling Kai she considered him her father was when she told him she was glad he walked her down the aisle at her wedding. But Maddie knew it was time for her to tell Kai that it was because of him that she was the person she was today—a fighter and a survivor.

Eager to leave and get out in the fresh air, Maddie gripped her hand on Annie's arm, and they left the way they came. Maddie was quiet on the bus ride back to the parking lot, but this time because she was relaxed and maybe even a little happy. Mom and Kai would be married in a couple months. All her life she'd been looking for that missing puzzle piece, but it wasn't missing after all. Kai had been there all along—loving her and protecting her like any good father would. Maddie rested her head against the window. It was going to be so amazing to be part of their wedding.

Annie seemed to understand Maddie's need for silence and only spoke to help her out of the seat. As they exited the bus, Maddie clasped her hand around Annie's arm and kept it there until they got to the parking lot.

Under the bright afternoon sun, Maddie took a deep breath. The crisp spring air washed over her face, making her drowsy. Utterly exhausted, Maddie only wanted to get in the car and doze as Dot drove them back to Memphis.

"I can't thank you enough for all you did to help me meet him," Maddie said, not sure if she should hug Annie or shake her hand.

As if reading Maddie's mind, Annie knew exactly what to do. She smiled and wrapped her arms around Maddie. "It's been a hell of a day. If you need anything at all, don't hesitate to call me." Annie ended the embrace. "Need help getting to your car?"

A frantic waving in the distance caught Maddie's eye. "No, thank you. I can see Dot coming over. I'll be fine from here on out."

They exchanged goodbyes, and Annie drove off in a sedan right as Dot rushed up, looking noticeably upset. Her eyes were wide and frightened, and her hair was mussed up.

Dot glanced at Maddie's phone, which she held tightly in her hand. "Hon, I'm so glad you're back. I don't usually look at someone's texts, but I was using your mobile to look up nearby bars when I saw a message come through. You also got a few missed calls that went to voicemail."

Maddie cocked her head. "Who called?"

"Mad, it's probably best that you read this after you're settled in the car."

"What is it? What's going on?"

Dot draped an arm over Maddie's shoulders and handed her the phone.

Maddie glanced at the text, the words "unexpectedly passed away" leaping off the screen.

An invisible force knocked the wind out of Maddie.

She couldn't breathe. She tried to make sense of what she'd read. Starkly aware of her own mortality for the past few years, she wasn't prepared for this. Light-headed and weak, she tried to take in a lungful of air but could only gasp. Not able to grasp the reality of this horrible news, she collapsed onto the ground and sobbed.

Crouched on her knees, Dot held Maddie's shaking body and rocked her gently. "Hon, let's get you in the car. Let's head back to Memphis."

"I need to go home. I need to get back to California. We have to fly back tonight."

"Okay, we'll see about getting an earlier flight once we get to the hotel. We can't make any arrangements from here."

Unable to stop the flood of tears, Maddie kneeled on the hard ground and rocked forward. She couldn't erase those words from her mind: unexpectedly passed away. Almost too much for her to bear, Maddie was certain her heart had been cleft in half.

Chapter Seventeen

San Clemente, California: April 2019

Maddie gazed at the golden rays of sunlight over the ocean, not yet ready to say goodbye. Over the years, she'd come to this beach many times, the ocean comforting her in times of sorrow and celebrating with her in moments of victory. For the past two weeks, waves of grief washed over her—the sadness at times unbearable. Maddie did her best to outwardly appear strong, but inside she had countless regrets and many words left unspoken.

Small waves lapped onto shore, the conditions perfect for paddle boarding or kayaking, but out in the distance, a few sets built in momentum. The memorial would soon begin. Several mourners congregated on the sand. Preferring to be alone for a few minutes, Maddie contemplated how life could change in an instant. Why hadn't she been the one who died? A few years ago, she expected to die within months of being told she had brain cancer. Six months to live. Grade four glioblastoma multiforme. No one lived long with that type of cancer. But here she was, four and a half years post-diagnosis and very much alive.

But was she truly living? Except for the moments she'd spent with Kendra or when Aria was born, Maddie had been teetering on a swaying tightrope—always fearful that the tumor would return and cut her life short.

Aria cooed in Taylor's arms. Maddie had been right; the baby looked a little like all of their families combined, although she clearly got her straight, brown hair from Taylor. Only two months old, Aria was already bright-eyed and almost always smiling. Taylor had taken to motherhood well, showering the baby with kisses and cuddles.

Taylor handed Aria to Braden's mom, then walked up

to Maddie and stood close. "Mom, they're almost ready to begin. Dad said you'll enter the water first, followed by me and Dad and then all the others."

As Maddie studied the breakers in the distance, her heart thudded hard, and her knees became weak. "They want me to be the lead surfer? If the swell picks up, there's no way I can paddle out past the waves."

Taylor linked her arm around Maddie's. "Mom, you got this. The waves won't get much bigger than this."

Maddie's eyes welled up with tears, and she had a hard time steadying her breath. She pulled Taylor into a sideways hug and squinted at the glaring light over the ocean. It was a perfect spring afternoon. The sun sat low in the horizon, and the air was crisp and fresh. Three yellow school buses and a few white vans arrived in the parking lot. A bunch of teens exited the vehicles and headed to the beach with surfboards and lots of gear.

Of all days for the ocean to be crowded with young surfers. Perhaps Maddie and the others should redirect them to a different surf break. "Must be spring break. The beach is gonna be crowded for the memorial."

Taylor rested her head on Maddie's shoulder. "No, they're here for the paddle-out. Surf teams from Laguna, Newport, and San Clemente came, and a couple more are on the way."

Maddie fought back the tears. She had no idea so many people wanted to pay their respects. The waves got larger, bringing with them a memory of how scared she was the first time she surfed, and how Kai put her at ease immediately. Maddie kneeled in the sand and applied another layer of wax on Kai's favorite surfboard as tears trickled down her face. Kai rode this board only two weeks ago. His passing shocked everyone. No one had expected he'd drop dead of a heart attack at such a young age.

There was no doubt Maddie was apprehensive about getting back on a surfboard, but she'd be safe with other surfers in the water. Matt from Monarch Bluffs had shown up after he'd seen her social media post. His presence was comforting, and Maddie knew he'd help should she encounter any difficulties in the breakers. When

Maddie took in all the people here for the paddle-out, she got even more choked up and brushed the tears from her eyes.

Well over a hundred people were gathered on the beach, ready to paddle into the water to honor Kai. People Maddie hadn't seen in years waited on shore, many of whom probably saw the newspaper articles or social media posts about Kai's memorial. Much more mature now than they were nearly twenty years ago, the entire surf team from Maddie's high school waited on the beach. Kai's cousin Mark had flown over a couple days ago and brought fresh leis from the islands. Though not able to join them in the water, Dot stood nearby and promised she'd cheer loudly during the paddle-out. Mom and Popo remained close by, both looking lost and heartbroken. Angela had sobbed for days after Kai's passing. Last night, she'd told Maddie that she didn't think she had any tears left, but more now trickled down her face as she stood on shore.

Maddie knew exactly how her mother felt and brushed away more tears of her own. What made today even harder was Maddie having to deliver the eulogy. This morning, she'd jotted down a few sentences to express what Kai meant to her—the words rapidly flooding out of her. Even so, she still wasn't sure what to say before everyone entered the water. Maddie studied two other sheets of paper she'd printed along with the eulogy. The first was filled with inspirational quotes. The second contained the various surfing slogans Kai would recite before he and Maddie would hit the waves, including a quote from Duke Kahanamoku, one of the greatest Hawaiian surfers of all time. Between all three pages, she hoped to pull something together that was meaningful and perfectly honored Kai's memory.

Additional surfers flooded from the parking lot to the sand. Drew and Taylor stood nearby with their surfboards. Mom and Popo waited on shore, ready to ride out in the boat provided by the marina. All the mourners wore brightly colored leis and held containers of rose petals. Stunned that yet more people had come to the memorial, Maddie knew she had to pull it together and be composed when she read the eulogy. They'd honored Kai's wishes to be cremated. Maddie would release some of his ashes during the paddle-out from a small plastic baggie tucked in her bathing suit top. She'd scatter the rest of Kai's remains this summer at his favorite surfing spot on the North Shore of Oahu.

Maddie slipped into her wetsuit. It was time to say a few words before leading everyone into the water, so she gripped Kai's board and retrieved her notes. With Angela on one side and Taylor on the other, Maddie scanned the crowd. There were people from way back during her teenage years and many who'd recently come into Kai's life. Mark approached Maddie and her immediate family and placed leis around their necks. Once again, Maddie fought back the tears, swallowing hard in order to breathe out her thanks. Mark nodded solemnly and headed to the water's edge, where he blew into a conch shell—the ethereal sound signaling the start of the ceremony. The crowd hushed, the only sound coming from the waves sloshing onto shore.

Maddie glanced at the mourners, then began to read her eulogy. "Over twenty years ago, on the cusp of a giant wave, you rode into our lives unexpectedly. Soon after, you welcomed us into your life as your *ohana*. You loved without limitations, taught us that the ocean could embrace us and teach us unlimited lessons. When I was a kid, you taught me to surf and instilled in me a love of the ocean. You always reminded me to face my fears, to never let *maka'u* stop me."

Choked up, Maddie paused and stared at the sentences written on the page, the words blurry from her tears. She ran her finger over the smooth koa wood beads of her bracelet, the gift from Kai that always made her calm and happy, no matter the situation.

She wiped the tears from her eyes and read more from the eulogy. "Like the faithfulness of the tides, you were always there. Your spirit lives in these waters, continuing to guide us on our journey. As Duke Kahanamoku once said, 'Out of water, I am nothing,' words Kai lived by every day. Today we return Kai's spirit to the ocean, where he will forever be part of these waters. And now, in the words we often heard from Kai: if in doubt, paddle out."

When Maddie turned to face the ocean, the crowd behind her cheered loudly. She stepped into the water, the gentle waves sloshing over her feet, and kept walking. Once up to her thighs, she hopped on Kai's board and sliced her hands through the surface as she headed to the surf zone. A small boat with other mourners motored past and quickly reached the area where the surfers would form their circle.

Well over a hundred surfers paddled through the whitewater. As Maddie floated inside the surf zone, a huge wall of water towered over her. When the wave grew in size, Maddie's breaths became shaky. Determined to not let fear stop her, she took a deep breath and braced herself for impact, but she instead paddled through the wave with ease, the breaker barely jostling her. Thrilled to be in the ocean, she sliced her hands through the water until she reached the boat where Mom and Popo and a few elders waited for the others.

Once she got past the surf line, Maddie sat atop the board and faced the shore. Taylor positioned herself next to her. The surfers formed a circle in the water. There were so many people that they had to widen the circumference and form a double row of surfers. Even more paddlers made their way to the circle, and the double row became a triple.

Rays of purple and amber filtered through the clouds, shining on people of all ages and walks of life who were here to celebrate Kai and all he'd given to the world. The outpouring of love and respect overwhelmed Maddie, and she again began to cry. There was no physical pain today. No headaches or sudden weakness. Today, the only pain was in her heart, tempered by how many people had shown up to honor someone she loved so dearly.

"This is exactly how Kai would've wanted to be remembered," Maddie murmured through her tears to Taylor.

Taylor nodded, wiping her cheeks. "That's for sure. He'd never want anyone to wallow in sadness over his passing."

It was time for the celebration to begin. Mark situated his board near the center of the circle and once again blew from the conch shell, the sound echoing out toward the ocean.

Mark then used a megaphone to carry his voice far. "Brothers and sisters, most of you know my cousin, Kenny Tamamoto, as Kai, a fitting name for someone so connected to the ocean. We all know that he wouldn't have wanted any of us to be sad about his passing. By the looks of things today, I see that he touched many lives, including Angela's and Maddie's. Before they toss their leis into the water, I'd like Maddie to say a few more words."

Maddie paddled to the inside of the circle and took the megaphone from Mark. There was no fear as she spoke to the crowd. "Thank you all for being here. I know Kai touched all of our lives. He taught me to love and respect the ocean and showed me that the waves and currents could teach me so much about life. He always told me there was nothing I couldn't handle. When I was young and just learning to surf, he'd often say, '*Mohala i ka wai ka maka o ka pua*,' which means, 'unfolded by the water are the faces of the flowers'." Maddie glanced at her mother, sitting in the boat, and nodded. They removed their leis and tossed them into the center of the circle. "As we toss our leis into the water, we celebrate Kai's life, grateful that his spirit will forever be part of the sea."

As she gazed at the two leis floating atop the water, Maddie felt a gentle pressure on her shoulder, as if someone had set their hand there. She looked behind her, expecting to see Taylor or another surfer nearby, but the others were several feet away. Maddie smiled, the tears springing to her eyes flowing not from sadness but from love. That had to have been Kai reminding her that he was here with her and always would be.

Everyone else tossed their leis and scattered their rose petals. A few of the leis and some of the flower petals floated away, folded into the waves and now becoming one with the ocean. Maddie reached inside the top of her wetsuit and pulled out the bag of Kai's ashes. She opened the bag and sprinkled the ashes into the water. The current quickly took them away—Kai's remains now forever part of the ocean he'd loved so much.

The sound of cheers and splashing became almost deafening, the noise likely echoing onto the beach. For a moment, Maddie could swear she heard Kai chanting the song he sang when he'd paddled out toward the breaking waves:

Ke ala nihi aʻe lā...Ka ʻuwea holuholu. The way is precarious, like a swaying tightrope.

Maddie knew she'd experience more scary moments as she went through routine screening exams and might one day face a reoccurrence of cancer or a kidney transplant, but she also knew she'd be able to balance on that swaying tightrope. Though not here to catch her, Kai would always be with her in spirit.

Full of gratitude at all Kai had given her over the years, how he'd been the best father she could have ever wanted, Maddie couldn't stop the tears which flowed from her eyes. Tears of joy. Tears of gratitude. Tears of grief. He'd taught her to face her fears, to embrace happiness when it came her way. She promised him she'd follow his teachings from now on, even if she hadn't always done so in the past.

The ceremony now over, the circle of surfers and mourners dispersed. Maddie slowly drifted closer to the surf zone. By now, the flowers had floated away. Angela and Popo waited in the boat a few yards away. Some of the surfers sat atop their boards; others cheered as they rode the breakers all the way to shore.

Taylor paddled closer to Maddie. "Mom, a good set is coming through. Think you can handle it?"

Each wave grew in magnitude, and the hair on the back of Maddie's neck stood up. Her breaths got shaky. "I'm not sure I have the strength to catch a wave. I'll wait until the next set and catch one of the smaller waves and ride it to shore."

"These aren't that big. You've ridden way bigger waves."

That was true. Maddie squinted at the setting sun as the breakers headed her way. "But I haven't surfed in years."

"Hey, once a surfer, always a surfer. But don't worry. I'll be with you. Let's catch the next one and ride it together."

Maddie swallowed hard as she nodded. Slicing her hands through the water, she paddled toward the breakers. She ducked under a frothing wall of water. On the other side of the tumbler, another wave formed in the distance. For a few moments, the breakers surged past as Maddie worked up the nerve to try and catch a wave. Then, she saw the cusp of a perfect wave just starting to break in the distance.

"This one's for Kai," she said as she wiped the tears from her face. As the wave approached, her heartbeat increased, and she forced herself to breathe slowly and evenly. When the water formed a crest behind her, Maddie paddled with all her might until her board caught the momentum of the wave. Right away, she popped up on her board and steadied herself as she rode the whitewash for a few seconds. Once she caught her breath, she angled the board slightly and zipped down the face. Taylor was riding the curl of the same wave and smiling brightly.

While the whitewater churned beneath her, Maddie also grinned as she gained momentum on the wave and rode all the way to shore. How thrilling it was to once again glide over the ocean—to feel one with the wave. Though she wanted to paddle back to the surf zone and ride another, she recognized how exhausted she was and hopped off her board.

She sloshed through the shallow water until she stood on the damp sand. Swarms of people congregated on the beach while they partied and honored Kai's memory. Drew had his arm wrapped around Angela's shoulders as they talked to Braden's parents. Angela's smile was tremulous, but it was good to see. Maddie wedged her board under her arm and started to head to the dry sand, but then she stopped. A woman on shore looked just like Kendra. Maddie took a few more slow steps closer to the beach. It was Kendra! Maddie's breath hitched in her chest. Had Kendra been here all along?

Maddie's heart was beating hard as she walked

toward Kendra, still unable to believe her eyes.

"Hi, Maddie." Kendra gave her a small smile and folded her arms. "It was cool watching you ride that wave. You're a really great surfer."

"Thanks." Maddie lowered her gaze. Weeks ago, she'd finally gotten over Kendra and had moved on, but right now she had no idea what to say to her.

"I probably shouldn't have come today. I should've contacted you weeks ago."

"No, it's okay." Maddie shook her head. The glaring sunlight over the ocean shone directly into her eyes, and she shaded them with a hand.

"I wanted to pay my respects." Kendra's voice was soft and gentle. "I'm so sorry about Kai."

"Thanks." Maddie wanted to show more appreciation for the support but instead blurted out the question that had been on her mind for months. "But how come you didn't text me back after you had your biopsy? Maybe your wife erased my texts. Or maybe you did see the messages and opted to not respond."

Kendra took one step closer to Maddie. "I shouldn't have lied to you when we were in Big Sur. I was an idiot to say I wasn't married. The thing is, I haven't been with Bree for years. I mean, not as far as us being partners. We don't live together and hardly ever see each other. She took me to get my biopsy only because I had no one else to help me. I had no idea she'd look at my texts."

Maddie set her surfboard on the sand. "I was really surprised when I found out that you've been married the whole time we were seeing each other."

"I'm only married to Bree on paper. Our investments are intricately tangled, and her insurance through the hospital is way better than what I could ever get."

That was something Maddie could understand, but she still had more questions. "Why did Bree read and respond to your texts? Why would she say she's your wife if you're not together?"

"Because she knows that legally, we *are* married. I guess maybe she feels she has a right to speak on my behalf."

Maddie nodded and folded her arms, only half aware

she was mirroring Kendra. "Sounds like marriage stuff to me."

"Maybe she still thinks she can meddle in my life. Also, because she's a pathologist, she wanted to be there when they did the biopsy so she could expedite the pathology results since the PET scan was inconclusive."

That didn't sound good. Maddie tried to steady her breathing. "So, your cancer is back?"

"No, but I did have a scare when they did the biopsy. Turns out it was just a benign nodule. How about you? Any changes in your scans or treatment plan?"

Maddie's breathing became even again. Feeling there'd be no harm in updating a fellow cancer survivor, Maddie figured she might as well get Kendra up to speed on her status. "My MRIs continue to show no changes. No new tumor growth, despite me not being on the anti-cancer drug for a while. I was on dialysis for months, but my kidney function has improved to where they're just monitoring me. After being told I might need a kidney transplant due to damage from the meds, I figured—"

"A kidney transplant? Oh, my God, I had no idea." Kendra stepped closer and loosely clasped her hand in Maddie's.

Although initially resistant to Kendra's touch, Maddie couldn't ignore the warmth flooding through her body. Sweet memories of their time together washed over her. Maddie returned the hold on Kendra's hand. "For now, they're just keeping a close eye on my kidney function. A lot has happened in the past few months. It turns out I've got two half-siblings." She filled in a wide-eyed Kendra on all the details. The words poured out of Maddie so fast that she barely took a breath in between sentences.

"Wow." Kendra shook her head slowly, as if trying to take in everything she'd just learned. "I don't know what to say. A half-brother and sister? That's huge."

Maddie nodded. "I haven't fully wrapped my head around having half-siblings. Kai's passing has taken all my focus lately."

"That's understandable." Kendra's expression turned thoughtful. "Have you contacted them?"

"Not yet. I don't know if I ever will." Maddie tipped her head to the side. "I'm curious to know more about them but hesitant at the same time. I wouldn't want them in my life if they're anything like my biological father."

"I get it. But they could be more like you than your biological father." Kendra gave Maddie's hand a little squeeze and smiled.

Maddie smiled back. Kendra always had a way of getting Maddie to see the positives. Over the past few months, she'd really missed Kendra's optimism. And missed so many other things about her as well. "Yeah, that's definitely possible. When I thought for sure I was going to need a kidney transplant, I figured I'd reach out to them, but now I may not need a kidney. At least, not anytime soon. But I've got half-siblings out there. It's hard to just carry on with my life without contacting them." Maddie laughed softly. "When I was a kid, I always wanted a sibling, and now I've got two who don't even know I exist."

"Give it time. Maybe someday you'll be ready to meet them."

"I'll consider that once things settle down." Maddie bit her lower lip. "I probably should've called you months ago to tell you about the possibility of me needing a kidney transplant and about being on dialysis, but I didn't want to be a burden."

Kendra cupped both hands around Maddie's and gazed at her. "You'd never be a burden to me. I care a lot about you. I had no idea you texted me the day I got my biopsy. I found out later that Bree erased your texts and her response to you. I don't know what you wrote to me that day, but Bree knows how I feel about you. I told her I'd met someone really special."

Maddie pulled her hand back. "Special? In her response to my text, she referred to me as your friend. Why would she not tell you about my texts?"

"Because that's Bree. She decides what's right for me." Kendra's tone was very bitter. "Dot reached out to me by email after Kai passed, saying how distraught you were. I confronted Bree about your texts and put a passcode lock on my phone."

It all made sense. But still... "I promised myself I'd never get involved with a married woman again."

"What if I wasn't married?" Kendra stepped closer and looked deep into Maddie's eyes. "Maddie, I like you. I mean, really like you. You're fun and intelligent, deeply caring and creative. I'm willing to officially divorce Bree to show you that I care about you...and that I want to be with you."

Maddie was tempted, but she needed more information before making her final decision. "I thought you said you never wanted to be involved with anyone ever again."

Kendra's hand lightly brushed Maddie's arm. "That changed when I met you. I hadn't expected to fall for you so fast. It was like we'd been together for years, yet we'd only just met. Things felt so right shortly after I met you, especially after the first time you spent the night with me."

That had been how Maddie felt, too. The connection was mind blowing. There was more to their relationship than great sex, though. The details about their cancer journeys, the long phone conversations late at night, the chats about their writing projects. Kendra's fingers on her skin still ignited that familiar warmth Maddie experienced the first time Kendra had touched her. Her stomach still did flip-flops while she listened to her speak. As the sunset reflected on Kendra's face, Maddie was once again struck by her beauty.

Maddie reached for Kendra's hand—comforted by her presence. The truth was that she never got over Kendra, despite proclaiming to others that she'd moved on. "Since we met, I haven't stopped thinking about you. Not one day goes by that I don't imagine your beautiful eyes gazing into mine."

Kendra's expression softened, and she squeezed Maddie's hand. "I haven't felt this way about someone in a long time. Can't remember if I was ever this crazy about anyone. I should've run after you months ago."

"Well, you're here now." Maddie laughed but quickly got serious. "But why would you want to be with me? I mean, you know the odds of my type of cancer. If the tumor comes back, there's likely not much they can do."

"I was drawn to you the moment I saw you. I spent way too long pushing people away, wearing a wedding ring to ward off potential girlfriends. When I met you in Big Sur, the connection was so powerful, something I couldn't ignore. Truth be told, it scared me. Probably why I didn't stay in touch or run after you."

When Maddie looked deep into Kendra's eyes, she knew the words were from the heart. Assuming what they'd experienced would only be a quick fling, Maddie hadn't planned to fall so hard for Kendra. "You know, ever since I met you, I've been trying to be better about living in the moment and facing my fears. I guess that whole carpe diem mentality kinda sunk in after that night with you in Big Sur. It's just that I'd never want you to fall too deep...since I don't exactly have the best odds with my type of cancer."

"I heard what you said before everyone went into the water. It was beautiful. I think everyone here today knows that anyone can die in an instant, even someone as healthy as Kai."

Maddie blinked away the sudden tears. "Seemingly healthy. He'd been putting off seeing a cardiologist for months. Turned out the heart attack was caused by a total blockage in his arteries."

"I'm so sorry," Kendra said softly. "I guess what I'm trying to say is, you and I probably face our mortality more than most people. In time, I could get some other type of cancer from all the radiation I had years ago. Or an MRI might show new tumor growth for you. Maddie, I want to cherish all the time with you that I can, no matter if it's a few decades or a few weeks."

A gust of wind blew a lock of hair over Maddie's face. In her mind, Kai's voice was telling her to face her fears. It was time to stop fretting about the future and finally take it day by day. "On the day you were getting your biopsy, I sent you a Woolf quote. It was in response to the text you'd sent me, the one about how you see me everywhere."

"What did you write?" Kendra asked, her face serious.

"It was another line following the quote you'd sent me. The words came from Woolf, but they were exactly how I feel. 'Life, I would tell you, would be impossible without you.'"

Kendra's eyes filled with tears. "I feel the same way. I know we haven't known each other for too long, but I can't ignore how I feel about you."

"Me neither." This time, Maddie's tears were from happiness. "Crazy as this might sound, maybe we both oughta stay legally married to our spouses. I mean, at least for the time being. Might as well make sure we're insured." If Kendra was willing to make adjustments and face her fears, then Maddie would do the same.

Kendra raised her brow. "You're sure?"

"I'm sure." And Maddie really was.

"So long as Bree doesn't meddle in my tests or treatment plans and as long as she's fine with me staying on her insurance, I wouldn't mind not having to file divorce papers or pay for mediocre insurance."

"I could get medical insurance as a part-time professor in the inmate education program, but I've also thought about returning to Southern California for a while. My mom's gonna need lots of support right now."

"My job is pretty mobile. I can write and edit anywhere, so long as I've got myove the beaches in Southern California. I could give you another swimming lesson." Maddie gave Kendra a sly s laptop."

"Anywhere, huh? You'd lmile.

"Sounds great."

"I might even help Kai's business partner with the surf shop for a while. He'll need someone to teach surfing for a few weeks during the summer."

Kendra tilted her head and grinned. "Maybe you could give me a surfing lesson."

"Only if it's a private lesson."

"How about in Hawaii?" Kendra had a sly look on her face. "We could spend a week on Maui and a few days on Molokai."

A huge smiled washed over Maddie's face. "Or spend a month in Hawaii. I'm planning to go to Oahu this summer, but we could also visit Maui and Molokai."

Kendra let out a quiet laugh. "That sounds amazing. If I end up being a confident enough swimmer, we could get certified to be scuba divers and go to that little crescent-shaped island off the coast of Maui."

"Molokini, it's a great spot to see lots of fish. Always wanted to go there." Maddie smiled again, struck by how radiant Kendra looked in the late afternoon light. She loved how adventurous Kendra was. In a matter of only a few months, Kendra had gone from being afraid of water to now wanting to scuba dive in the deep ocean. Maddie leaned over and kissed Kendra softly on the lips. She reached for Kendra's hand and looked deep into her eyes. "You're even more beautiful than I remembered. I'm glad you're with me right now…and that you'll be with me later."

Kendra pulled Maddie's hand up to her lips and kissed each knuckle. "I hope you know that once I put my arms around you tonight, I'm not gonna let you go."

Kendra's words made Maddie ache with desire. "That makes two of us."

Now grateful that Kendra had come here today, Maddie understood the importance of enjoying any and all little daily miracles. And she knew it was crucial to not let fear get in the way. How stunning Kendra looked in the amber glow of the sunset, her beauty enhanced by the struggles she'd been through. Maddie and Kendra had many more adventures to enjoy together. As she gazed at Kendra, she couldn't stop smiling. She knew she could never let her go. Not now. Not ever again.

A loud voice in the distance caught her attention. It was Drew, calling out to Dot, and it returned Maddie to the moment. Kai's memorial was officially over. Some people were tidying up, and some were heading to the parking lot. Others were gathered in small groups. Taylor had an arm around Angela as Popo handed them both another tissue. Maddie needed to rejoin her family, and she needed to introduce them all to Kendra.

As the breakers continued to surge toward shore, Maddie said a silent goodbye to Kai and vowed to live in the moment and enjoy whatever time she had left. She slipped her hand in Kendra's and kissed her softly on the lips. Right now, everything felt right and safe. Though she wasn't certain what the future entailed, she had today—and many more tomorrows. In this moment, Maddie knew that life would indeed be impossible without Kendra by her side.

Acknowledgements

First and foremost, I would like to thank my readers and fellow authors who have encouraged me as I continue to write my books, this one especially. This novel is a labor of love. It might have taken a long time to be released to the world, but here it is at last. I couldn't have finished *Uncharted Waters* without the support from other writers who offered countless words of encouragement.

I would like to thank Patty Schramm from Flashpoint Publications for helping me get this book published. To my amazing editor, Zee Ahmad: There are not enough words to express to you how grateful I am that you poured heart and soul into editing my book. You push me to be a better writer, and I am incredibly lucky that you're my editor. I am grateful also to Ann McMan for creating such an amazing book cover.

I am deeply indebted to my beta readers—Nicole Falconer, Robert Falconer, Jennifer Fenwick, Sallyanne Monti, and Lisa Turnbull. You provided valuable feedback during the revision process.

I also want to recognize the Laguna Beach Marine Safety Department and the Morro Bay Harbor Department for the helpful information your guards provided about ocean rescue procedures.

Additionally, I express my gratitude to the *Sun* magazine and to Esalen Institute in Big Sur for providing a safe and beautiful location where I first worked on this book.

I'm grateful for assistance from Diane Gillespie and Vara Neverow (from the International Virginia Woolf Society) in guiding me in the right direction to get permission to use excerpts from Virginia Woolf's novels.

Excerpts from TO THE LIGHTHOUSE by Virginia Woolf. Copyright © 1927 by Houghton Mifflin Harcourt Publishing Company, renewed 1954 by Leonard Woolf. Reprinted by permission of Houghton Mifflin Harcourt Publishing Company.

The passages from Woolf's *To the Lighthouse* are also included with permission from The Society of Authors as the Literary Representative of the Estate of Virginia Woolf at 84 Drayton Gardens, London SWO 2SB, UK.

In addition, I wish to say a special mahalo nui loa to Zenna Hurley MacGregor and Greg Kahn for their help in coming up with the right Hawaiian phrases used in my book, and to my father, Robert Beers, for teaching me about Hawaiian customs and traditions that he learned as a boy growing up in Hawaii.

A special thank you goes out to Nancy Carnevale, Stephanie Hathaway, and Tara Kubicka-Miller for helping me to better understand what a cancer patient goes through. Sharing your personal experiences with me years ago helped me when I was in the initial phases of writing this book.

Additionally, I am especially grateful for the help from Karen Sandore, one of the best nurses in the medical field. Thank you for the helpful information about meds and medical procedures.

A special thank you out goes to my brother Greg: You were always just a text away when I needed you to research medical information. I also thank you for closely reading the chapters dealing with medical jargon and making sure my information was as accurate as possible.

To my circle of close friends: Thank you for your continual support of my writing endeavors. You remind me to never stop dreaming.

And to Kat: Thank you for your unwavering love and support as I write my novels.

Books by Lynnette Beers

Just Beyond the Shining River

After she gave up a promising career as an artist and turned her back on her British roots, Gemma Oldfield settled into life in Los Angeles to be with the woman who'd captured her heart. When things don't go as planned, Gemma buries herself in her work as a Hollywood set decorator–all the while clinging to the hope that the passion with her lover can be rekindled. But she must temporarily leave L.A. behind and return to England after her grandmother's unexpected passing.

Once there, she discovers shocking secrets she could never have foreseen. When she finds hundreds of letters written from a mysterious person dating as far back as the 1930s, Gemma embarks upon a quest to understand why her grandmother took so many secrets to her grave.

In her pursuit to learn more about her grandmother's past, Gemma meets an intriguing woman who has the potential to change the course of her life forever. But can Gemma open her heart to love again? Will she stay in England for a new beginning or return to the States to the life she knew before?

Saving Sam

As an experienced San Diego lifeguard, Sam Cleveland has been trained to save others. On what becomes the most treacherous beach day ever, she battles the sea as her ability as a lifeguard is tested. While she risks her life to rescue swimmers from the rough surf, her world comes crashing down when she learns that her brother Robert has been in a serious accident. She then must leave San Diego and the young woman she's recently started dating to return to her hometown—a place that holds a horrid memory from her childhood.

Once back in Mississippi, Sam sits vigil at Robert's bedside. Always protective when Sam was a child, Robert clings to life as investigators search for the person responsible for his accident. As she faces the possibility of losing her brother, Sam is reminded that her hometown holds an unspeakable secret that she and Robert vowed to always keep buried.

On the hunt for the man who intentionally harmed Robert is Lieutenant Annie Wright—the woman who captured Sam's heart years ago. Now just friends, Sam and Annie work together to find the person responsible for Robert's injuries. But as painful childhood memories resurface, so do old feelings of love. Will Sam choose to move forward with the chance at new romance in San Diego, or will she return to the comfort of familiar love with Annie in Mississippi?

Caught Inside

Maddie Fong is painfully aware of being the outsider at her new Southern California high school. Teased for being different, she does her best to adapt to her new life. Raised by a single mom, Maddie retreats by burying herself in books and dreaming of a different life. But one day she and her mother meet an intriguing man from Hawaii who introduces Maddie to surfing—which ignites in her the sense of new and exciting possibilities.

But can Maddie overcome her intense fear of water to ride the waves? And if she summons up the courage to learn to surf, will it help her win the attention of a sweet girl from school named Ally Flores? Once Maddie adjusts to life in a beachside town and starts college, she learns that love and bravery might not be enough for her to reach her dreams and find happiness. When she encounters unexpected obstacles that could change the course of her life forever, Maddie faces tough decisions as she has to choose what's most important to her. But she is determined to never give up—no matter what it takes.

Bringing Rainbow Stories to Life

Flashpoint Publications welcomes submissions from writers of every color and books featuring characters of every color. In addition, Flashpoint Publications encourages job applicants of every color whenever a staff position becomes available. We believe that EVERYONE is entitled to a seat at our table.

Visit us at our website: www.flashpointpublications.com

9 781619 295711